THE LIES BENEATH

THE WESTWICK UNIVERSITY DUET
BOOK 1

BRI BLACKWOOD

BRETAGEY PRESS

First Digital Edition: March 2023

Cover Designed by Shepard Originals

Edited by: Chrisandra Corrections

Sisters Get Lit.erary

EAL Editing Services

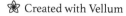 Created with Vellum

For those that will do whatever it takes to get what they desire.

NOTE FROM THE AUTHOR

Hello!

Thank you for taking the time to read this book. The Lies Beneath is a dark college billionaire enemies-to-lovers forbidden romance. It is not recommended for minors and contains situations that are dubious and could be triggering.

For a more detailed trigger and content warning list, you can find it on my website.

It isn't a standalone and the next book in the series is The Truth Between.

BLURB

Privilege has its secrets...

Westwick University is known for its prestige and pedigree for hundreds of years.

Many people would die to come here...

And some have come here and died.

There are lies buried within these walls that the world doesn't know about.

But I do.

It's what happens when your family has gone to the same college for generations.

Stories and secrets are passed down, making me yearn to know more.

I'm determined to discover if each and every one is true, but I'm distracted.

Because my new professor has taken a particular interest in me.

Or so I think.

I shouldn't be tempted because anything with him is forbidden.

But the way that he only has eyes for me has set me on edge.

I can't tell if there is something there or if I'm making it all up in my head.

Why would a billionaire, who is known for his solitary life after the death of his wife, want to teach here?

There's so much I don't know.

But I know that lies do nothing but lead to more lies.

And when I uncover the truth, the world will implode.

PLAYLIST

Lift Me Up - Rihanna
Young and Beautiful - Lana Del Ray
This is Why - Paramore
Sacrifice - Bebe Rexha
Vigilante Shit - Taylor Swift
You're Not Here - Akira Yamaoka
Everybody Wants To Rule The World - Lorde
My Love Will Never Die - AG, Claire Wyndham
How Villains Are Made - Madalen Duke
Shallow - Tommie Profitt, Fleurie
Devil Doesn't Bargain - Alec Benjamin

The playlist can be found on Spotify.

1

IRIS

The rush of air that left my lungs rattled my bones. Every single muscle in my body felt as if it was on fire. I was clearly working some muscles that I didn't know I had. Without a doubt, I would be hurting even more in the morning. What made it worse was that I couldn't stop now, although I wanted to.

Why the fuck had I packed so much?

Not being able to deal with the load anymore, I placed the box on the closest banister to me. I leaned against the stairwell wall, allowing it and the railing to bear most of the weight of the box I'd been carrying. It gave me a moment to catch my breath as I tried to help my body come to terms with the physical exertion I was inflicting on it.

I reminded myself that all of this was for the betterment of my family. The apologies that we deserved were long overdue, and, deep down, I couldn't wait until I proved everyone wrong. I'd be accomplishing something that no one before me had managed to do. Failure wasn't an option, and my determination to show everyone how wrong they were wouldn't allow me to fail.

This year, I was going to be living in Payne Hall. It was something I'd had fantasies about doing when I was younger. Even before I'd found how monumental Eddison Payne was to my family, the thought of living here had been my dream. While I was living in Payne this year, it wasn't to be confused with the pain that was shooting through what felt like every nerve in my body.

Moving into one of Westwick University's oldest dormitories meant I had to climb up a million stairs in order to make it to my room. I spent most of that time muttering every curse I could think of, and wondering why, in all this time, hadn't someone thought about adding an elevator to this building.

Maybe I needed to take a breather. I could rest for a bit and use the time to check on Gran. With a loud groan, I shifted the box's weight so that it was once again back on me, and I continued up the stairs.

As I struggled with the box, I was still shit talking to myself for not choosing another box or bag to bring upstairs. It would have been an immeasurable help because then I wouldn't have had to take so many trips downstairs or ask for help. Yes, there were people there that were supposed to help with moving in, but I preferred to do things myself.

I was quickly learning that, without a doubt, I would have no issue staying in shape if I had to deal with climbing these shadowy stairs every day.

Speaking of shadows, this building had plenty of them. I wasn't sure if they'd ever replaced the windows here, based on how old they looked, and the light they allowed in was minimal. I knew the dormitory was considered a historical building—it was one of the oldest dorms on campus—and I was convinced that this place hadn't seen a large-scale renovation ever. Then again, what did I know?

Everything about this place screamed that it had been around for centuries. I was sure these walls could tell hundreds of stories, while its doors had kept the secrets of the thousands of students who had come before me. The black iron gate standing near the entrance had signs of wear and tear from years of standing against the elements. Green moss grew on the building's gray brick walls, and I could see where people thought that this property gave off the vibes of an old castle. Although the structure itself looked somewhat dilapidated, the lawn was well maintained, thanks to the college's landscaping team. I couldn't help but notice the irony in where their priorities lay.

Sure, the aesthetic of the building was cool, and I couldn't help but wonder if Payne Hall was haunted, but that wasn't the reason I was here.

Once you passed through the front doors, you were immediately greeted by a statue that stood in the center of the building's foyer. The name on the plaque in front of it said Eddison Payne. Throughout my time on Westwick's campus, I'd found myself drawn to the statue, to the point where I'd snuck into this dorm several times just to catch a glimpse. I'd always suspected that I would live in Payne Hall as a student, given my family's history, but seeing this statue solidified it.

Why I was drawn to this statue didn't make much sense to anyone outside of my family. Seeing Eddison Payne standing there with a bunch of papers and a notepad in hand, that was the key to everything, I just knew it, and I had evidence to prove it.

But where the hell were those papers?

A lot of questions surrounded the mystery of where Payne's papers might be. Nothing indicated that they had ever been found, although some suspected they might have been buried somewhere in this building. Apparently, he'd spent a lot of time here when he was a student, so if he'd left anything, the chances that they were somewhere in here were high. Then again, the likelihood that they might have been destroyed was also very high.

I finished the trek up the staircase and my muscles burned the entire way. It took me a minute to maneuver the box so that I could open the door that would lead me out of the stairwell. You would think with it being move-in weekend, that someone would have made sure that it was easy to get from your car to your room.

With a heavy sigh, I yanked the door open before fixing my grip on the box and walking as quickly as I could through the door. Once I'd overcome that obstacle, I took a quick look around, without stopping any of the progress I was making toward putting this box down in my room. It was easy to see the resemblance between some of the other dorms I'd seen on campus and other buildings within this part of New York State, including the Chevalier Manor on the Brentson University campus. I knew that was for good reason.

Rumor had it that Westwick and Brentson were built around the same time because their founders hated each other, and both wanted their own schools just to have another way to compete with each other. Why else would there be a need to build two colleges so close together during that same time period?

As I turned the corner and reached the hall that my room was on, I felt a surge of energy pass through my body. I was almost there and then I could drop this box down and shove it into a corner of the room where I probably wouldn't even bother to open it for the entirety of the school year.

I was so focused on getting to my room that I didn't notice someone else in the hall until the person had already passed me.

"Iris, it's good to see you again!"

"Fuck," I mumbled under my breath as my steps faltered. It took me another second to gather myself before I turned around.

I readjusted my hold on the box to look at a girl I didn't recognize. Her deep brown eyes sparkled as she stared at me, and her golden-brown skin glowed without any help from the sun. But nothing about her rang any bells for me. Despite the fact she obviously knew who I was, I was drawing a blank on her and her name.

Where had we met before? Westwick was a decent-sized school, so we could have met at some point, but I couldn't, for the life of me, recall when we had. Though, I tended to remember the faces of those who tormented me over the ones who wanted to exchange niceties.

The smile that was displayed on her face was wide, but I couldn't tell if it was genuine. What I was sure of was that her sunny personality, fake or not, was the direct opposite of everything else in this building.

She tucked a strand of her black hair behind her ear

before she looked down at the box in my hands. "Can I help you with that?"

I hesitated as a debate waged within me. Her help was wanted, but I wanted to deal with this on my own. After going back and forth with myself for a split second, I decided that I'd be an idiot not to say yes. After my quick nod, she hurried over to me and took some of the weight of the box off of me.

Relief flooded my veins with the transfer of some of the load. I wanted to shake out every limb to make sure that I still had feeling in them, but that would need to wait until I got to my room.

"This *is* heavy. Where's your room?"

"Down this hall. All the way at the end."

The helpful stranger started walking backwards, helping me carry the heaviest box known to humankind down the hallway. It took a few seconds for us to sync our movements to the point where we both had no issue handling the box. We took our time walking though, to prevent either one of us from tripping or the box from falling.

When we reached the doorway of my room, she walked in first and together, we placed the box down in a space that wasn't occupied by anything else.

"Oh, there you are, honey."

I turned and came face-to-face with Gran. She was standing near the window, and I wouldn't have been surprised if she was looking out of it when we walked in. I'd often found her staring outside, and I'm sure being here brought back a lot of memories. I assumed reminiscing was what had her looking out now, as there wasn't much to see outside on this cloudy, dreary day besides all of the students moving back to Westwick.

Gran gave me a small smile before looking at the other person in the room. "Thank you so much for helping Iris get that box up here."

"It wasn't a problem. I'm Aria. It's lovely to meet you."

I watched as Aria stuck her hand out to shake my grandmother's hand. Knowing her name didn't help me remember her though.

Gran gave her a warm smile and said, "I usually don't do handshakes. If it's alright, I'd like to give you a hug."

After Aria gave a small nod, my grandmother opened up her arms. Gran was always willing to give out hugs, especially to those who needed it. I didn't know if this hug was because of Aria's good deed or if Gran thought she needed a hug. Hell, it could have been both.

Watching Aria and Gran embrace was awkward because the familiarity of the gesture made it seem as if she knew this stranger more than I did. When the hug ended, Aria gave my grandmother a bright grin before turning to me.

"We should grab lunch sometime when you're settled in."

Her request was simple enough, and I sensed nothing but friendliness from her, but everything about our interaction threw me through loop after loop, as if I was on the world's largest roller coaster. None of this was making sense.

In fact, I was becoming irritated with Aria. I knew that if I'd met her before, I would have recognized her face at the very least, even if her name escaped me.

"Uh... that's not a good—"

"Aria, we need to go now." Another girl I didn't recognize was now standing at my door. She didn't bother looking over at me or Gran. I was happy to be ignored.

Aria turned to me after giving Gran a small nod. "I'm glad

you chose to live in Payne Hall. It's an excellent choice. And I'm sure we'll see each other around a lot, since I live here as well."

With that, she turned on her heel and walked out of my room, taking her friend with her.

"Interesting girl."

I looked over my shoulder at Gran. Her friendly expression had changed into one that was more serious, but it didn't give me an idea about what she might be thinking.

"I have no idea who she was. She acted as if we knew each other, but I swear I've never seen her before."

"I picked up on that, dear," Gran said as she walked over to my bed. "You should be careful about her."

It made it all the more interesting as to why Gran gave her a hug.

"Why do you say that?" I didn't want to say what I was thinking before Gran told me her thoughts. I wanted her unbiased opinion.

"Her energy was strange and I'm not sure why, but as I've said before, you'll attract more bees with honey than with vinegar. I think that is how the saying goes. Anyway, back in my day, Payne Hall wasn't a good choice. While I understand why you chose to live here, it doesn't mean that an outsider would know that. So why did she refer to it as such?"

I shrugged, but Gran was right. Anyone who knew Westwick knew that staying in Payne wasn't an "excellent choice." While its location was optimal because it wasn't too far away from most things on Westwick's campus, it was still far enough out that it was slightly isolated. Not to mention all the stairs and that the place was rumored to be haunted.

But that was a story for a different day.

For most, Payne Hall was the last option. The only reason why students ended up staying here was because they got unlucky in the room draw and were forced to, well, except for me.

"Gran, you don't need to make my bed."

Gran had been fluffing my pillow before she stopped what she was doing to look over at me. "I want to, sweetheart. I wasn't able to do any of the heavy lifting. The least I can do is make your dorm room homier."

None of this was a surprise. Gran had always done her best to make sure I felt at home. Whether it was making a homemade meal most nights so that there was dinner on the table or helping me learn how to drive when I turned sixteen. Although I saw less of her when I was a kid, she did everything she could to take care of me when my parents died around my thirteenth birthday. She'd been with me when we were delivered the news.

I remember that night like it was yesterday. Gran did everything she could to calm me down, even though she was suffering through a huge loss too. My shock quickly turned into sobbing when we found out that Mom and Dad had been murdered in a botched robbery attempt after attending a party in New York City.

While she'd shed some tears, she refused to break down in her grief. It wasn't until she thought I was asleep that I heard her wails, calling out for daughter and son in-law to walk through our front door. The sorrow that I heard from her that night would stay with me forever.

Their deaths left a hole in my heart that would never be filled, although Gran tried her best. I knew how fortunate I was to have her in my life, and I didn't take a second of that for granted because we were all each other had. That was just another reason I was so determined to find Payne's rumored letters, and any other documentation there might be that could help us prove our case.

"Okay. I won't try to stop you."

"I'm almost done anyway."

I scoffed and folded my arms across my chest as I watched her finish making my bed. My stomach growled loudly, and I could feel my cheeks grow hot. I'm glad it chose now to make that noise, versus when Aria was in the room.

"Why don't we stop for a bit and grab some lunch before we come back here and unpack your things?"

"That sounds like a great plan, Gran. Hey, that almost rhymed."

Gran chuckled as she walked over to me and pulled me into her warm embrace. I soaked every moment of it in because I knew that once she left, it would be the last time I would get one for a while.

"Are you sure you don't want to keep Margaret's diary and papers with you?"

The diary and papers were the reason why I was here, but I shook my head against her chest. "No. I took some photos with my phone so I can look at them later. I'd rather you have them so that we know they're safe. I made notes, and if I need anything, I'll call. Look here."

I broke our hug and grabbed my phone. I swiped to my photo app and once I'd clicked on the icon, it took a second for it to load. I moved my phone so Gran could see the screen and I showed her the images that I took.

"Great, but don't just call me when you need to ask questions pertaining to that, okay? I want to hear from you more than that."

She pulled her body back slightly so that she could look down at me and gave me a bright smile. A few seconds later, she stepped away from me. I patted my jeans in an attempt to find the key to my room so that I could lock the door behind us. After Gran had walked out of the room, I took a moment to look around, eyeing everything that still needed to be done.

At least my room didn't seem to have any dust or spider webs, but I made a note to make sure that I cleaned every surface with a disinfectant wipe before I unpacked.

A flicker of light came from underneath my closet door and caught my attention. What the hell was that?

"Are you coming, dear?"

I waited for a moment to see if the light would reappear, but it didn't. "Y-yes, I am."

I stood there for another second to see if anything would change, but nothing happened. Telling myself it was just my imagination, I closed the door behind me. However, thoughts of what I'd seen didn't leave my mind for the rest of the day.

2

IRIS

I refused to fight the yawn that left my lips as I tightened my ponytail. It was a crime to be up this early in the morning, but if I couldn't get back to sleep, I needed to do something productive.

And for whatever reason, I'd chosen to go for a morning jog.

As I got out of bed and turned on my ceiling light, a small smile appeared on my face as I thought about Gran. She would probably ask me a dozen questions about why I was voluntarily up so early. She'd also be wondering if something was wrong with me.

Jogging wasn't in my list of tools that I used when I couldn't fall asleep. Falling and staying asleep wasn't usually a problem for me; I thrived on staying up as late as I could and then waking up at the last moment to do whatever I needed to do to get ready for the day.

Running helped me forget about my problems temporarily and helped to keep my anxiety and depression more under control. While it didn't always work, it was still a useful tool to have in my arsenal. It was something that was always there for me when life had gone to shit. It just wasn't something I usually did at six in the morning.

I did fight against the next yawn, as I adjusted the pink sports bra I'd thrown on. There was still a slight burn in my muscles from moving my things into my room two days ago. I checked the temperature, and it was warm enough to throw on only a t-shirt. I needed to enjoy this warmer weather before it became cold as fuck in no time at all.

My gaze landed on my closet as I bit the corner of my lip. I walked over to the place where I saw the light a couple of days ago. No matter what I told myself, I couldn't shake that moment from my consciousness. I bent down to examine the area where I'd thought I'd seen the light again. I ran a hand along the floor, hoping that this time I would notice something different. There were some cracks and holes that I could feel, but there was no light that I could see. I was convinced that my eyes hadn't been playing tricks on me though.

There was nothing there. Just like there hadn't been anything there when I checked the other ninety thousand times. I'd tried my damnedest to recreate the light reflection, but I hadn't been able to. None of that did anything to alleviate the creepy factor of this situation.

It took a bit longer than planned for me to draw my attention away from my closet. I needed to get in the right headspace for this excursion and I had several things I needed to do before I took off.

Stretching my body in an attempt to prevent injury took a few minutes, and, after, I put my sneakers on and grabbed my key. I decided to leave my phone in my room to discourage distraction. While I enjoyed listening to music when running, I'd found that I also enjoyed listening to nature. Having the opportunity to immerse myself into my environment, even for a short period of time, was relaxing in a way. It allowed me to spend my time thinking, instead of drowning out my thoughts with music. This wasn't to say I would never listen to music again while running, but I liked the change of pace.

I lightly jogged down the stairs and glanced at the statue of Payne before I walked to the front door. I took my time opening the door, trying to stay quiet. No reason to wake up anyone lucky enough to still be sleeping.

Once I was outside, the first thing I was greeted with was a gentle breeze. It felt wonderful against my exposed skin, wrapping me up in its cool embrace. I looked around to see if anyone was in the area. Finding no one, I walked down the steps to Payne Hall and began my jog.

It felt wonderful as I ran down the road, making sure to avoid areas that had cobblestone. I could run on them if I wanted to, but it made me nervous, so I tended to avoid it where I could.

I glanced at Chevalier Manor as I ran past. I made sure not to stare for too long because I refused to give in to my anger. This run was all about serenity and attaining peace, not gaining any stress.

As my feet hit the cement, my vision became laser-focused, and the only thing that mattered was running for as long as I could. Because of how early it was, there were only a couple of people out and about. I briefly wondered why the hell they were up because you couldn't have paid me money to be up right now if I had been able to sleep.

The breeze that met my skin grew the faster I went and

suddenly, a rush of adrenaline pumped through my body. I didn't have any idea where I was going, even though I knew this campus like the back of my hand. I was just determined to go wherever my body took me.

My speed picked up and something told me to take a left turn rather than continue down the path I was on. It took about thirty seconds before it finally became clear where I was headed. I was running toward the ravine that served as the northern border of Westwick's campus.

In the time I'd been here, I rarely came out this way. Mostly because I'd never found a reason to, but there was something else that was cause for concern.

Just over the ravine was a decrepit old house that students tended to avoid. I didn't know anyone who knew who the owners of the property were, but because it was private property, no one wanted to trespass or bother the owners. That wasn't the only reason the students avoided it though.

Much like everything else in a two-mile radius of this campus, there were rumors about it being haunted. I couldn't confirm or deny, but I tended to err on the side of caution.

An old tale stated that a guy was dared to run up to the house, knock on the door, and run away. The person knocked and the door opened. They went inside and were never seen from again. Now, if that was true or not is left up to the discretion of the person listening to the story.

My eyes were trained on the house up ahead as I felt my speed increase. Unlike the upkeep around the common areas that Westwick paid for, this area had weeds that, from a distance, looked like they would reach my knees. The house looked worn down, with chipped paint and siding hanging on by a thread. The exterior of the home needed some fixing up, but from where I was, I couldn't tell if the interior was in a similar condition.

My breathing came in short pants as my lungs were starting to feel like they were on fire. It took a couple of seconds for me to slow down, and I came to a stop just before the ravine and bent down in an attempt to catch my breath. My legs had taken over completely, and I hadn't realized how fast I was traveling until I was forced to stop for a breather. I shouldn't have been running as fast as I had been and now, I was paying the price.

It felt great to have my blood pumping after a serious workout. I stood up and rested my arms on my head as I tried to bring my breathing and heart rate down. Normally, the adrenaline that rushed through my veins would have slowed down as my heart tried to find its normal rhythm again. But it didn't.

Deep breaths. Take deep breaths, Iris.

Remembering to control my breath while running sometimes became a problem. And right now it was more important to focus on catching my breath instead of the energy and slight panic that filled me.

When my breathing was almost back to normal, I looked at the structure just across the way from where I stood. In addition to the house that I'd been focusing on as I was running, it seemed as if there was a shed or something in the backyard. I tried to squint to see if that would help me confirm any of the details I thought I was seeing.

I debated hopping across the ravine to get a closer look at the house, but quickly decided against it. Instead, I walked along the water, forgoing the opportunity to return to the walkway so that I could start heading back to campus.

I walked until I could get a clear view of the front of the mysterious house. Everything about the house yelled *deserted,* but if you looked past the current state of its upkeep, you could kind of see that the house was beautiful in its heyday. Although the rest of the house looked run-down, it seemed as if someone had recently taken the time to paint the front door a light gray. Maybe the owner was in the process of renovating the house.

I'd been standing there long enough. If anyone saw me right now, they'd probably think I was attempting to do something nefarious. It was then that I reached for my phone to check the time before heading back to campus.

"Fuck," I muttered to myself as I remembered I'd left it back in my dorm. So much for wanting to take a scenic run through campus. As I continued to roll my eyes at myself for not bringing my phone with me on this run, the front door opened about a third of the way. Well, unless my eyes were playing tricks on me anyway.

I was beginning to wonder if I needed to see an optometrist since this was the second time in the last few days that I was wondering if I was seeing something strange.

But when a prickly sensation floated along my skin, causing goose bumps to form, I knew I wasn't wrong. The door shifted slightly, and I took a step back. Although I was yards away from the front door, I still felt the urge to put as much distance between me and whoever—or whatever—was there as I could.

I swallowed hard and took another step back. The adrenaline that should have lessened as a result of my heart rate returning to normal, ramped back up.

No one could tell me that I wasn't being watched.

Everything in me told me to run in the opposite direction, but it was as if I was frozen in place. My lip trembled as I willed myself to walk away, but my body wouldn't cooperate. I was drawn to this house for some weird reason, and there was nothing I could do about it.

The door opened a smidge more, but I still could barely see inside of the house, and I couldn't see who was holding the door open. If there was someone holding the door open at all.

This is how I die. Staring at an old house that may or may not be haunted.

As if the world heard my thoughts, a strong gust of wind came out of nowhere and made me shiver. Suddenly, the shirt and shorts that I decided to wear for my run weren't warm enough. There was now a chill in the air, but I wasn't sure if it was from a change in the weather, or from the scene that was unfolding in front of me.

The door moved again, opening more before it suddenly slammed shut. I didn't hear the impact of the door meeting the doorframe as much as I would have if I'd been closer, but there was no doubt in my mind that it had caused a loud banging that must have left whoever closed it with ringing in their ears.

Then again, that was *if* it was a person.

That thought was the push I needed to turn around and run back toward the trail I'd left. Damn any soreness that I might have had or how quickly I might get out of breath this time. Nothing mattered but getting the fuck away from whatever that was.

The same momentum that drew me to the home took me away from it. There was no denying that fear had taken over and the only way to calm it down was to get the hell away from this property.

The temptation to see if something was behind me was strong, but I resisted. It would do nothing but slow me down and that was the last thing I needed.

I ran most of the way back to my dormitory. I didn't slow down until I laid eyes on Payne Hall, and then my body began to feel worn out. The yearning to get away from that house across the ravine had become all-consuming, and now my body was paying the price for it.

My breathing was labored as I walked up the front stairs to my dorm. This time, instead of being more cautious about waking someone up as I opened the front door, I yanked it open and slipped inside.

When the door clicked behind me, the sigh I let out was enormous. I immediately sat down on the floor. The weight of my body became too much, and I laid back. I didn't care if anyone walked up on me and thought what I was doing was strange. Making myself move right now would be comical at best, and unless someone came around and decided to carry me, there was no way I was making it up those stairs right now.

I closed my eyes and laid completely still except for the movement of my chest rising and falling. When I opened my eyes, I found myself staring up at the ceiling, studying some of the intricate details someone had painted there. It was harder to see what the drawing was, due to age and the state of the painting, but it was obvious that someone had taken a lot of time and effort to do this.

When I moved my head back slightly, my gaze landed on Payne's statue, standing there in all its glory. It felt as if he were mocking me from beyond the grave, laughing at how I'd been frightened of something I hadn't seen.

Standing just behind it was a door I hadn't noticed when I snuck in here last year. That was something I wanted to explore when I had more strength and energy. The unknown of what lies behind that door was what made every nerve in my body become frazzled.

After a few deep breaths, I finally felt strong enough to move, so I sat up. It took a couple more minutes before I felt as if I wouldn't pass out. I made my way to my feet and walked toward the statue.

I took my eyes off of the sculpture and focused on the door to the rear of it. Deep down, I knew I shouldn't be doing this, but I couldn't help my curiosity. I put my hand on the doorknob and twisted it, but it didn't budge.

I tried pulling on the door and nothing changed. Even when I pulled as hard as I could, the door didn't move. It felt as if it was sealed shut.

With one final glance, I walked away because I didn't have any more time to waste, and I still had a small journey that I needed to conquer before I made it to my room. But at least it would put more distance between me and that old fucking house.

As I made my way toward the stairs that would lead me to my floor, I thought about how the only thing in my future was a shower and getting back into bed. After what I'd just been through, I'd earned it.

3

SOREN

A small tree branch snapped under the weight of my shoe as I walked across the cobblestone street, but I didn't bother to look down. It wasn't worth wasting the time or the energy. Instead, my body propelled ahead, determined to walk up the stairs and into the building in front of me. My brisk walk had nothing to do with my being late. It had everything to do with my resolve to get this over and done with.

I paused for a second to take in the Chevalier Manor on Westwick University's campus. The building that was standing before me brought back a lot of good memories and some bad.

Once I climbed the steps, I stood in front of a heavy, dark-brown wooden door. It was a door I'd stood in front of many times before, but this time was different. It was the first time I'd been back in a while. Since before everything had gotten completely fucked up.

As I moved to knock on the door, it swung open. A man I didn't recognize stood in front of me, but didn't attempt to move out of the way so that I could walk in. He looked to be on the younger side, so I suspected he wasn't too many years removed from college.

"Name." Suspicion filled his gaze as he studied me. He was trying to remember if he'd seen me before and I already knew the answer to that was no.

The confidence that radiated off of him was laughable at best. It was this false sense of bravado that I knew would come crashing down once I told him who I was. His reaction was over the top, and, if I wanted to, I'd have no problem taking him out. And I wouldn't break a sweat doing so.

I understood why he was glaring at me. The meeting had already begun and now I was attempting to enter the premises. Could I have come early? Yes, but I also wanted to make an entrance. It was time to announce that I was back.

"Grant."

Realization hit him like someone had dropped a bucket of ice water on his body. His expression turned almost comical. His narrowed stare suddenly widened, and his mouth dropped open. I kept my face neutral. *Weren't expecting that, were you?*

He scrambled to get out of my way. I dipped my head in acknowledgement and walked through the doorway. He didn't make a peep, just how I preferred it.

Silence filled up the foyer as soon as he closed the door behind me. I looked over my shoulder and the guard at the door turned, facing the front door as if he was too afraid to look in my direction. We were the only ones standing here, but he didn't dare make a sound nor did he make a move. I had to admit that it was rude of him not to even bother attempting to point me in the direction I needed to go, but I understood his fear.

He was concerned about pissing me off and what might happen if he did. *Good.*

Shifting my gaze from him, I took in the foyer. It soon became apparent that nothing much had changed on the inside either and that things were frozen in time. The dark gray paint on the walls almost looked black. That was the same color that had been on the walls when I was a student at Westwick. It was obvious that the paint had been touched up over the years in order to not appear run-down, but the look and feel were still the same.

I took a step and the creaky wooden floor groaned under my foot as the weight was applied to it. It was obvious that the floorboards were old, the polish had worn off and was due to be redone.

I walked down the hall until I reached the second door on the left. Having the fucker standing guard at the front of the manor's help wouldn't have made much of a difference anyway because I knew exactly where I was going. There was only one place in the home that would be large enough to hold a meeting of this caliber.

I opened the door and entered another hallway, much shorter than the one I'd just been in. This hallway was illuminated by candles and only contained a set of midnight-black doors that were slightly darker than the color of the walls. No one was standing near the entrance to the door I approached, but I suspected there might be someone on the other side.

I turned the doorknob without thinking and pushed it open slightly. I could see into the room more than I expected. I shifted my body so that I could observe what was occurring.

From what I could see, those that were in my line of vision were facing forward and paying attention to the speaker at the front of the room.

I pushed the door open enough to slide through before closing it behind me. The light click of the door latch seemed to be only heard by me because everyone else's attention remained transfixed on the person who was currently talking.

I shouldn't feel any hesitancy because I should trust every man in this room. After all, we belonged to the same organization and had pledged allegiance to supporting its overall mission. A couple of years ago, I wouldn't have been watching every breath that the people in the room before me took, but this was what a long time in isolation would get you.

The mood was serious. Most of the meetings that I'd attended before my absence had a similar tone, so this wasn't a departure from the norm. But standing here while I listened for my name to be announced wasn't normal.

Being alone was what I wanted. It was what I craved. Yet now, I was standing in a hallway waiting to walk into a room of about fifty people.

Forty-nine of those people weren't expecting me. However, Parker Townsend, Chairman of the New York City branch of the Chevaliers, was. After all, he was the person who would be making the announcement. Not even Ioan, who was standing to Parker's left, knew what was about to happen.

The agreement had been that, while I took a leave of absence, Ioan would step up and help Parker where Parker needed him to. That position would be terminated, effective immediately, upon my return.

Parker and I had kept in touch during my absence, and I would help him out here and there when he absolutely needed me, but Parker was more than able to take care of most matters himself, along with some of the other Chevaliers he'd brought into his circle of trust. But some things became too large for even him and his team to overcome.

That was where I came in.

I'd been standing in the shadows, waiting to make my entrance. It was where I felt most comfortable. I spent most of my time watching and waiting. But my attendance at tonight's meeting had been a long time coming.

My return to the Chevaliers had been long awaited, but everything was different now. Being back felt strange, and I debated for a long time whether I wanted to return at all.

No one would have blamed me if I hadn't.

Deep down, I knew I would always come back. Whispers had floated around about what my next moves would be, but I made sure that very few people knew what my plans were. That allowed me to move in silence and not be disturbed. That was very important in my line of work.

I looked around the Chevalier Manor and memories of my time here flooded my senses. Not much has changed since I was a student here. There was something about being back at Westwick, even temporarily, that fueled me. Returning to my alma mater and being involved with the Chevaliers again had lit a small fire within me. Signs of life had begun to emerge, and I wasn't sure how I felt about it.

A life I thought had long been dead and buried right along with my wife.

That was just one reason why it had been necessary for

me to take the time away, but now I was back and ready to continue my duties.

Serving as the right-hand man of the Chairman of the Chevaliers was an honor, and I didn't regret it for a second. Watching over the investments and business interests of the company that bore my name by day and maintaining order by any means necessary for the Chevaliers by night had made me feel more alive than anything else ever had.

Until both cost me the woman I was supposed to protect.

My gaze landed on a flickering candle just outside of the room I was about to enter. It danced due to a slight breeze in the air. This candle and the many others that lined this hall lit up the space, providing the only light that we had. Sure, there were other lights that could have been turned on, but it was important that during this meeting, we used candlelight.

It was what the founders of the Chevaliers did, and it was a tradition that we liked to uphold.

We'd decided to hold our alum meeting at one of the first collegiate Chevalier chapters in the world. This would be much tamer than any ritual or initiation process that we had, which made it an excellent time to introduce me back into the fold.

Parker cleared his throat, and I knew that the time had come. The crowd in the room followed his gaze and all eyes were now on me. The shift in the room was palpable. The murmurs that filled the room stopped. It was quiet enough to hear my footsteps as I walked up to the front of the room.

Parker's lips twitched slightly before he said, "Welcome back."

I shook Parker's hand and gave him a slight nod. I also shook Ioan's hand before turning to speak to Parker.

"It's good to be back." And I meant it.

Parker's eyes studied mine for a moment, and I made sure not to give anything away. I trusted him the most out of everyone else in this room, but that wasn't saying much. We shared a mostly cordial relationship with an emphasis on maintaining the equilibrium that the Chevaliers had in the state. There was always the opportunity to go for more, to boost our standing, but once you'd reached a certain limit, there were no external competitions.

The various mafia families and other organizations in New York had nothing on the Chevaliers. They might say differently, but we knew the truth. If all of the families joined up to come at us, then maybe they would have a shot. The chances of that happening, especially with the way things were right now, were slim to none.

I turned and faced everyone else in the room. Their eyes were trained on Parker, Ioan, and me.

Parker broke the silence. "As I said, we are well aware of the threats that are being thrown at our organization and now that we are fully staffed again, we are more than equipped to contain any challenge."

I nodded, agreeing with him entirely. We were prepared for anything and everything and no one here needed to worry about anything less.

Parker answered a few more questions before dismissing everyone in the room. Instead of leaving with the crowd, I stayed behind, choosing to wait until Parker finished talking to the stragglers who'd wanted to speak with him after the meeting. A couple of the newer people to join the New York City chapter looked at me warily.

I didn't recognize them, but it was obvious that they knew

who I was. I heard one of them mumble my name under his breath. It made me fight back a grin because my reputation preceded me.

Excellent.

"Grant."

I turned my head to look at Ioan. "If there is anything I can do to help with your transition back into your role, let me know."

"Thanks. I appreciate it."

Ioan stood there for a second longer than necessary, before he, too, left the room.

Parker quickly wrapped up the conversations and answered the questions that were asked of him. Once we were alone, he grabbed his papers and stuffed them into his briefcase more haphazardly than I expected.

"Everything okay with you?"

My question was met with silence. I cleared my throat and Parker looked up at me.

"Sorry. Yes, everything is fine."

"Doesn't seem that way."

Parker shrugged. "Every job has its ups and downs."

I couldn't argue with him about that. "Fill me in."

"Just like old times?"

There was a slight spark in his words. Although he wouldn't admit it out loud, I knew that he missed me being around more. Being on the top of the Chevaliers was a lonely job and many of the things you knew, you couldn't share. Some of those things he did end up sharing with me and a select few others eased the burden, but I knew there was a lot I didn't know.

I preferred it that way. The less I knew, the better it was, especially when it came to the instances when I needed to protect the interests of the Chevaliers... by any means necessary.

I stared down at his watch and tilted my head slightly. "Another new watch?"

Parker stopped his movements and slowly turned to face me. "Have you been tracking me?"

I shrugged my shoulders. "Or maybe I have an excellent memory."

Parker's eyes shot to the ceiling before closing. I watched as he tried to calm himself down while I tried to control the urge to smirk.

When Parker finally looked at me again, he said, "I'm happy that you're on my team and just choose to fuck with me, instead of being a part of one of your jobs."

"I'll take that as a compliment."

"As you should."

I crossed my foot over the other and leaned against the wall. "If you do truly want to know, I saw you, Ace Bolton, and Kingston Cross together."

Parker nodded. "Ah. I was meeting with them to discuss... some matters pertaining to the Chevaliers at Brentson University."

"I'm surprised Ace isn't here tonight. Do you have him doing something else?"

He shrugged but chose not to elaborate and I didn't push him for more information. I was only mildly curious, but if it had nothing to do with the work I needed to do for our organization, it didn't matter to me.

"You were wearing a watch with a dark green wristband with gold accents and that isn't the same watch you're wearing now." I gestured to his left wrist with what looked to be a watch with a black wristband. I wasn't completely sure given the lack of light in the room though.

Parker's gaze narrowed. "I'm not going to ask how you saw my wrist from wherever you were standing. Your attention to detail is impeccable."

"It's a lovely trait to have."

"Does that help you when deciding what art pieces you want to add to your collection?"

Although his question slightly surprised me, he had a good point. My attention to detail did help me select the art pieces that I liked and pick out the ones that would be coming home with me.

Parker grabbed his bag and walked toward the entrance of the room, and I was by his side in a flash. He opened the door and gestured for me to go first, but I shook my head and held the door for him instead.

Once we'd walked through the house and arrived back at the front door, the guard standing at the door looked at us and his eyes widened. I got a small sense of satisfaction from his fear as his eyes jumped between Parker and me.

He quickly opened the door and turned his head to stare at the ground. As we left the building, he refused to look us in the eye again.

Parker didn't say a word, but he didn't have to. I knew he noticed the weirdness that occurred between the guard and me though.

As we walked to the small parking lot where our cars were located, the crowd that had been inside of the Chevalier Manor had dispersed and we were left with students wandering around, going to who knows where.

"You know if you want to..."

Parker's voice faded to the background as my eyes landed on a student walking toward me. With nothing but the reflection of the streetlights on the angles of her face, I could see that she was stunning. Her dark hair was up in a ponytail and her clothes shouted that she was a student at Westwick. There was no doubt that she was at least a decade younger than me, probably more.

I continued to stare at her, willing her to look up at me. But she didn't. She was so engrossed in telling whoever was on the other end of the phone about her laptop, that she wasn't paying attention to anyone or anything else. I could see the scene that was about to unfold in front of me. Although I had plenty of time to move out of the way, something within me refused. And what I'd predicted in my mind happened in real time.

"Oof," she said right after we made an impact. I could hear whoever she was talking to yelling on the other end of the phone.

My hands landed on her forearms as I tried to steady her. Her body grew rigid at my touch. Her eyes remained closed for longer than required and I wondered if she'd hurt herself when we collided. Her eyes sprung open, and I watched as she stared at my chest before slowly tilting her head up so that I could get a good look at her face.

I found myself searching every inch of her face. I could see that her eyes were a lighter shade, potentially blue, but it was too dark to confirm their color. They also showed some tiredness in them, and I thought about what could be the cause. I didn't think classes had started yet, so was it school related?

Her skin appeared to be in between fair and olive, but the light from the streetlamp might have been deceptive. What I did know was that it all looked familiar. Too familiar, including the haunted look that pierced through her gaze. After I'd had my fill, my eyes zeroed in on her lips that now formed the shape of the letter 'O.'

What I wouldn't give to bite that piece of flesh. When a small sound left her mouth, my thoughts cleared, and my gaze narrowed.

"Watch yourself. Would hate to see you get hurt." My words were low with a sarcastic bite. I wasn't sure if she'd heard me. I looked at Parker briefly, who was taking in the entire exchange, but his face didn't indicate how he felt.

It became obvious that she did in fact hear me and she seemed to be caught off guard. It didn't take her long to recover. "I obviously didn't mean to run into you. There is no need to be a dick."

She seemed more shocked by the words that came out of her mouth than I was. But even with the accusatory tone her voice took on, I noticed she hadn't made any moves to remove my hands, which were still on her arms.

Interesting.

I didn't speak for a second, and the only sound between the two of us was her friend yelling her name in an attempt to make sure that she was okay. It also answered one of the questions I'd had in relation to her.

Iris. Her name was Iris.

"Heed my warning." My comment was as much for her as it was for me because our minor interaction had caused a tangled web of thoughts for me.

Love at first sight? Didn't exist.

But this, this was something else entirely. And I was determined to explore it.

I removed my hands from her arms and let her go. As I walked around her, the back of my hand touched hers. The spark I felt as our hands touched told me all I needed to know.

The only thing I wanted was her. And I'd made a promise to myself that I would always get what I wanted.

4

IRIS

I gritted my teeth as a low rumble threatened to leave my throat. If anyone could see what I was doing right now, they wouldn't know what to think.

"You son of a—"

I cut my own words off as it took every ounce of control to not snap on my laptop. It was an older model but had done well for me up until now. While I'd been trying to download my syllabus for the Principles of Marketing, it decided that now would be the perfect time to freeze on me.

The device would give me a moment of reprieve and then it would freeze again, keeping me in a cycle of hope and despair. Was it fucking with me because it knew that I'd been daydreaming about purchasing a brand-new laptop that I couldn't actually afford just weeks ago?

At least this wasn't the worst time for it to happen. It could have pulled this when I needed to take a test online or was writing a paper that I hadn't saved in a while. So, I should be thankful for that.

I kind of was. But still, it was a huge inconvenience, one I didn't want to have.

I'd spent most of the last hour trying to slowly prepare for classes while browsing the internet for things that could distract me from doing what I should have been doing. I chalked it up to the little adventure I took on my morning jog scaring the productivity for the day out of me, and now all my brain had enough energy to do was small tasks or zone out into space. Thankfully, there hadn't been anything really important that I needed to do today or else I would have been fucked.

When my stomach growled, I finally gave up on what I was trying to do. It must have been the universe's way of saying quit while you're ahead, even though I felt like I was on a slow descent into hell.

I stretched, lifting my arms above my head as I did so. I needed to get some food quickly. It would be more of a hassle to drive somewhere and pick something up than going to grab something on campus. But could I make it there in time?

My gaze flew to the clock on my laptop before I did a double take and rolled my eyes. Was it really that late? I wasn't sure if the time was frozen on it too. I grabbed my phone and saw that it was indeed as late as I feared, which meant I only had about twenty minutes to get to the food court and grab something before it closed for the night.

I snatched my black hoodie with Westwick University written across the front off my bed, and threw it on over the t-shirt I was wearing. That would hopefully be enough to keep me warm.

I grabbed my wallet, shoes, and phone as I slipped into my sneakers. Taking the time to undo my shoelaces was out of the question. I quickly locked my door behind me before nearly running out into the hallway. Our dining hall was about a seven-minute walk from Payne Hall so every moment was precious.

As I walked down the stairs, I spotted Payne's statue. Eddison Payne was one of the official founders of the Chevaliers. He, Theodore Cyrus, and Otto Frederick had crafted the secret society. All of the members, those alive and dead, had taken an oath to support the good of this organization. In return, members reaped the benefits of all, especially monetarily. While Brentson University was the birthplace of the first Chevalier collegiate chapter, Westwick was home to the second.

And how did I know all of this?

Most of the tales of Chevaliers were not known to the general public, which was obviously the box I should fall into. What made me different was that I'd had stories told to me and letters that had been passed down for generations that filled me in on some of the goings on. Now, while I trusted my ancestors, it wouldn't surprise me if parts of the story had been changed and that was just one of the reasons I was determined to find the truth.

Because my great-great-great-great grandmother, Margaret Turner, should have been listed as a founding member of the Chevaliers right along with Eddison Payne, Theodore Cyrus, and Otto Frederick.

That fact would change the Chevaliers as we knew it. We would have a claim to the same protections that were given to descendants of the founders. The Chevaliers wouldn't call us liars and do what they could to punish us for speaking out. Some things were more subtle than others, but the punishments were still being enacted all the same. My family members who'd also attended and graduated from Westwick had tried to do the same, with little to no success. I needed to show, beyond a doubt, that everyone who called us liars and who did everything in their power to discredit us was full of shit.

It would also call into question why women weren't allowed to go through the process of becoming full-fledged members of the secret society. Not that this shouldn't have been called out long before now. It would bring forth many of the lies that were told to keep women from joining. These were just a couple of reasons why I was highly invested in finding anything that might change the narrative with one of the most powerful organizations in the world.

Now, it was up to me. Nothing was going to stop me from proving that we'd been right all of this time and that we deserved, at minimum, an apology among other things.

A brisk breeze greeted me when I walked out of my dorm, and I shivered slightly. My hoodie was doing a lot of the heavy lifting to keep me warm, but I was still chilly.

That gave me even more incentive to get to our food hall as quickly as possible. With my attention completely on getting the food that my stomach so desperately needed, I jumped about a foot in the air when my phone rang.

I pulled the phone out of my pocket and glanced down at the screen. I read over the name that appeared twice before putting the phone to my ear.

"Hey."

"Hey yourself."

"I'm shocked you called me," I said as I stuffed my other hand in the front pocket of my hoodie. It brushed up against my wallet and keys, which I'd haphazardly placed in there, so it made them easier to carry.

Bianca Henson, my best friend of two years, and I mostly communicated by text message because neither one of us liked talking to anyone on the phone. It was something that we quickly got into the habit of doing after we exchanged phone numbers during a summer camp we both briefly attended. I usually saved my phone calls for Gran because she wasn't huge on texting and sometimes it was easier for both of us just to talk versus type.

"Decided to do something different. Are you settled in at Westwick?"

It was then I realized that I hadn't reached out to Bianca since I'd been back on campus. I could blame myself and think that I'm a shitty friend, but with everything going on and being super busy, contacting anyone had been the last thing on my mind.

I hadn't told Bianca much about what I'd hoped to accomplish when it came to clearing my family's name. Of course, she knew some things about it, given how involved her family was with the Chevaliers, but I tended to avoid mentioning it at all costs because, as much as it pained me to say, I didn't trust her with this. She knew things I hadn't told anyone else, but this matter I kept close to the chest.

I sighed as I picked up my pace. "Yeah. Well, things could be better, but I won't complain too much. Heading to grab some food before everything shuts down."

"Spill. Do I need a glass of wine?"

I scoffed. "No. You shouldn't be drinking alcohol anyway."

I said it in a teasing tone, but I was somewhat concerned about her. Yes, I knew that, as college students, we did drink, but I noticed at the end of last year, she'd started drinking more heavily at parties or mentioned alcohol more. I didn't know everything that she was doing because we didn't go to the same school, nor did I live with her.

None of that meant I wasn't concerned about her well-being.

"Never stopped me anyway. I won't get anything, but you're not getting out of this. Tell me what's up."

I could hear her fiddling around with something in the background and I wondered if she was settling in for me to tell her a story. If she could have, I'm sure she would have popped some popcorn to eat on the side too.

"It's nothing that serious. My laptop is being a pain in the ass and I'm hoping that doesn't mean that it's going to die soon or need to be repaired. It's not under warranty anymore and I can only imagine how much it would cost. It would definitely make things tighter for me unless I got a job in town or on campus."

"Ouch. Hopefully it's just a one-time thing and not a sign of things to come."

I could hear it in her voice. Bianca wanted to offer to buy me a new laptop, but she knew I would be offended if she did. I'd worked my ass off to get here and I had several scholarships that helped make this college more affordable for Gran and me.

Gran helped where she could, but with her living on a fixed income, I didn't want to burden her further. She deserved for this to be her golden years and for her not to be worried about how much money she had or if she would need to drastically cut the things she needed in order to make ends meet.

"I'm sure everything will be—"

My words died on my lips because I walked into something hard. It didn't feel quite like a brick wall, but the impact had shaken me up.

"Oof," I said right after I walked into whatever it was. Opening my eyes was the last thing on my mind because I was worried about what I might find if I did. Walking into something was embarrassing enough and although nighttime had fallen, there were still some people walking around and the potential for someone seeing me do what I did was high.

Fuck.

I was wobbly for a split second before and not opening my eyes made it worse. I could hear Bianca talking on the other line, asking me if everything was okay because I'd stop talking mid-sentence. As I was trying to decide what to do next, I felt something grab a hold of my arms. That was enough for me to force my eyes open.

I found myself staring into a dark colored coat. Had I really been so caught up in my conversation with Bianca that I didn't realize that there was a person in front of me? How trapped up in my own head had I been?

I could feel his gaze on me and the heavy weight of it all made me timid in a way I'd never felt before.

My eyes slowly made their way from the person's chest up to the person's face. If I thought I had any chance of getting out of this situation without wanting to melt into a puddle on the floor, all thoughts of that had vanished now.

The first thing that called out to me was that he was older. While there were students who weren't in their late teens to early twenties here, he looked out of place. From what I could see of this guy's face, his features were like he'd walked straight off of a magazine cover, but there was no way he could entice anyone to buy what he was selling. Between his piercing gaze and the eerie aura that surrounded him, fear—not joy—filled my emotions.

My mind was telling me to get away from him as quickly as possible, but it was as if I was frozen in place. I was too busy staring at him and he seemed just as engrossed by me.

It was odd for me. While I'd gotten attention from boys in high school and my freshmen year, nothing compared to this.

He didn't blink as he studied every inch of my face. It was as if he wanted to commit all of it to memory. What he was doing was unnerving and should have made me want to run away in hopes of never seeing the man in front of me again. When he looked at my lips for several seconds too long, I gasped, and his eyes shot up to mine. It was as if he'd been caught in a haze and had just woken up.

But now he was glaring at me, and I wasn't sure if it was the quick shift in his mood or our bodies slamming into each other that made me dizzy. I wanted to apologize because I assumed I was at fault due to my not paying attention, but before I could get the words out, he spoke first.

"Watch yourself. Would hate to see you get hurt."

The deepness of his voice made my cheeks hot, but because his words were soft, I questioned whether I'd heard him correctly. When I realized that I had, it crushed any fantasies my brain wanted to conjure up. It was as if I'd been splashed with ice cold water as a prank, and my reaction was to strike back as quickly as possible.

"I obviously didn't mean to run into you. There is no need to be a dick." Did I mean to say that? Not really, but I meant every word. I'd made a promise to myself that I would do more speaking up, especially when I knew that something was uncalled for. He wasn't going to get away with being rude to me.

"Heed my warning."

Did people say heed anymore? This time, I was stunned into silence as I replayed those three words on repeat in my head.

The man in front of me dropped his hands and shifted his body slightly so that he could walk around me. As he walked away from me, our hands touched slightly, and I jerked my hand in response. I couldn't help but turn to watch him. It was then that I noticed that he wasn't alone. Another guy was standing a few feet away, to my left. Neither one turned around to look back at me as I stared at them.

What the hell were these men doing hanging around a college campus? A thousand thoughts ran through my mind about why they might be here before Bianca's yell brought me out of whatever stupor this guy had put me in.

"Iris!"

"Hey, yeah. I'm here."

"What the hell happened? Your voice was muffled, and I couldn't tell what was going on."

I felt bad about making Bianca worry. "I ran into someone because I zoned out while I was talking to you."

The sigh that left Bianca's lips was comical and would have made me chuckle if it were any other time. But I was still reeling from my encounter with the creep. Speaking of, both men walked to a dark sedan and the guy I hadn't spoken to got in.

The jerk that talked to me took one final glance at me

before walking away, into the shadows where I assumed he came from. It was odd that he didn't have a car, but that wasn't my concern.

All that I could hope for was that he would never appear on Westwick's campus again. Or that he had a one-way ticket to hell.

"You would do that," Bianca said.

Her voice broke me out of the trance I'd briefly been put in once more. However, this time, I turned around and began to walk even faster. This distraction had made me even later, and I needed to get to the dining hall as soon as possible. Thankfully, I wasn't too far away, and I should have several minutes to spare.

"Anyway, what were we talking about?"

"I don't remember." Bianca let out a yawn before she continued. "I think my panicking made me tired."

This time I did crack a small smile. "Or you were already tired. It is kind of late."

"True, but I'll stay on the phone with you until you get back to your room."

I had planned on asking her if we could talk until I was back at Payne, so I was beyond glad that she offered. Although I didn't want to admit it to myself, let alone anyone else, the encounter I'd just had left me a little weirded out.

"Thanks. Now tell me what's new with you."

As Bianca began to tell me about what had happened at Brentson, I couldn't help but hope that I would never see that prick again.

5

IRIS

The morning after next, I felt around for my phone to turn off my alarm that was currently blaring. It was the first day of class and I wasn't too proud to admit that I was nervous.

But at least the sun was out; a complete one-eighty from what I'd experienced over the last few days. Ever since I'd moved back to Westwick, the weather had been somewhat dreary, and it had gotten to the point where I wondered if it was a bad omen.

Maybe I was wrong.

I glanced at my phone again to confirm that I had about an hour before class. That would give me plenty of time to get dressed and be out the door on time.

Instead of focusing on pulling myself together, I walked over to the desk in my room and pressed a key to take my computer out of sleep mode. But nothing appeared on the screen.

I pressed another key to see if that would cause a change, but I was greeted with the same result.

"This can't be happening," I mumbled to myself. I held down the power button and said a silent prayer, but I still got nothing.

I held back all of the curse words that threatened to roll off my tongue. After I'd gotten back to my room and hung up with Bianca, I didn't bother with my computer in hopes that, maybe if I left it alone, it would magically fix itself. I was convinced the device was openly mocking me at this point.

I ran a hand through my bed hair and the urge to pull hard on my strands was real. After all, it would temporarily take away the frustration I felt about my laptop giving me problems.

This was something I didn't have time to deal with. I'd already planned on bringing a pen and notebook to class, so not having to bring my laptop would free up some space physically, but mentally I would be thinking about the damn thing until I found a solution.

I didn't have enough money to buy one outright. Would it be possible to get a payment plan or something that would allow me to pay for a new computer over time? Or maybe Westwick had some type of program where I could buy a new or refurbished laptop to get me through classes?

Add that to my never-ending to-do list.

For now, it looked as if I would be spending a lot of time working at the library. Not that it was a bad thing because, hopefully, that gave me a place where I could concentrate.

But I couldn't dwell on that now. I needed to get ready for class.

It didn't take me too long to shower, get dressed, and to quickly throw my things into my book bag. I dug around and found a pair of headphones. This morning I chose to listen to music instead of nature because the last thing I wanted or needed was to speak to anyone on the way to class.

Was that weird? Maybe, but I wasn't about to change now. With my headphones firmly planted in my ear and my book bag over one shoulder, I locked my door and left my dorm.

The walk to class went just how I planned, with me not having to talk to anyone. I did acknowledge a couple of people that I recognized with a small nod, but other than that, I refused to be bothered.

I was a few minutes early to class, yet I still wasn't the first to arrive. I wasn't surprised to find that several people had also decided to be overachievers, but I was pretty sure that as the year went on, the likelihood of all of these people continuing to arrive early would diminish.

My first class of the semester was Principles of Marketing. This course was the one I was looking forward to most. I hoped it lived up to the expectations that I built for it in my head or else it would be a huge let down.

Professor Clyde Hamby was already standing at the front of the room, and he smiled at each student as they entered the classroom. He gave us a couple of minutes to get settled before he began class.

Professor Hamby walked us through the introduction of the class as well as the syllabus. I wasn't excited about the group projects he wanted us to do, but I would make do. I hated that I had to socialize with other people, but I was determined to do whatever it took to get a good grade.

Class went about as well as expected. I was still excited about what this course would bring. As soon as I walked out of class though, the only thing I could think about was what the hell I was going to do about my laptop.

The ringing of my phone jolted me out of my thoughts of despair. I pulled the device out of my book bag and stared at my screen for a second before I answered. I didn't recognize the number. The only thing I knew was that based on the area code, it seemed as if the person was from Westwick.

"Hello?" Confusion laced my voice, and I didn't bother trying to hide it.

"Is this Iris Bennington?"

A greeting would have been a nice way to start the conversation, but I didn't want to get into it because I didn't recognize the voice on the other end of the line. "It is. Who is asking?"

"My name is Sam and I work in the post office on campus. We have a package for you that you need to sign for."

"Are you sure you have the right person?" Embarrassment clouded my thoughts as the question left my lips. Heat rose up through my cheeks and I knew that I had to be blushing by now. Of course he had the right person. He'd said my name.

"Yes, this package is for you, and we want to get it to you as soon as possible. We left a package slip in your mailbox."

Okay...

"I'll be there in a few minutes." I disconnected the call before I could say something else that would embarrass me further.

Thankfully, my next class wasn't for a couple of hours, so I had plenty of time to head to the campus post office and grab whatever the package was. If I needed to drop it off at my room, I had enough time to do that too.

Anticipation began to build the closer I got to the post office. I wondered if Gran sent something as a surprise. It wouldn't be the first time she'd done so and getting gifts from her always made my days better. But I never remembered getting something that required a signature for me to pick it up.

What the heck could it be?

My question would soon be answered, and I walked toward the wall where all of the student mailboxes were located. I found my number and fished my keys out of my bag. Once I had my mailbox open, I found a white envelope and the mail slip that Sam mentioned.

On the way to the front desk to pick up my package, I opened the envelope and found a sweet card and message from Gran.

> *Iris,*
> *I hope your first day of classes has gone well.*
> *Call me when you have a chance.*
>
> *Love always,*
> *Gran*

Her note was so sweet, but not completely unexpected. She'd sent me a card for the first day of classes last year and throughout my freshman year. Sometimes they were themed, and other times they were just cards that she would send randomly to let me know that she was thinking of me.

But there was no mention of a package, which led me to believe that it wasn't from Gran. The only other person I thought it might be from was Bianca, but she usually didn't send surprises. Instead, she would randomly drive to Westwick so that we could hang out in person instead of just communicating through text or talking on the phone.

I stuffed the card into my bag and, with the package slip in my hand, I walked around the corner to the package pick-up window, but there was no one there. I waited a second to see if anyone would materialize, but no one did.

Although it made me want to cringe, I rang the small silver bell on the counter. I felt awkward having to summon someone, but I didn't want to waste any more time.

A guy came out from behind several rows of stacked card-board boxes. His blond hair was slightly in his face and, as if he knew I was thinking about it, he swept it to the side. He had to be around my age, so it was easy to assume that he was a student at Westwick as well. I could feel his eyes on me as he walked closer, and I tucked a piece of hair behind my ear as I waited for him to approach.

"How may I help you?" he asked, as he leaned forward on his elbows and gave me his full and undivided attention.

"Uh..." I said, suddenly feeling unsure about myself. I wasn't sure if that was due to him staring at me or being concerned about what this package was. With a deep breath, I was finally able to get the words out. "I received a phone call about me needing to sign for and pick up a package."

I put the package slip down on the counter and the guy picked it up.

"Ah, Iris. I'm Sam, the guy who called you. Your package is right here."

Sam checked something off on the piece of paper and put it to the side before walking away. I looked up and checked the time on the clock in the mailroom and saw that, while it felt like time was flying by, it hadn't been. In fact, not much time had passed at all.

When Sam came back into view, my mouth dropped open in shock. There was no way I was seeing what I thought I was seeing, right?

I waited for him to set the white, sleek box on the counter so that I could confirm what I was seeing. My eyes weren't seeing things. Unless someone was punking me, that box indicated that there was a brand-new laptop in there.

Sam gestured to the object between us. "See? This is why I had to call you."

I nodded my head slowly as I struggled to find the words to say. This couldn't be happening to me.

Sam pulled out a clipboard and said, "You just need to sign here on this line, and you'll be good to go."

I was able to comprehend what he said through the massive fog that was clouding my brain and scrawled my signature on the line he pointed to. It took more mental energy than it should have for me to grab the box and mumble a thank you before I walked away from the counter with the laptop clutched to my chest.

The walk back to my dorm passed by in a blur, and soon, I found myself locking my door behind me. I placed the box down on my desk, next to my defunct laptop, as if it were a newborn.

There were so many thoughts crashing through my mind at one time that it was hard to make sense of any of them. I didn't know what to react to first.

As if I were moving on autopilot, I grabbed the box, determined to unbox whatever was inside. I couldn't prevent the gasp that left my lips as I was able to confirm that the post office had been right to assume that there was something very expensive in this package.

This laptop looked to be top of the line and had to retail for thousands of dollars. I only knew because I'd looked at new computers a couple of weeks ago.

I stared at the device for way longer than necessary and I chalked it up to still being in shock. With a shaky hand, I reached out to touch the thin layer of styrofoam covering what I assumed was its cool surface. My brain was still trying to process what was going on in front of me and accept that this was actually real.

Normally, I would have been excited just to have a new laptop. However, I felt anything but because of the mysterious circumstances surrounding how I came to have this device. There was a boulder in my stomach, weighing me down.

If I'd thought my old laptop was messing with me before, I realized I was dead wrong. This new one had entered my life and had thrown my world off balance.

As if the puzzle pieces of my brain had finally clicked together, I grabbed my phone and called Bianca. When the call didn't immediately go to voicemail, the nerves in my body went into overdrive. Hopefully, she wasn't in class or busy doing something else that would prevent her from answering the phone.

When I heard her accept the call, the question that was sitting on the tip of my tongue tore through me before she could say hello. "Did you buy me a laptop and send it here?"

Bianca didn't respond and I didn't know whether that was a good thing or bad thing. What I did know was this did nothing but leave me in suspense.

"No, Iris. I didn't send you anything. What's going on?"

A piercing shiver shot through my body as I replayed her words over again in my mind. Deep down, I'd known she hadn't sent it. It was way too expensive if it was not refurbished and nothing I saw indicated that it was. However, that was the only lead I had.

If not Gran or Bianca, who had sent the laptop?

6

SOREN

The smell of firewood filled my nostrils as it provided one of two sources of light in my office. The sizzling and snapping coming from my stone fireplace were the only lively thing in this house at the moment. It also served as background noise that brought me solace. The only other sound was the clacking of keys as my fingers flew across the keyboard, determined to make sure that everything I wanted to find had been found.

The dinging of my email brought my attention away from the research I was doing. I hated being disturbed, but I was waiting for one very special email. It was the only reason I had the tab open. It was the only email that would be sent to this random email address anyway.

The small sound icon was slowly fading after alerting me that the ping had come from that tab, and I couldn't fight the grin as I clicked over to that page. My lips widened when I read the subject of the email.

Your Order Has Been Delivered.

Excellent. Now I needed to wait for her to collect the package. I intentionally hadn't tried to disguise the packaging that the laptop would be delivered in because I hoped that whatever employee was at the campus post office would realize just how valuable the package was and would call her immediately. It would only be a matter of time before I got the alert that she'd turned on the laptop and was setting the computer up to her liking.

What she didn't know was that, not only had I customized the device, but I made it easier for me to be able to virtually track every move she made. It was important for me to get to know her. The real her. Not the façade she chose to put on for the general public or to her classmates.

I pulled my hands away from the keyboard and my desk groaned as a result. Everything in this house made a noise one way or another. It had to be from the burden it carried due to the secrets it held.

I cracked each finger on both of my hands. The temporary pause in my research gave me time to think over the things I knew and how it all connected to a bigger picture.

Iris.

I could spend more time scouring for photos of her, but the image of her that I had from our meeting would forever be ingrained in my brain. My research over the last day or so was forming a profile on her. While there was so much I knew, there was also so much I didn't. The only way I was going to find out more was to get closer to her.

If I'd thought being back at Chevalier Manor had lit a spark within me, running into her had set my body ablaze. My cravings were insatiable when it came to finding out every last detail about her. Most people wouldn't understand, but that didn't concern me in the slightest. I would be relentless in my pursuit to know all of her secrets, no matter the cost or consequences.

The high-pitched ring of my office phone shattered any thoughts I was having of her. The first disturbance I'd been expecting. This one was a complete surprise, and I didn't appreciate it one bit.

When I saw who it was, I didn't hesitate to answer.

"Parker. To what do I owe this pleasure?"

"I have something I want you to look into for me. It shouldn't take up too much of your time and would be a great way to get back into the swing of things."

I didn't need to be eased back into anything. However, I was curious, but I needed more information. It wasn't often that Parker called on me, especially after what happened, so I couldn't help but wonder what this was about.

"Tell me more," I said as I got more comfortable in my office chair. The squeak that followed was annoying, but not irritating enough for me to buy a new one.

"The Turner family."

That wasn't exactly telling me more, but I'd allow it. I waited a beat to see if he would continue but he didn't. If this was a way for him to trigger my curiosity, he'd done his job.

"What about them?"

"An issue has come up."

That made me sit up, forcing another noise from the chair. Out of the corner of my eye, I saw something move near my bookcase, but when I looked over there, I didn't see a thing.

Same shit, different day.

I could have tried to convince myself that I'd imagined it, but it was a lie. This was what life was like in this house, and I'd come to terms with that.

I shifted my attention back to Parker's phone call. "You're being vague."

"That's by design. I wanted to make sure that you're in this and not about to half-ass it."

"When have I ever half-assed anything, Parker?" My question came out sterner than intended, but my frustration was becoming more apparent. He needed to spill what background information he had and what he needed me to do, so I could get off the phone and wrap my head around the problem and solve it.

"One of the Turner heirs has moved into Payne Hall. I suspect that wasn't a coincidence."

Given everything I knew about the Chevaliers and about that dorm, this wasn't by chance. No one who attended Westwick intentionally picked it as their dormitory.

At least, not when I'd attended. If that changed in the years since I was there, I'd be surprised.

"You think they're still passing down the story that Margaret Turner is one of the founders of this chapter of the Chevaliers?"

Parker wasted no time in answering me. "Over the years, we know the family has come up with one reason or another as to why they should be credited with creating the Chevaliers. I don't think they've, all of sudden, stopped with this newest generation."

"I couldn't agree more. So, you want me to track down the

heir and kill them?" That would take care of the problem immediately.

"That's a bit drastic. For now, I think you should just track her. If you notice anything suspicious, let me know. I trust your discretion."

"Her?" I shouldn't have automatically assumed that the person he was talking about was a man, but I had. Very much wrong on my part.

"Yes, her name is Iris Bennington. I'll send a photo of her once we get off the phone."

The entire world came to a halt. My body froze in place, stunned by his admission. I knew that Parker rarely made mistakes, but this had to be one. Or he was fucking with me because he knew that I'd just paid for her laptop. I'd known her name, but hadn't come across anything that had indicated that she was a part of the Turner family, yet.

Parker spoke, but it sounded as if he was far away. It took a moment for my brain to recalibrate and for me to piece together something to say.

Before I could utter a word, Parker spoke first. "Did you hear what I said?"

I cleared my throat and said, "I did. Loud and clear." My voice was unwavering and represented everything that I didn't feel right now.

I don't like surprises and I hadn't been expecting this.

I cleared my throat again, pushing any other thoughts I had about this arrangement to the side. "Is there anything else that we need to talk about in regard to this?"

"That was it. I'll send you her picture in a minute, and I want you to tell me everything you find out about her."

"You got it."

Parker paused before he said, "And if things get dicey, you know what you have to do."

He'd given me permission to take her out if need be. When this call had started, I was ready to get my hands dirty with a fresh kill. But once he'd told me who my target was, that changed everything.

What Parker didn't know was that I'd already done my research on her. What could be found about her online had been completed, making me already several steps ahead of him. However, there was always more to see, more to find. I intended on keeping that little detail to myself.

"Is there anything else you have for me?"

"No. As I said, this shouldn't take too long so let's wrap this up as quickly as possible."

"You got it." I placed the receiver back on its cradle and waited.

When my cellphone vibrated about a minute after Parker and I hung up, I knew what it was. A text message that would show Iris Bennington's face. I couldn't help but chuckle when I realized that it would have been just as easy for Parker to have called me on this phone versus calling me on the office one.

The notification forced my cellphone's screen to light up, providing another source of light in the room. I pushed back from my heavy wooden desk to give myself more room before grabbing the device.

My phone recognized it was me, and soon I saw a photo of Iris blown up on the screen. The darkness that surrounded her the night I met her had somewhat concealed her beauty, but this picture didn't fully capture it either. There was some-thing about watching her in motion that made her ethereal.

The night replayed over and over in my mind and I couldn't get enough.

But the stakes were a lot higher now.

And we were about to get to know each other a whole lot better.

7

IRIS

A heavy sigh left my lips as my hand cramped up once again. I tossed my pen down and flexed my fingers, trying to work out the stiffness. This was irritating and I knew there was an easy fix. My eyes darted between my notebook on my lap and the computer on my desk. It would be easier for me to take notes on a laptop than writing right now. I had a more than capable alternative waiting for me and it was only a few feet away.

Yet I'd been stubborn enough to carry on with what I was doing. I'd tried to ignore the pain, but it didn't work.

Although it was now after dinner, nothing I'd done in the last few hours had changed the way I felt about the laptop that was mysteriously sent to me. Even in the dull light that came from the small lamp in my room, the laptop felt as if it was imposing, a larger than life item that made everything shrink in comparison. It was still there, taunting me, because I knew how much easier things would be if I'd just use the fucking thing.

With a big huff, I flung my notebook, and it landed at the

end of my bed. It took no time for me to walk over to my desk, throw myself down in my hard wooden chair, and turn on the laptop. My nerves were wrecked as I went through the process of setting up the computer. It was pretty painless, if I had to be honest with myself, but not knowing who sent the computer weighed heavily on my mind.

I'd created different scenarios about how I'd come to be in possession of this expensive piece of equipment, but none of them made sense. When the laptop was finished updating and the setup was complete, I could feel myself start to feel giddy as mixed emotions swam through me. It was the first time since all of this happened that I'd felt excited about the prospect of having a new laptop to get me through my sophomore year, not to mention some of the extracurriculars I planned on doing. It was well worth whatever feelings I was having about how I'd come to have this thing.

The difference between my old computer and this one was night and day. Having something that worked quickly and smoothly was a huge change. It felt as if I'd been brought into the twenty-first century when I'd been operating in the nineteenth. Adjusting to this would take some time, but I was excited.

I opened up the web browser and began downloading the apps and programs that I would need for class. While I waited for the downloads to complete, I found myself researching more into Payne Hall, reading over many of the documents that I'd already found during previous searches before coming to live in the dorm.

Payne was rumored to have been intent on keeping records of everything. While I wasn't one hundred percent sure, I still felt confident that he would have written down who the original founders of the Chevaliers were. If I couldn't have access to any of their founding documents, this was the next best thing. Somehow and some way I would be able to prove Margaret Turner was involved in the founding of the Chevaliers.

I was so engrossed in what I was doing that I jumped when my ringtone went off. The sound was notifying me that someone had sent a text. When had I turned the volume on my phone up to full blast?

> Unknown Number: Did you like the present I sent to you?

I'd seen this all play out before. This was the beginning of how every person in a horror movie ended up stabbed in the throat and lying on the ground bleeding out. My reflexes took over and I immediately put my phone, screen side down, on my desk. Deciding to ignore it wasn't my finest hour, but this was where we were.

I didn't need an astrophysicist to tell me that this was the person who sent me the laptop. But would the creepiness factor with all of this outweigh my desire to know who the hell this was and how they got my number?

As if my phone knew it was the topic of my obsession as I wondered who was texting me, my ringtone rang again. I'd forgotten to adjust the volume, but this time, I'd been expecting it. I tapped my fingers on my desk as I debated with myself about whether I was going to read the message or not.

The common saying, "curiosity killed the cat" crept into my head before it began flashing like a warning sign. Everything about this was shouting a red flag, yet my fingers stopped tapping on the hard surface. I moved my hand to where it was now hovering over the phone, trembling slightly. My shaking could have been due to my position, but I was willing to bet it had more to do with what I might find in that text.

My heart pounded in my chest as I grabbed the phone and checked the notification. I released the breath I'd been holding when I read what the message said.

> Unknown Number: Was it not to your liking?

The message seemed innocent enough, but it wasn't just because of the manner in which I got the laptop. There was also the fact that I didn't know who this was.

My fingers flew across my phone's screen before I could stop them.

> Me: Do you make it a habit of sending expensive gifts to someone you don't know?

It wasn't my best comeback, but it was the best thing I could think of given the circumstances. My brain was still trying to recover from this delivery that ended up at my campus's mailroom for me.

> Unknown Number: I can spend my money however I choose, petal.

> Me: Who the fuck is this?

> Unknown Number: You'll soon find out.

> Me: The hell I will. I'm calling the police and consider yourself blocked.

I followed through with my threat and blocked the number, hoping that would be the end of it. But I still didn't know what the hell to do with the laptop in front of me.

Throwing it in the trash was ridiculous, but I wasn't comfortable with keeping it. My fingers threaded through my hair, and I pulled on it in frustration. What should I do? What could I do? I knew yanking my hair wasn't going to solve anything, but it did temporarily distract me enough that I wasn't thinking about the situation.

Would going to the police solve anything? The likelihood of anyone believing me or taking the time to research my claims was slim because they had more pressing things to investigate. Then again, having a record of what was occurring could be beneficial.

> Unknown Number: You won't like what will happen if you go to the police.

> Me: How many numbers do you have? I'm calling the police.

I exited out of my texting app to find the non-emergency number for the police. As I found it, my phone rang. I recognized the first three numbers and knew it was the asshole who sent me the laptop.

In another life, it would have been comical to be referring to someone who sent me an expensive laptop as an asshole, but nothing about this was remotely funny. I sent the call to voicemail and continued trying to make my phone call when my ringtone played again. If this person wanted to talk to me so bad, then so be it.

I answered the phone but didn't give the person on the

other end of the phone an opportunity to speak. "Listen here, fucker. You're going to leave me alone one way or another. I'm going to call the police and they're going to pay your ass a visit. Got it?"

"3621 Ely Garden. Centerview, New York."

The blood that flowed through me caused a frosty chill, making me feel as if my whole body had turned into a sheet of ice. I recognized the address before he finished saying it. It was my grandmother's. He'd recited it as if the words were etched in his memory or he'd written it down.

I wanted to believe this was a joke or a sick prank, but there was no way I had heard him incorrectly. More questions flew through my mind at a rapid pace. Had he been there before? How had he found her? We didn't share a last name because my mother took my father's when they married. A sickly feeling festered in my stomach, and I wished I hadn't answered the phone.

He already knew where I was, and now, he confirmed that he knew where Gran was. What the hell did he have planned and why was he doing all of this?

"Now that I have your attention, once again, you will not call or go to the police. I would hate to have to pay a visit to your grandmother. Understand?"

The first time he'd spoken, I was in shock that he'd known my grandmother's location. This time, I listened to his voice more closely. His voice was deep and menacing, his threat laced through every word he spoke. The promise of him taking away the most important and precious person in my life, without him thinking twice about it, was prominent. It was as if things were already set in motion and I couldn't do a thing to stop them. The whole thing pissed me off, but I was also disappointed in myself because he sounded familiar, and I couldn't place it.

"Do. You. Understand?"

It was easy to pick up on his irritation and his sternness. I needed to tread lightly. "Y-yes. I understand."

"Excellent. Now, did you like the laptop?"

His tone this time was softer, and if he hadn't just threatened my grandmother, I might feel differently. However, his asking me about the computer again made me feel disgusted, but I played it cool. "Yeah, it's great."

"Excellent, I hope you get a lot of use out of it," he said as his voice took on a lighter note. "I'll see you soon."

I heard three beeps on the other end of the line, signaling that he'd hung up the phone on me.

THE NEXT MORNING, I rushed out of my room like my ass was on fire. I was eager to find out more about this laptop and I needed to do it before I had to go to class.

It made more sense to wait until after I was done with class for the day, but today, I had a class that ended just as our tech department would be closing up shop, and I was too impatient to wait until tomorrow.

I was desperate for any information I could get, and I needed it now.

Uncertainty surrounded this whole situation as I didn't know what challenges I would face or how I should prepare myself. I had no idea what he wanted or why he'd chosen me. It felt as if I was a pawn in his game that I didn't know I was playing.

There was also a lingering question about whether I should go to the police or not. His threat against my grandmother had scared me to my core, but not going to the authorities left me with a bigger target on my back. I needed to make a decision, and soon.

Based on the voice on the phone yesterday, I thought I was looking for a man who didn't sound old but didn't sound like he was my age either. If I had to guess with the limited amount of information I had, I would think he was in his thirties or forties.

Nothing in the box had given away who sent it. I'd spent the rest of the evening going through the device to the best of my ability, looking for any files or applications that might provide a hint as to who the sender was. Heck, I was also trying to find out if some sort of tracker was available on the device as well. I turned off the laptop's location services so if I did lose it at some point, I was screwed.

All in all, it probably made more sense to throw the laptop out or try to trade it in. And maybe my laziness was winning out here, but I really wanted to keep this high-powered machine. After using it and performing multiple searches on it, I concluded what I already knew: it was light years ahead of my old computer.

The speed that it operated without lagging was much less frustrating. Being able to accomplish tasks quickly and efficiently was much less stressful. I had more confidence in this machine and trusted that it wouldn't randomly freeze, increasing the chances of me losing my work.

There was no way that I could give it up. Not now. Not ever.

"Iris?"

I paused just as I was about to open the door to walk out of Payne Hall. I turned and found Aria standing behind me. It was the first time I'd seen her since I moved in. Which, even with me not being the biggest fan of socializing, was strange. I hadn't been a hermit since I arrived, although I wanted to be, so I was surprised I hadn't run into her again.

"Is everything alright?"

"Um," I tried to think of a lie quickly. "Yes. I'm having issues with my computer and wanted to see if I could drop it off at IT Services before class."

"Oh, then I don't want to stop you."

"Thanks!" I said as I spun around and pushed the front door open. I wasn't sure how to end that conversation without it being awkward, so I continued on my way.

With my interaction with Aria pushed to the depths of my brain, all of my focus was on getting to IT Services. The walk to their building passed quickly, and I found myself standing at the front desk.

"What is it I can do for you?" The guy at the front desk asked the question without taking his eyes off of the computer screen in front of him. In spite of my current distress, I was mildly impressed that he was able to multitask this way.

"I'm hoping to have an antivirus software put on my laptop." The words fell out of my mouth in a jumbled mess. Throughout all of this time, I hadn't pieced together a reason for being here outside of me wanting them to do a deep dive into my computer and see if they could find the fucker that's stalking me, because I didn't want to give up the computer he bought me.

I mentally shook my head at myself because it didn't sound logical to me either.

"I can send you the link to download the antivirus software. I hate that you had to come all the way here for that."

Fuck. It was obvious that I wasn't prepared, and I didn't want to make the trip down here for nothing.

"I've been having trouble connecting to the campus's Wi-Fi too, so I didn't know if maybe I downloaded something I shouldn't have. Like a virus or malware."

I was throwing out every word I knew about computers in an effort to appeal to the student sitting here. Maybe it was the desperation in my voice that got his attention, or my shitty vocabulary when it came to tech terms, but he finally looked at me.

"I'll write up a ticket and take the computer. All I need you to do is leave your password for the laptop with us and check back around 4:45 p.m. We should be done working on it by then."

What were the odds that I might get my laptop back the same day? Probably almost zero, but I would take what I could get. "That would be great."

I did as I was told and found myself smiling as I left tech services. Even if I didn't find what I was looking for, at least I'd taken steps in the right direction.

Campus security wasn't far from where I was, and I debated for a second whether I should go there or not. When my feet started walking in the direction of their building instead of toward my next class, I knew I had my answer. Despite being terrified of what would happen to my grandmother and me, I needed to report this.

My walk was temporarily interrupted by my phone

vibrating. I snatched it from the pocket of my hoodie and saw that I had a new text.

> Bianca: Want to meet up at Beyond the Page this evening?

I smiled as I typed up my reply.

> Me: Give me a time and I'll be there. I have so much to fill you in on.

> Bianca: Excellent. I'll text you in about an hour.

I smiled to myself. Things were starting to slightly look up now and it was something I so desperately needed.

8

SOREN

Out of the corner of my eye, I could see the sun setting, radiating a warm, orangish glow. The sky decided that this wasn't enough and added pinkish clouds to the mix. It made the scene before me a fitting end to a picture-perfect movie, but this was anything but.

I was sitting in my Porsche Taycan in Brentson with only my thoughts to keep me company. There was a lot of power in silence. Many people couldn't stand to be alone with their thoughts, but it was where I thrived. It allowed me to focus and dissect every problem and solution that needed to be handled. That was why I enjoyed it.

Being by myself was always the goal. It allowed me to breathe without restriction. Not having to answer to anyone again was always in the back of my mind, given my upbringing. What people tended to have an issue with was having to be alone with one's own feelings. I could see how that would be frightening. It forced you to come to terms with things that you didn't want to face, but that wasn't a concern for me. I had nothing to fear when it came to my views, because I didn't have anything to be afraid of.

Not anymore. Because there was nothing else anyone could take from me.

Well, except this. My little secret.

I'd been staring out of my car window for the last thirty minutes and was more than willing to stay out here, in this exact same position, for as long as it took. My eyes refused to stray from the scene unfolding in front me. It was one of the most wholesome things I'd seen in my life.

There was plenty that I needed to do but sitting here and watching as Iris sat across from her friend, Bianca Henson, chatting and sipping from a mug, was something I didn't want to miss. This moment showed her in a completely different light.

This outing was obviously something she needed. The small smile on her lips, the lack of tension in her shoulders, were all signs that pointed to her being much calmer than earlier today. She looked relaxed and at ease, happy, as if the weight of the mission that had been bestowed on her wasn't something she was thinking about on a regular basis.

I knew she was. I could tell by tracking her every move on the new laptop I bought her. It was cute that she'd taken it to the campus's IT and had them digging around the computer. They were no match for the level of security I'd put on that device. This didn't mean that they were incompetent in their jobs, but the applications that had been installed on the computer were simply way out of their league.

If I had to guess, she was trying to find more information about the computer and, therefore, more information about how it was made and see if there was anything that linked back to the sender of the laptop. They didn't find a thing and they never would.

To be honest, I thought she would have tried to pawn or toss the computer out after our interaction on the phone, but I guessed she needed that laptop more than she let on. It was a huge convenience for her to be able to work from her room. I guessed the advantages of having this high-powered device outweighed any of the disadvantages.

That was fine by me.

I'd been contemplating what to do about her going to campus security and telling them all about me. It was a cute effort, a bold move I was willing to admit. But it was something she would pay for dearly.

I'd also debated with myself whether it would have been worth walking into the coffee shop and watching her up close. There were plenty of tables around and slipping in would have been easy. Sitting in my car won out because I wanted to give her some space to breathe, to feel safe. And then I would snatch that security blanket she'd created away, leaving her feeling vulnerable.

And that was exactly where I wanted her.

Iris rose from her seat as I leaned back into mine to get a better view of her. Her long brown hair cascaded down her shoulders. The dark blue jeans and black cardigan over a white t-shirt was different from what I was beginning to piece together as her normal wardrobe.

I'd seen her on campus this morning on the way to class, and she'd had on black leggings and a Westwick University hoodie. Iris hadn't bothered to look up or she would have seen me walking several feet behind her, watching her every move. I saw when she'd put her headphones in her ears, intent on ignoring the world around her. She checked her phone, I assume as a result of a text message or phone call being received, and soon she was typing away. I debated whether it was Bianca setting up tonight's outing, but I couldn't confirm because I hadn't been tracking her phone.

Yet.

She picked up the mug that she'd been drinking from and tipped the remaining liquid into her mouth. I assumed it was a cup of decaf coffee because she tended to not drink caffeine after four p.m. if she could avoid it.

The amount that I'd learned about her in such a short period of time would terrify most people, but I was determined. I would know everything there was to know about her, and I had extra motivation because I'd missed the part where she was connected to the family that continued to perpetuate the belief that they were heirs of an unnamed founder of the Chevaliers.

I wonder, given Bianca's connection to the Chevaliers, if Iris has come clean about what she was trying to do by living in Payne Hall this year?

The touch screen display in my car lit up, alerting me that someone was trying to call me. It was fitting that Parker's name appeared just as I was thinking about the Chevaliers. I was irritated that he was taking my attention away from watching Iris, but it must have been important if he was calling me. As I cleared my throat, I reached out to touch the screen, accepting the call.

"Yeah?"

"Why do you sound out of breath?"

"Rushing to the phone," I lied with ease. I didn't want to admit that I'd become breathless from staring at Iris. That was something I didn't want to admit to now or potentially ever.

"Ah, okay." Parker doubted my answer, but he probably wouldn't question it anyway.

"There's something I wanted to fill you in on about the Turner/Bennington case."

I sat up straighter as if that would help me hear Parker better. At least it gave me a better view of Iris. "I'm listening."

"You aren't the only one keeping tabs on Iris."

"Wait a minute. I haven't seen anyone suspicious around her since you told me to watch her."

It was true. I didn't have surveillance on her twenty-four seven, but when I was around her, I'd watched our surroundings. No one near her had been paying special attention to her, or I would have started doing my research on them.

"I should rephrase it. You aren't the only one who will be keeping tabs on her. Word on the street is that Finn Welch knows what she is trying to do, and they want her to succeed in finding Payne's documents because he plans on stealing it."

I'd heard of Finn Welch before, but I hadn't done any business with him. I wasn't a fan of his name being mentioned in the same sentence as Iris, let alone him tracking her.

"To do what with?"

"We haven't figured that out yet, but we know he and others have become very interested. One option is that selling anything related to our founding or secrets about our organization could be very lucrative."

It made sense, but I didn't respond. I let his comment

hang in the air as my gaze turned back to the woman sitting in the coffee shop before me.

My mission had shifted. The silence that I craved was about to be disturbed. I didn't want anything less than to hear each and every one of the people who wanted to come after Iris screaming bloody murder, wishing that I could just end it all right there right now. No one was going to touch a strand on her head as long as I was walking this Earth.

9

IRIS

My shallow breathing was all I could hear as I laid in silence. Terror had set in and made itself at home. I hadn't expected my feelings to go away, given that nothing was resolved, but the panic that sat in the pit of my stomach was almost debilitating.

Fear had tightened its hold on me and refused to let go.

This feeling wasn't unfamiliar. I'd had plenty of instances when my anxiety and depression had kicked in. Some occasions when it hit me were more prevalent than others. I hated when I would have an episode, but sometimes it was unavoidable. I'd hoped that my going to campus security, and their promises to work with local authorities as well as patrol around here more, would have settled the fear. It was still present, but not as bad as it had been several years ago.

The lowest I remember feeling was when I got the news that my parents weren't coming home. I remembered staring out the window of my childhood home on and off for days, hoping that the news I'd heard was false. I had been convinced my parents would be driving up to our home and parking in our driveway. That everything I'd been told about their deaths was a lie.

Because how could this be real? Why was this my reality now?

My hopes and dreams weren't answered. My parents were gone and sleep still escaped me.

The only light that filled my room came from the moon. The soft, white light casted an eerie glow over my room that was fitting for Payne Hall. I could say that the amount of light shining in through my large window was the reason I was staying awake, but I'd only be lying to myself.

The reason I was still awake was because I was scared. I was terrified but was justified in that feeling. My stalker's threat ran through my mind like a song on repeat. If anything happened to my grandmother I would be beside myself with grief. And if it happened because of me?

I wouldn't know what I would do with myself because she was all that I had left.

Dark thoughts had filled my mind after my parents' tragic death. Ending it all had been an option that I'd thought about taking. I wasn't sure what had made me not go through with it, but I was still here. And now I had to deal with a stalker who threatened me yet sent me expensive gifts.

My current predicament was the only thing I could think of. When I should be focused on my first week of classes, I was stuck thinking about how I'd stumbled into whatever this was.

Lying in bed did nothing to ease my worries. Not that I'd expected it to, but I hoped that need and the desire for sleep would have won, and I could forget about what happened for at least a fraction of a second.

But I couldn't sleep. No matter what I tried to do, sleep wouldn't come, and I was left staring at my ceiling, hoping that darkness would overcome me for the night.

Instead, I was replaying the text messages and phone conversation in my mind as if it were a music playlist I couldn't get enough of. Except I wanted to forget everything that had happened regarding this over the last few days and go back to the way things were before.

A dull ache formed on the lower left side of my stomach. It was a warning of what was to come if I couldn't keep my anxiety about this under control.

I closed my eyes once I'd gotten tired of staring up at a ceiling that I could only see due to the moonlight that was caressing it through my window. I took several deep breaths as I tried to calm myself down. Sometimes I could sleep through the pain if it wasn't that bad, but I had no idea if this incident would be similar to the others.

Too bad counting sheep or counting each dollar that my textbooks cost had failed me. I focused on what I could do to get this guy to leave me alone and relieve this ache that I felt.

The thought of bringing Bianca into this made my stomach turn. She had enough shit going on with her father's political career. It almost felt selfish to ask her, but I did know that she had familial connections that she might be able to call on for me. Perks of growing up in a family that did everything to make sure that they got, and maintained, power on the local level. It was only a matter of time before her father wanted to level up his political career. I was sure that his connection to the Chevaliers would probably make that dream a reality sooner rather than later.

My eyes sprung open as an idea populated in my mind. If I could prove that I was an heir of one of the founders of the Chevaliers, then maybe they would protect me from whoever my newfound stalker was.

I understood that this was a huge stretch because I didn't know what was going to happen once I revealed the truth. Hell, maybe I'd end up dead because of the secrets I would be unleashing into the world.

It would disturb the equilibrium that the Chevaliers created. Most people didn't know that the society existed, and maybe that was for the best. The power they held and could release at will was scary enough as it was, so there was a great chance that I would end up dead.

Those thoughts also forced fear into my veins. It would be easy for me to give up on what I wanted to find and choose not to unravel decades of secrets, but deep down, I knew that I would always regret that. So, I had no choice but to accept the consequences that would bear down on me as a result of what I found.

Because there was no way I was keeping quiet about any of this if I was given an opportunity.

When the pain didn't lessen, instead choosing to become sharper, I made a decision. Although I didn't want to, I slowly got out of bed and walked over to the top drawer of my dresser. I opened it quickly and took out the pill bottle I kept in there in case of emergencies. I emptied a pill into my hand and put the bottle back in its resting place for safe keeping. It took two steps for me to retrieve a water bottle that I'd had in my book bag, and I used it to aid in my taking of the pill.

It would take several minutes for the pill to take effect, but it was the right choice for me. I didn't like to take that pill often, but sometimes it was necessary. It would not only make the pain I was feeling go away, but it would also make me feel drowsy enough to fall asleep and that was something I was looking forward to.

I got back into bed and settled in under the covers. Of course, my brain was still spiraling, but all would be well in just a few minutes.

I almost jumped out of bed again because I couldn't recall if I'd set an alarm for tomorrow morning. It took a second for me to remember that I had. If I hadn't, the likelihood of me missing class increased exponentially, and that was the last thing I wanted.

I turned onto my side and pulled my covers up over my body. I closed my eyes again, determined that, this time, I would fall asleep. The urge to check the time was there, but I'd plugged my phone into an outlet near my desk. I'd done it to encourage myself to get out of bed in the morning because I suspected that I would have trouble sleeping.

Excellent prediction, Iris.

Turning my brain off was harder than I thought it would be, but exhaustion became my only thought. I could feel my eyelids growing heavy and soon the darkness welcomed me, and I was all too pleased to fully embrace it.

I could hear a faint sound but I couldn't make out what or where it was. Grogginess consumed me and confusion flooded my brain.

Was I awake? I couldn't be, right? There was no way that it was time to wake up yet.

When I heard the creaking of wood in the direction of my door, my doubts started to fade as consciousness came filtering back in. In my hazy state, the only thing I could think of in my room that was made of wood was the door-frame that encased my doorway. Was someone standing just outside my door?

I struggled to open my eyes because my eyelids weren't cooperating with me. Thankfully, my hands were, and I brought them to my face as I tried to wipe the sleep from my eyes. I knew that I was still groggy from not only sleep, but from the medicine I took.

When I was finally able to open them, I wiped my hair from my face, accidentally yanking on a strand. If I hadn't confirmed that I was awake before, the pain I briefly felt told me that I was. Thankfully, I didn't hear anything else, and now I was annoyed because I could have tried to fall back into a deep sleep. It took several moments before I could confirm that the sleepy haze I'd been in had now cleared.

I glanced around and it took me a second to realize that the moonlight that had been coming in through the window was nowhere to be found. I suspected a cloud was blocking the moon, making it almost pitch black in my room. That did little to soothe me.

All of my motions stopped when I heard something touch the doorknob. I hadn't been imagining it. Any semblance of sleep that I hoped to get was now out the window. There was someone standing outside of my door. Or maybe it was some*thing.*

I specifically remembered locking the door before I went

to bed, so someone was about to be in for a surprise when they realized that the door wouldn't open.

Or so I thought.

I heard the doorknob turn, and I knew I was in trouble. Whatever it was, I knew I didn't want to risk attempting to get to my phone which was sitting on my desk across the room.

There was no way I was going to be able to get around the person and there was a chance that someone might hear me scream or the ensuing scuffle, but could I rely on that to save me?

I moved my hands so that they were at my sides, and I did my best to slow my heartbeat, even though it felt as if it was beating one hundred miles a minute. Every second it took for this standstill to end, the harder it became to steady my heart rate.

Time slowed as I waited for what was to come next. I'd been worried about not having a light source due to the lack of moonlight, but I could use that to my advantage. Pretending to be asleep was the best option I had because I didn't know what was going to walk through that door.

Nothing could pry my gaze away from the door. I narrowed my eyes, in hopes that, if the person could see my face, they wouldn't know I was awake, watching their every move.

As I watched the door, it slowly opened, letting the dim light from the hallway into my room. I couldn't see much besides the silhouette of a large figure filling up my doorway. As loudly as I could hear my heart pounding in my ears, I was convinced that the person standing a few feet away could hear it too.

I held my breath as the person stepped into my room. I

wished that the moon would show itself, revealing the face that was concealed by the shadows.

Mother nature wasn't on my side because as the stranger took another step toward me, the moonlight remained hidden by the clouds. I slowly closed my eyes just in case my intruder got close enough to notice that I wasn't asleep.

With my eyesight gone, the rest of my senses kicked into overdrive. I could hear the person walking closer. I couldn't tell exactly what they were doing, but when I felt the lightness of his breath near my ear, I knew I'd been found out.

"I know you're awake." His voice sliced through the stillness in the air like a sword piercing through flesh. "Don't even attempt to scream for help. No one's going to come, anyway."

A chill traveled through my body because I recognized the voice immediately. It came as no surprise to me that this was the man who sent me the laptop and called me on the phone to confirm that I liked it, further stroking his own ego. It took every ounce of control for me not to react. I was going to maintain my "sleep" state for as long as possible. Not only was I afraid of addressing the stranger in my room, but remaining quiet just might save my life.

"Don't you know how to follow directions?"

The jig was up because I'd jerked hard at his words. My eyes sprung open as the hairs on my arm stood at attention. The puzzle pieces were starting to fall into place as I took in the man before me.

Although his face was still partially hidden, my memory was able to paint the picture of the man in front of me. I'd run into him the other night when I was rushing to get food before Westwick's dining hall closed for the evening.

I'd also been talking to Bianca about my laptop, which, if

he'd overheard me, made sense of how this expensive piece of equipment ended up in my mailbox so soon after my old one started acting up. What none of this explained was why.

Slowly, the moonlight that I currently had a love-hate relationship with was creeping out from behind a cloud, shining more light into my bedroom. When I could see more of his face, it was just as I'd imagined.

His dark wavy hair was perfectly styled as if he'd just done it. His eyes were darker than I'd imagined, and I couldn't help but wonder if they were black. The way he had no problem breaking and entering places that he shouldn't be in, as well as threatening to harm people who did nothing to him, made me think that his eyes were as dark as his soul.

I was so busy staring at him that I didn't notice that he'd moved his hand. He didn't say a word before he ran a finger across my neck. I flinched at his touch before I batted away his hand.

"Answer me. Or did you not understand what I said?"

I swallowed hard as I tried to piece together something to say. "I heard you and I know how to follow directions." My voice was barely above a whisper.

"Yet, you didn't listen."

"What do you mean I didn't listen?" The things he was saying didn't make any sense and I wasn't sure if it was because of the words coming out of his mouth or because I'd just woken up.

"You reported me to campus security."

How the hell did he know? I was stunned into silence. It shouldn't be public information. Unless he knew I'd done it because he'd been watching me.

"I could show you the photo I took outside of your grandmother's house this morning. She seems to be a lovely woman and I would hate to see her get hurt."

"Don't you fucking touch her." Tears welled up in my eyes and I hated myself for it. I dared any of them to betray me by falling because I didn't want him to see me cry.

He shrugged off my threat as if it didn't mean a thing. "I warned you not to say a word to the police and since the police will work with campus security about all of this"—he gestured between the both of us with his hand— "you clearly didn't listen. When I told you to watch yourself, what I was warning you was that you should be careful of one thing. Me."

Everything happened so fast. I saw a hint of silver as he grabbed one of the straps of my tank top and sliced the strap in half. He did the same thing with the other, baring my breasts to his hungry gaze. I gasped in surprise and wanted to yell, but my scream was caught in my throat.

I was afraid to feel the coolness of the blade that would soon turn to red heat because he'd planned on slicing my skin. But the feeling of him stabbing me never came.

Instead, I found myself watching him as he placed the blade on one of my nipples, staring at it as it pebbled up due to the chill in the air and of the blade. I wanted to fight back, but the risk of getting cut was too great. My stalker had the opposite reaction that I did, choosing to lick his lips at this exact moment.

"I've been waiting for what has felt like forever."

He dragged the tip of the blade to my other breast and gave it the same treatment. I was frozen in fear. I prayed to myself that someone would come by and see this. I might be embarrassed by the current state I was in, but it would be more than worth it to get him to stop. For now, all I could do was brace myself for the nightmare that would occur.

I held my breath as he removed the knife from my skin before he replaced it with his gloved finger. I could still see that he was holding the knife out of the corner of my eye, ripping the idea of screaming for help again from my brain. If I did, I had no doubts that he would slit my throat.

He didn't say another word as he removed the knife completely from my line of sight and it wasn't until I heard it touch the windowsill, that I felt comfortable with the idea of yelling for help. Then he rendered me speechless when he took my nipple into his mouth.

A moan left my lips, it took every ounce of control not to cover my mouth. I wasn't supposed to be enjoying this. This asshole was stalking me and threatening me and my grandmother.

Just as quickly as it started, he let my nipple drop out of his mouth with a loud pop.

A smirk appeared on his lips before he uttered, "See you soon, petal."

He left more quietly than he came, locking my door behind him. I expected a sense of relief to wash over me, but there was none to be found. I scrambled out of bed, grabbed my desk chair, and stuck it under the doorknob. Was it a fire hazard? Yes. But did it also make me feel more secure? Also yes.

I yanked open a drawer and removed the scraps of the tank top that were left and pulled a long-sleeved shirt on. I weighed whether I should keep the chair there or not before finally deciding to do so. Even if it didn't keep my stalker out, it would at least make a loud enough noise that would wake me up in case he did return.

I crawled back into bed. There was nothing but dread hitting me in every direction because the stranger who had no intention of leaving me alone, not only knew how easy it was to get me but knew how quickly I would respond to his touch.

10

IRIS

When my alarm went off the next morning, there was no need for it. The job that it was supposed to do was pointless because I never went back to sleep. My late-night visit had kept me up for hours, twisting and turning. I couldn't count how many times I replayed what happened in my mind. I'd debated calling Bianca and telling her what happened, but I refrained for fear that it would lead him to her.

The way he had no fear about making threats to human life, walked into my dormitory, opened my door, and touched me as if I was one of his possessions, increased my anxiety significantly. It was as if all of my nightmares had come together and manifested themselves within this man. What scared me more though was, deep down, I got the feeling that this had only just begun.

My thoughts swirled to the point that they were suffocating as more questions than answers were found. The next thing I knew, I was watching the sun creep up over the horizon, announcing that a new day had begun. And the last thing I wanted to do was get out of bed and go to class.

There was at least one thing on my side, however. As luck would have it, I only had one class today, and I figured I could half-ass it and then come back to my room and go to bed. Thankfully, there shouldn't be any quizzes today or else I'd truly be fucked.

Chances were that the asshole wouldn't try to come around here during the middle of the day. There were too many students and personnel wandering around, and he might draw attention to himself.

Then again, was that just me trying to hype myself up and create a false sense of security? When it all came down to it, would it stop him?

Yes, he'd chosen to break into my dormitory in the middle of the night but even then, there was a chance that someone was walking around and could have seen him. When he came inside, he didn't bother closing my door. Anyone could have looked in and saw what was happening, but he obviously hadn't cared.

Add that to the *shit that made me more afraid of this guy* column. But, if we came into contact with each other again, I wouldn't show any fear because I didn't want to show him any of my weaknesses. I didn't know what he would do with any of that knowledge, but whatever he would do, he would use it to his advantage.

I rubbed my eyes and slowly got out of bed. Deep down, I knew I should be moving faster, but my body was on autopilot. I threw on my hoodie and switched out my pajama pants for some black leggings. I used my fingers to do some sort of detangling job before quickly tossing my hair into a high ponytail. I called it a win when I looked only half asleep when I checked my face out in the camera on my phone.

I'd only have enough time to run to the bathroom and brush my teeth before I needed to be out the door to class. With a heavy sigh, I snatched my toothbrush and toothpaste off my dresser and dragged my tired body to the bathroom.

As I was brushing my teeth, I made plans for what I would do for the rest of the day. Homework needed to get started, but I also needed to get a move on trying to find the papers that Payne supposedly left behind.

I took a few extra seconds to splash water on my face and then wiped off the excess, waking me up temporarily. Rinsing off my toothbrush took a couple more seconds and I left the shared bathroom in a huff.

When I opened the door, a breeze followed me, causing a white piece of paper to blow across the room. I almost didn't notice it in my current state. I dropped my toothbrush off before I picked up the paper and my book bag for class. Even though I had no time, I skimmed the note because, thankfully, it was short.

> *Iris,*
> *I was hoping to grab lunch or something with you. Here's my phone number if you want to meet up:*
> *516-555-4834.*
>
> *Aria*

I grabbed my phone and stuffed it, and the note, in the front pocket of my hoodie. I told myself I'd deal with the message from Aria later and left my room without another glance.

As I walked to class, all I could think about was the note from Aria. It was as if that piece of paper was seared in my brain because I didn't know what to make of it. Sure, it could just be someone trying to be nice and make friends, but my paranoia had other thoughts. Why would she want to be friends with me? What was in this for her?

I should try to shove the thoughts I was having about Aria into a corner of my brain, but I chalked it up to my stalker forcing me to be on edge more than I'd ever been in my life. The trauma I'd suffered in my life was one thing. Although I'd wished for my parents to come back, deep down, I knew that there was no chance of that happening. The unknown with this situation was causing a different slew of emotions that I wasn't sure I was prepared to face. I was currently living my life in a panic state because I didn't know when my stalker would show up again.

The only thing I knew was that it was just a matter of time. If he was going through all of this to prove a point, he wasn't about to give up on it now. With that in mind, I looked around as I walked along, I found nothing of interest. No one was looking at me or even looking in my general direction for that matter. The streets were the same, nothing was different about the buildings on campus.

It felt... normal. I needed that.

Once I settled into the fact that no one was there to get me, the rest of my walk to class was uneventful. I felt as if I was running on autopilot. I barely remembered climbing the stairs up to the front doors to enter the building where this class was being held. Nothing out of the ordinary happened when I placed my bag down next to my desk and slid into the chair. When class began, I knew what was going to happen. Zoning out was definitely in my future, and if I could make it out of here without drawing attention to myself, it would be a miracle.

Throughout the whole class, I fought to keep my eyes open, choosing to focus on random spots in the room in an attempt to look engaged in the discussion that was going on. At this particular moment, I couldn't care less.

I wasn't sure how I avoided getting caught spacing out, but I did, because when my professor dismissed us, he hadn't said a word. To say I was grateful was an understatement. Maybe after the shit I went through last night, luck was now on my side. At the very least, it felt as if I was being granted a well-deserved break.

I was exhausted, but was able to pull together a final burst of energy that got me back to my dorm room. When I locked the door behind me, the only thing I bothered to do was drop my bag and take off my shoes. I climbed into my bed without another thought and fell asleep.

I HEARD a bang in the distance and my eyes popped open. My heart was rapidly beating. The slightly disoriented feeling that came about as a result of sleeping clouded my judgment. It took some time for me to realize where I was. I quickly took stock of the room I was in.

Sunlight was still shining in through my window. My desk was in the corner with both laptops sitting on it. My door was still closed which meant I didn't have any visitors.

Or they'd been kind enough to close the door behind them when leaving. I was grateful to find that I was still in my room.

But what had woken me up?

I didn't see anything out of place or that would give a hint as to what might have been the culprit. Chalking it up to someone dropping something in another room, I sat up in bed and stretched. I reached for my phone to check the time. My eyes widened when I realized just how much time had flown by.

The nap refreshed me more than I thought it would. I'd always felt groggy after a nap, but maybe the lack of sleep gave way for the two-hour nap I took to reinvigorate me. It was enough to energize me to take care of some of the things I knew I needed to do.

I shoved my body off my bed and walked over to my desk. There was still plenty of schoolwork I needed to do, but there was something I wanted to do first.

I took the piece of paper that had been burning a hole in my pocket since I received it this morning. I reread the note multiple times before I added the phone number to my phone and sent a text message.

> Me: Hey, Aria. It's me, Iris. Just wanted to send you a quick message so you had my number, and we can schedule time to hang out.

I put my phone on Do Not Disturb and turned it so that it was screen down on my desk. I still hesitated when I pressed a key on my new laptop and watched as its screen came to life. It took me some time, but I figured out how to find my old playlists that I used to listen to music. With that on, I opened my math textbook and set forth with doing what I assumed would be the hardest homework for me to do.

My brain didn't automatically connect with all of the rules and concepts in math and doing it first would mean getting it out of the way. I would be so happy when I was done with learning it and couldn't wait to say goodbye to math class forever.

But hoping and wishing wouldn't get my math homework done, so I settled down and got to work.

With all of my focus on my homework, it didn't take long for me to lose track of time. A loud knock on the door ended my concentration and forced me to jolt in my seat.

Who could that be?

Once again, I hadn't been expecting anyone and now this was the second unannounced visit in less than twenty-four hours.

"Who is it?" I asked, hoping that someone would respond. As my luck would have it, no one did.

As I stood up from my desk, I debated with myself how easy it would be for me to buy something I could use to protect myself. It was now obvious that security here wasn't top notch if someone had the ability to walk into my room without issue.

"Who is it?" I asked again, wondering if the person on the other side of the door heard me. But I still didn't get a response.

I crept up to the door with my phone and put my ear against it to see if I could hear anyone on the other side. Hearing nothing, I put my hand on the doorknob and turned.

There wasn't a person on the other side of the door, but there was something there.

Instead of a person standing there, there was a flower sitting in a pot. But it wasn't just any flower.

It was a yellow iris. It was obvious that it was a play on my name, but I knew that different colored irises meant different things. I brought the flower inside and placed it on my desk, before looking up what yellow irises meant again. It had been a while since I'd researched it.

When I saw that a yellow iris could be symbolic for a friendship or a deep relationship, I wasn't surprised. There was no note, but I knew exactly who it was from.

My stalker.

11

SOREN

One of my phones vibrated on my desk and before it could do it a second time, I threw my coat on. It was go-time, and I refused to delay myself further, so putting my coat on would save me a few seconds.

Not that there was much for me to prepare to do because I'd only been home for an hour. I'd been tending to more important matters like watching Iris from afar. I'd left her once I knew she was safely back in her dorm room and more than likely staying in for the night.

It had been days since I appeared in her room in the middle of the night. Over the last few days, I'd implemented some of the plans that I'd come up with to keep tabs on her. Some she might come across, but others would never be found and that was probably for the best. That, plus taking care of things at Grant Enterprises, made it easier to stay away from her.

Staying far away for now was my best bet. I wanted to lull her into a false sense of security. Making her think that I'd forgotten about her was intentional because, when I did show up, she'd be caught off guard. That was right where I wanted her. Not expecting a thing made her vulnerable and that's what I wanted her to be.

I checked the phone that I'd been using to track my first target to make sure that my assumption was right. And it was.

Finn Welch was home.

Thank fuck.

Sometimes patience was a key component of my job. It didn't matter if you were waiting for some evidence or a small tip that would help you connect the dots and find the motherfucker you were looking for.

The latter was what had happened tonight, but the time it took for that to happen hadn't been pretty.

I was used to getting what I wanted when I wanted it. Having to wait for people to do their jobs meant there was less work that I had to do, but sometimes the job wouldn't happen in a timely fashion. That was the hand I was dealt because there was something more important that I had to do. Watching Iris was, by far, the most important thing I had to do. Everything else came second, which meant that I had to employ someone to hunt down the first guy on my list.

Finn did a number of different jobs for various organizations in the city, some legal, some not. Rumor had it that he was searching for "the woman who could bring the Chevaliers to their knees" because having access to her would be worth a fortune on the black market. Especially to us because keeping Iris from finding anything related to Payne meant keeping the status quo within the Chevaliers.

I believed the rumors to be true. When you were on top, people would do anything to bring you down. And by taking him out, not only was I protecting Iris, but I was also taking out a threat against the Chevaliers.

A two-for-one special. I almost felt guilty about having such a deal. Almost.

I walked out of my office and into my foyer. No one greeted me in my foyer because there was no one here. I was the only occupant of this old creaky house and refused to hire staff because it wasn't a priority, not to mention, I preferred to be alone.

I opened my own door and locked it before I jogged down the stairs and walked to my Porsche. Within a couple of minutes, I was driving down my long, winding driveway and on my way to Finn's house.

The drive was fairly easy though his house was about an hour away from my own. None of the precautions I'd put in place with Iris had gone off, nor had I gotten any notifications from Finn's home alerting me that he'd left.

This was perfect.

I parked a distance away from Finn's home, choosing to walk as a way to avoid drawing attention to myself before I approached him. Although I didn't give a fuck about whether I surprised him or not because the result would be the same, I preferred to keep every advantage that I had.

After parking, I stepped out of my car and began walking toward Finn's estate. If this evening proved one thing, it was that fall was on its way. Outside of the noises created by the brisk breeze and the sounds of my shoes crushing leaves as I walked to my destination, I was surrounded by silence, just like I preferred.

Once again, instead of choosing to walk right up to Finn's front door, I walked around the perimeter of the house searching for an entrance point. My search didn't take long, and I found a side entrance that was open.

What were the odds that it would be this easy? I assumed this was open in case he'd locked himself out, which now worked to my advantage. I now had a way of getting in here, hopefully without drawing attention to myself.

During my initial research, I found a floor plan of the house. While I waited until Finn returned, I studied it, making note of where the primary rooms, including the primary bedroom and bathroom, were.

I slid inside the entrance and waited. I listened to see if I could hear which part of the house he was in so I knew where I needed to go. I recalled the map of the floor plan in my head and when I heard what sounded like a crash, I knew he was in the kitchen.

I silently walked up the stairs and leaned forward so that I could see into the kitchen. When I saw the fridge was open, I answered the only question in my mind.

While he was preoccupied, I snuck into the kitchen and found where all of the kitchen knives were. I turned my attention back to the man at hand and spoke. "Word on the street is that you're on the hunt for someone."

Finn flipped around and regarded me curiously, but there was no fear in his eyes. Yet. "Ah. Now it makes sense why you're here unannounced. Iris Bennington is looking for Chevalier shit and you don't want her to find it."

He said it with so much certainty that no one else would have doubted it. But I knew better. There was no way that was accurate. I'd been following her since I'd run into her and the most she'd done was some research into Payne. But I was interested in finding out more.

"Keep talking."

"Why should I? Wouldn't it be easier to take her rather than come all the way over here? After all, she's just a defenseless girl, unlike me."

He raised his shirt, showing off the gun at his waist. I clenched and unclenched my fists but made sure to keep my expression neutral. It was cute that he thought that was going to stop me. He also underestimated me, and that would be his downfall.

"What do you know about her?"

"Asking me when you have all the resources that you and the Chevaliers could buy is rich."

I took a step toward him. "Something or someone told you about her and I want to know why. Then we can focus on who is spearheading this. After that? I want to know who else is after her, because I know you're not the only one."

Finn gritted his teeth in anger. "You think you're running shit in my house? You're on my turf now! Has all the time you spent in your house since Eden was murdered—"

I took another step forward, this time drawing my pistol and pointing it directly at Finn's head. "Watch where the fuck you're going with this. Trust me, this isn't the road you want to travel down."

I hadn't intended on pulling my weapon, but I refused to have that moment let me down. I'd already decided that he wasn't going to be able to take the easy way out of this before I'd arrived, and I wouldn't miss the chance now to make him suffer, especially after the comment he made about Eden.

His punishment would be even more heinous now and my excitement about it threatened to bubble up to the surface. He wasn't prepared for what I was about to do, and I reveled in that fact.

Finn thought I pulled my gun out as a warning, but that wasn't the case. I'd shown it to him in order to tease him. He was going to wish that I'd used my gun to take him out, but I refused to give him what he wanted.

"You're not going to do shit." Finn pulled out his gun too and I let him. It would have been easy for me to shoot him in a limb to halt his movements, but this would be more fun.

Doubting what I would and wouldn't do was the second mistake he made. The first? Turning his focus on Iris because he wanted to be seen as the top man in the area. That was when he became nothing but a dead man living on borrowed time.

"Put the gun down," I said calmly. I felt every bit of that tranquility too because I knew how this was going to end.

When I saw the slight shake in the hand that was aiming the gun at me, I knew his nerves were getting to him. If he was planning on shooting at me, he better not miss. The smarter decision would be to put the gun down and cooperate. He would still end up dead, but I would at least let him die with some dignity.

That thought fled my mind when a loud bang bounced off of every wall in this room.

Finn took the shot but didn't have the outcome he expected. His eyes widened when he realized he put too much faith in himself and missed. The bullet was lodged somewhere, probably in the wall behind me, but I remained unscathed.

"Is this really how you want to go out?" I was genuinely

curious because this seemed to be a fool's errand. A smirk played on my lips as I said, "It's my turn."

Finn was shaking like a leaf as I took my shot. I hit my intended target. Finn's wrist.

When he dropped the gun and doubled over in pain, I kicked his gun out of the way and put mine away while approaching him. I unzipped my coat, letting it hang open, so I had easy access to several of the other weapons I'd brought with me that I hadn't had the opportunity to play with.

"Now, are you going to give me the answers I want, or are you going to make this more difficult on yourself?"

"Fuck... you," he said as he winced, trying to breathe through the pain of having been shot.

"Wrong answer."

Everything happened so quickly that I couldn't tell if Finn's mouth had dropped open in surprise or from pain. Maybe it was a mixture of the two.

First, I pulled a zip tie out and grabbed Finn's wrist and attached it to the door handle of the fridge. Once he was secured, I pulled out one of the knives I'd been carrying and grabbed his other wrist. He screamed in pain as I slammed his arm on the kitchen counter closest to where we were standing just before I pressed the blade to his thumb. It would have been easy to make this end as quickly as possible for him, but I wanted him to feel every ounce of pain.

Finn attempted to fight against my grip, but it was no use. I watched with a sick fascination as the knife cut through flesh and bone until the finger was no longer attached to his hand. While I preferred silence, hearing his screams brought me great joy.

Watching the blood leak from where his appendage had

been was thrilling. It had been so long since I'd done this, that I forgot how it made me feel. The exhilaration that flowed through my veins had been missing since Eden's death. The evening that I'd fucked everything up.

This, in a way, felt like the start of redemption.

I leaned in close to his ear, in an attempt for him to hear me over all of the yelling he was doing, and said, "How does that feel? Describe every feeling you're having right now."

He didn't say a word. The only noises emanating from his lips were sounds of agony. I couldn't help but wonder if or when he'd go into a state of shock.

"I'm in so much... pain."

I reached over and grabbed a white kitchen towel for him to place it over his hand. That was me being nice for a moment if you will. The towel only remained its original color for so long before it turned a crimson red.

I shrugged, not giving a damn if he was hurting or not. "It will all end if you tell me what you know about Iris Bennington."

It was a bold-faced lie, but he didn't have to know that.

Finn opened his mouth and then snapped it shut. He followed through with the same motions again as his eyes squeezed shut. Was the pain becoming unbearable? Good.

"How did you find out about Iris?"

He swallowed hard before he replied, "Because there is a large bounty on her head. We're supposed to leave her alone until she finds whatever proof there is that her ancestor is also a founder of the Chevaliers. But If she succeeds, she's dead."

Finn struggled to speak, but I was able to understand every single word. If he was right, whoever offered up the cash wanted Iris to do the dirty work and then they would swoop in at the end and take whatever she found and do who knows what with it. "Who issued the bounty?"

"No one knows, but it's over ten million dollars."

Understandable as to why people from every corner of the world would want to throw their hat in the ring to get a piece of this action. "Who else is keeping track of her?"

Finn shrugged before he hissed. I guessed the motion caused more pain to shoot through his arm. It meant nothing to me.

"You know who else is watching her. It wouldn't make sense for you to not be tracking your competition given the large sum of money that is at stake."

When his whining stopped and he looked over at me for the briefest of moments, I knew that I was right. I yanked the towel from his hand and slowly removed his index finger. The howling that left his mouth came from deep within his throat as if it were being released from the depths of his soul.

That was if he had one.

I tossed the towel that now had a deep pink hue to it, back on his hand and pulled out my phone. I found what I wanted on it and said, "Tell me who else."

I pressed the big red circle on my phone's screen and held it up to his mouth. I wanted to make sure I caught every single name he said.

Finn sucked in a deep breath before he rattled off several names. Some of them I'd heard of, and some of them I hadn't. I wondered if they came into this line of work while I was on hiatus.

"Good job. That wasn't so hard now, was it?"

Tears streamed down his cheeks as he slowly nodded. I

moved the knife to the side and although he was still in pain, I watched as he visibly relaxed. Ah, another mistake he'd made, because I wasn't done with him yet.

I grabbed Finn by the mouth, and I smirked when I felt his tears land on my fingertips. "You know, I should cut your tongue out for what you said to me earlier."

If I thought his eyes had grown wide before, they were likely to pop out of his head now.

"B-but..." His stuttering made my smile widen.

"But," I said, doing my best to help him with the word. "I'm not going to. Instead, it's obvious that you don't like listening and doing as you're told, so I have something better in mind."

I leaned forward, grabbed my knife, and brought it up to his ear. The theme of the night was that slow and steady wins the prize, and, in this case, my prize was his ear.

Feeling him thrash next to me as I sliced off his ear was thrilling. Every move I made to get the ear off until it fell on the counter with a smack was more exhilarating than buying a new company and adding it to my already robust arsenal of entities. This was why I did this.

But it became too much for Finn.

He fell to the floor with a loud thud, his hand still zip-tied to the metal handle.

This time, his blood had gotten on my jacket. I was anything but amused, but I understood it was just another hazard of the job at hand.

Finn didn't know what to do with himself, as he was bleeding from several points of his body. Part of me wanted to stop and memorialize the scene in front of me, including the look of terror on his face and the screeching that was coming from his mouth, but I didn't want to waste another second on this piece of shit.

"I'm bored of all of this. Goodbye, Finn."

"But you said—"

But his words were cut short because I'd finally slit his throat. I'm sure he was still praying for me to turn my gun on him, but his hopes were in vain. I glanced to my left and walked over to a chair to watch as he rolled around on the floor. That was going to leave a mark. The last thing he would ever see is me, staring across the room at him. Watching as life fled from his eyes brought me nothing but joy that I refused to show.

I closed my eyes for a second as silence returned. It was as if, for this moment, everything was right in my world because I could finally breathe again. Then again, the air smelled metallic as Finn bled out on his linoleum floor. While it would have been nice to continue to stare at the masterpiece I'd created, it was time for me to leave.

But before I left, I pulled out the burner phone from earlier and found the camera app. The flash of light from the burner phone was the last I would see of him. When I finished, I closed the door behind me. What was done, was done, and I had no regrets.

The only things I bothered to clean were my knife and the blood on my jacket. I could have tried to clean up the mess I'd made, but I didn't give a shit. Whoever found his body should take it as a warning if they, too, were trying to harm Iris.

I returned home about an hour later. The long shower that I took to wash the gunk of the day off of me was long overdue. Once that was complete, I stepped out of the bathroom in nothing but a pair of pajama bottoms and made my way to my office. As I enjoyed the whiskey that I poured, I sent the photos that I took to myself and saved them in a special hard drive that was connected to my computer. Once the transfer was made, I shut down the device, much like I'd emptied thoughts of Finn from my brain.

With a clear mind, the only thing that mattered was Iris.

It was time to pay her another visit.

12

IRIS

I paused outside of the front door and took a deep breath. It was foolish because it was lunchtime at West-wick University, meaning that a ton of people were walking in and out of the dining hall to grab food.

To avoid causing a bottleneck behind me, I forced myself to move. One foot in front of the other was what I had to repeatedly tell myself in order for me to get to my destination.

I walked to the entrance of the dining hall and swiped my ID card so that I would be granted entry. I pocketed the piece of plastic and looked around the room to see if I spotted Aria. When I didn't see her at first, I walked around the room to see if I could find her but came up short.

I reminded myself, as I found a table where the two of us could sit, that there was a chance that she was running late. A quick glance at my phone told me that I had no notifications so I was left to wonder if she would show up or stand me up.

It was my own self-doubts creeping in. It felt weird for someone to be going out of their way to be friendly to me. It made me think that there were ulterior motives behind her actions and it was something that I couldn't shake.

This was ridiculous, and I was no longer in high school. It was just lunch with someone who wanted to be friends. Why should I be worried?

The flower that I received, and my stalker's ability to make me think that he was hiding behind every corner, didn't help my mental state either. Thankfully, I hadn't seen him in days.

The first twenty-four hours that flew by without hearing anything from him was anything but peaceful. I found myself checking underneath my bed and in my closet multiple times that day because I was convinced that he was hiding in my room. By day two, it hit me like a ton of bricks that he had no need to hide because he was bold enough to do everything that he'd done so far. Hiding didn't seem like his style.

That also led me to believe that he wasn't scared of anything or anyone. Even with his threats, I'd been debating with myself whether or not it was worth going to the police. After all, I'd done nothing wrong and for whatever reason this man had chosen me as the person he needed to stalk.

If he indeed decided to leave me alone, it would take a while for me to stop looking over my shoulder for what felt like every second of every day.

I checked my phone again and still saw nothing from Aria. I would give her another few minutes to either text me or show up before I ate lunch by myself. There was no way I was going to waste a meal that I already paid for.

I played a quick game on my phone while I waited and heard some rustling near me. I looked up and found Aria a couple of feet away.

"Oh my gosh. I'm so sorry I was late. I woke up late for

class and then left my phone. Today has been comically bad," she said as she plopped down in the seat in front of me.

I gave her a small smile and waved her off. "It's not a big deal. Shit happens."

"That it does..." Aria's voice trailed off as she looked around the room before turning back to me. "Do you want to get lunch and then we'll meet back here?"

That sounded good. I pushed my chair back and stood up.

"You know, when I thought of this plan, I didn't expect to have to get up again so fast," Aria said.

I chuckled as Aria groaned and took her time getting back to her feet. We went our separate ways to go and grab the food we wanted. It didn't take me long to grab a sandwich with a salad, and when I walked back to the table, I found Aria already sitting there again. I assumed she hadn't been there long because she was just spreading a napkin across her lap as I was putting my lunch tray down.

We both dug into our meals and didn't talk much while we were eating. Our silence didn't do anything to ease the wariness that I felt, but I was determined to stick it out. Obviously, leaving now would make things even worse because I would have to make up a lie about why I needed to leave. Knowing me, I would end up stuttering, further incriminating myself.

A small chuckle escaped my lips that I hoped Aria didn't hear. Being in my brain was a whole lot of fun.

Aria took her napkin from her lap and wiped her lips. "So, you're probably wondering why I wanted to get lunch with you."

I nodded, happy that I didn't have to be the one to broach

the subject. It would have been too awkward for me to handle. That was saying something when, at times, I was the poster child for awkwardness.

"We had a class together during freshman year and I was hoping to get to know someone that also got stuck living in Payne Hall."

I had no recollection of the class we shared last year. Then again, I didn't pay much attention to the people in my classes because I preferred to stay to myself. I also wasn't about to say I'd intentionally chosen to live in Payne Hall. She didn't have any reason to know that. "You don't know anyone living in Payne Hall either?"

Aria shook her head. "No. My friend Beth was helping me move in, but she lives across campus. I was supposed to live with her, but something malfunctioned and she got put into a single instead of a double. And I was forced to move into Payne Hall as a result."

I'd never heard of Westwick's housing selection process getting things that wrong before, but that didn't mean it hadn't happened. "That's so shitty. I'm sorry."

"It's fine, and there is nothing I can do about it now."

She had a good point. There was no reason for us to belabor the point because what was done, was done.

"How are your classes going so far?" I was proud of myself for carrying on the conversation. I contributed that to not feeling nearly as nervous as I had before.

Aria took a sip of her soda before she responded to my question. "So far so good. Not looking forward to all of the work that I have to do, but I don't want to fail."

"What classes are you taking?"

Aria and I talked about the classes we were taking and

some of the events that we'd heard would be taking place on campus. Our conversation was fun. It felt nice to have someone I could connect with and talk to. So far, this felt more genuine than anyone else that I'd talked to who lived on campus.

Now, I would still say this whole experience was out of my comfort zone, and that I wouldn't be diverging any of my deep dark secrets to her any time soon, but it was nice to have a friendly face on campus.

As we were finishing up our lunch and began to pack our things to leave, Aria said, "Did you hear about the secret masquerade party that is supposedly happening on campus this year?"

I paused what I was doing and did a double take. "I have two questions. Say what? And if it's a secret, how do you know about it?"

"Touché. I guess it's not a secret that it's happening anymore, but it's supposedly the first time this party is happening in decades, and no one knows who hosts the event."

Her explanation did nothing to clear up my confusion. "How does no one know who hosts the party? Are there no guests at the party? Then is it even a party?"

Aria picked up her book bag and put the straps over her shoulders. "Somebody must know who hosts the party, but no one says who it is. And I'm not sure how you secure an invite to this party, but I'm going to do my damnedest to figure out a way to get in."

I picked up my book bag as well and followed up with my lunch tray. "But why?"

"It's on my bucket list of items that I want to accomplish

before I leave Westwick. If I don't score an invite this year, I don't know what I'll do because I don't know if it'll happen again."

Could I really fault her for trying? If that was something she wanted to do, who was I to judge?

"Well, if I can help you in any way, let me know."

Aria chuckled. "You look like you'd rather saw off your hand than go to anything like that."

"It's not that. It's that I genuinely don't think I can help you in this situation."

"It's cool. I'm just telling you about the party because it is something that is supposed to happen on campus."

I nodded and walked over to drop my lunch tray off so that my dishes could be cleaned. Aria followed suit and together we walked out of the dining hall.

Aria cleared her throat. "Are you headed back to the dorm?"

"Yeah. I have about an hour before my next class."

"Same. We can walk back together. By the way, I had a great time at lunch."

"I did too." And that was the truth. I'd enjoyed the company even if it had only been for a short period of time.

Aria and I were a few feet away from the front doors leading into the dining hall when Aria said, "Shit, I left my ID card at our table. I'll be right back."

Before I could respond, Aria turned on her heel and jogged back into the dining hall. I was left looking at her before I heard someone say, "Excuse me."

I quickly apologized and moved out of the way. It shouldn't take Aria long to collect her ID as long as no one had taken it. I tucked a piece of hair behind my ear as I stared at the door, waiting for Aria to walk back out.

Suddenly, I shivered as the hairs on the back of my neck rose. It felt as if someone was staring at me, which automatically made me think of one thing. I was afraid of what I might find if I glanced around.

I swallowed hard and looked up. I blinked rapidly three times as I watched Sam coming toward me. Our eyes immediately connected, and he gave me a small grin.

Had I been transported into an alternate reality? I didn't think he would recognize me. After all, we'd only interacted at the post office once, and that was days ago. I mentally kicked myself because I couldn't just stand there and stare at him. My brain finally acknowledged that he was intending to be friendly, so I waved at him as he walked by. It was just my luck that Aria caught our interaction as she was walking out of the dining hall to catch up with me.

"I didn't realize you know Sam," she said when she was a couple of feet from me. The smile on her face told me that she was thinking something she shouldn't be.

"I don't know him, per se, but we did meet at the mailroom after he called me about a package that had been delivered for me."

"Hmm."

"Aria, it's nothing. He was nice to me and was doing his job. Nothing more, nothing less."

"Okay. I'll see if you say the same thing in a few weeks."

I gave her a weird look before I started walking again with a renewed determination to get to my dorm. It took a couple of steps for Aria to catch up, and when we reached the street we needed to cross to head to Payne Hall, I looked up and found a fancy sports car parked on the street. That was strange because there was supposed to be no parking here. That's what the parking lots on campus were for.

As we approached, the driver's side window lowered, and my eyes widened.

It was him.

I looked down, refusing to acknowledge him any more than I already had, and continued my conversation with Aria. I did my best to hide the fact that he'd scared the shit out of me.

I started speed-walking, causing Aria to walk faster to keep up with me. I could feel his eyes burning a hole into my soul with every step I took and as soon as we were safely inside Payne Hall, I let out a sigh of relief without her realizing it.

When she didn't ask anything about what had just occurred, I considered how close I was to running into him and having to explain myself to a stranger. The whole thing would have been a disaster and was one I'd only barely missed.

13

IRIS

I folded my body into a stretch that served two purposes: to loosen my hamstrings and to double-check my laces. It would be one of the last things I did before I took off running.

The last thing I wanted to do was run at the end of a long day, but this was an exception. I wanted to get as far away as possible.

No.

I *needed* to get away. It was important to put an emphasis on that.

It didn't matter that it was for just a short period of time. Everything within me screamed for this release, and I owed it to myself to do so.

The pavement under my feet became my salvation as adrenaline flowed through my veins. It helped to fuel me and allowed me to push away all of the thoughts from today. It allowed me to focus on the only thing that mattered.

Me.

My body kept a measured pace as I ran down the sidewalk. I knew that no one would disagree with me over the beauty of the pink and orange colors that painted the sky right now. The crisp breeze helped to cool down my over-heating body as I made every attempt to burn off this excess energy. The crunch of fallen leaves under my sneakers left me feeling satisfied. I did my best to avoid any tree branches that might be on the ground as well, as a result of the changing seasons.

I debated taking the path down to the old house I'd seen on one of my first runs, but quickly nixed the idea. It was getting dark, and I didn't want to travel too far away from Payne Hall because I would need to cover that same ground when I wanted to come back home.

No matter what I did, thoughts of my stalker tended to not be far from my mind. Running gave me an outlet to avoid my current issues, yet nothing I did shifted my focus from that problem.

Having him show up today had been both unexpected and expected. I'd been wandering around campus waiting for him to appear in my room again. I hadn't expected him to appear in public nor had I thought he would take this long to make his presence known.

Thankfully, he didn't approach while I was walking with Aria back to Payne Hall. Instead, he chose to watch me from his car and Aria didn't notice.

But I did.

It was as if my body was attuned to the frequency that he gave. My paranoia fed into it, but I wasn't sure how to feel when I realized just how different my reaction was from when Sam was looking at me to when I noticed that my stalker had shown up once again.

It didn't help that I knew that my stalker was a danger to me, versus Sam who hadn't shown the same tendencies. That line of thinking led me to purchasing a bat after my last class of the day, and now I want to be better prepared for when he showed up again because deep down, I knew it wasn't a matter of *if*, it was a matter of *when*.

Too bad I wasn't able to bring it all with me. At least this time, I made sure to bring my cellphone in case I needed to call for help.

But so far, so good. There were enough people still out and about, going about their day, that I didn't feel as if I was alone.

Speaking of feeling alone, maybe it wouldn't hurt to invite Aria along on one of my runs. Then again, I didn't know if she liked running. But it wouldn't hurt to ask, and, in my opinion, it would be a great way to reach out to her and show that I was also invested in forming a friendship.

I gave myself a mental high five. One point for me. Zero points for my awkwardness.

I continued to run until I reached my cutoff point. I slowed my pace to a light jog before coming to a stop near the iron gate that served as the entrance to campus. Darkness was quickly approaching, and I wanted to be back in my dorm before the streetlights turned on.

I checked the time on my phone and turned my body so that I was facing my university's campus. From the outside looking in, the campus looked to be filled with rich history and architecture that looked as if it belonged in a horror movie. During the day, Westwick looked like your stereotypical college campus. But when darkness fell, the shadows grew and became more imposing. The streetlights provided some light, but not enough to shake the feeling that someone might be lurking behind every corner.

And right now especially, that wasn't a chance that I wanted to take.

With that motivation, I took off jogging back to Payne Hall. Before I started my run, I'd decided that an easy pace was ideal because I knew what would happen when I returned. I found that once I knew I was on my way home, my body would take over and start running at a pace that wouldn't have been anywhere near sustainable had I not taken it easy when I first started out. It was as if the draw to get home as soon as possible would put an extra pep in my step, and I would take off running in order to get home in time, even if I didn't have a set time that I needed to be there.

Just like my journey to the entrance of Westwick University, my return to my dorm was uneventful. I walked through the front doors and immediately noticed the flickering lights that lit up the foyer. They hadn't been on when I left and I didn't remember them being that dull when I'd arrived back home last night.

What the hell was going on?

I jumped when I saw a slight movement out of the corner of my eye and was surprised at what I found. The door next to Payne's statue was cracked open.

The last time I had wandered over there, it was sealed shut. I was beginning to wonder if I'd imagined the whole damn thing and the door could have been easily opened the whole damn time.

Every warning signal was going off in my head. They were telling me to walk upstairs and go to my room, but I couldn't. I refused to listen because none of this made sense. I knew for a fact that I struggled to open that door and now, all of a sudden, it was slightly ajar.

No, this might be the opportunity I was looking for and I wasn't about to squander it. I looked around to see if anyone else was nearby. Seeing no one, I walked around Payne's bronzed statue and over to the door. A shaky hand grasped the doorknob and after waiting a beat, I slowly opened the door and found myself staring down into the black abyss. Before I could open the door even a quarter of the way and pull out my phone so that I could shine a light through the doorway, the door's weight suddenly became too much to hold and there was nothing I could do except get out of the way before the door slammed on me. I took a step and tried to open the door again, but it wouldn't budge. It was as if I was having a moment of déjà vu.

If I wasn't creeped out by what had just happened, I might have laughed at my luck. This must have been a sign that I shouldn't enter or look at whatever was down there, and I needed to listen to that advice.

Deciding not to spend a second longer on this, I walked over to the stairwell, and just as I was about to walk up the stairs, the lights in the foyer became brighter. There was no way that any of this was a coincidence. I didn't have an explanation for it, but this wasn't happening by happenstance. I needed to see what was in that doorway.

I took the steps up to my floor two at a time, determined to get back to my room as quickly as possible. My mind spiraled down different rabbit holes about what all of this could mean. Was this related to finding Payne's missing letters and documents? What the hell had suddenly made the door too heavy for me to pull?

I almost walked past my room because I was so lost in thought. I wanted to check the doorknob first to make sure that it wasn't unlocked before placing my key into the lock. If it had been unlocked, there was no way that I was going in there because I knew that I locked the door before I left. If it was open, it more than likely meant that someone had broken in once again.

When I couldn't twist the knob, the tension in my shoulders eased. This was, hopefully, a sign that no one had entered my room. I unlocked the door and immediately turned on the lights.

Nothing looked to be disturbed.

My bed was still as messy as I'd left it. Both laptops were still there. I was pretty confident that no one had been in here since I'd left.

I grabbed my shower caddy with my bath essentials, a towel, my robe, and my baseball bat. It was a struggle to make sure that I didn't drop everything. Before I walked out, I looked down the hallway and noticed that there was no one walking around on my floor.

Good.

Because I was about to do something that more than likely would look very weird to anyone that spotted me. It wouldn't be the strangest thing someone had seen me do, but I would like to save myself from having to get any strange looks or answering questions.

Once I had a firm grasp on the things I needed, I slipped into my shower shoes, walked into the hallway, locked my door, and headed to the bathroom.

As I stepped into the bathroom, I looked around to see if anyone else was in there. It was mostly to make sure that my unwanted visitor wasn't lurking in a shower stall or something. Thankfully, the room was well lit enough that it made it easy to confirm that no one was in the room.

After I made sure that the coast was clear, I quickly debated with myself about whether it was worth locking the bathroom door so I could ensure that no one else would follow me in. I decided against it because that wouldn't be fair to anyone else who might want to bathe while I was in here. It was also still early enough in the evening that I felt as if the chances of my stalker appearing were slim.

The fact that I needed to deal with this, and that I had someone who had decided to make it their mission to be my stalker, was still mind-blowing.

I turned the shower head on and stripped as I waited for the water to heat up. This shower was nothing like the one at my Gran's house, but it did the job. Having the water beat down on me felt wonderful on my tired, achy muscles. After the excitement of the day, I needed something to calm me down. Fear mixed with adrenaline was one hell of a combo, and it would take a lot for me to come down off of that high.

I watched as the remnants of the water from my shower swirled down the drain. The relaxing nature of it loosened my body, giving me an opportunity to just stand here and breathe without restriction. The weight of everything that was on my shoulders felt lighter and I was grateful, but I suspected it was only a temporary fix.

After I finished my shower, I put my robe over my body and wrapped my hair to help it dry. I grabbed my shower caddy, my running clothes and baseball bat, and walked back to my room, unlocking it.

As I was putting things away, I realized that I left my shampoo in the shower stall.

"Fuck," I muttered to myself. I needed to run back to the bathroom and collect it. I took my towel off my head and shook my hair out before dropping it into my laundry basket and left my room.

It took me about a minute to travel to and from the bathroom, and when I opened the door, I screamed.

There was a man standing near my window with his back toward the door. When I yelled, he turned around and my eyes widened.

"Looking for this?" he asked, as he held up the baseball bat in his hand. A dark smile took over his face, sending a shiver down my spine.

Seeing me earlier today hadn't been enough for him. My stalker had now made it obvious that we had unfinished business that needed to be attended to.

Immediately.

14

IRIS

My brain struggled to process what was happening in front of me. It couldn't comprehend that I was seeing what I knew I was.

I knew I should be afraid of what he might do to me if given the chance. Well, if he were to take that chance because he had no problem taking what he wanted. What was fueling my rage was his audacity.

"Get out of my room."

The only change in his stance was that his lip twitched as he slapped his hand with the bat. "No."

I wasn't surprised that he refused. I should have known when he didn't act out this afternoon that he had something else up his sleeve. "Your threats mean nothing to me and I will call campus security again. Or hell, maybe this time I'll go to the police myself." The fact that they still hadn't caught him and this man had broken into my room multiple times was alarming.

"Go ahead and do it, but my *promise* still stands. Every single word of it."

I wanted to call his bluff, but I didn't know if I could because I didn't think he was lying. I needed to shift gears and change the direction of this conversation. Another option was to find a way out of here as soon as possible.

"Why are you doing this?" My tone was softer than when I demanded that he leave my room and that was by design. "What can I do to make this all end?"

It took a lot to swallow my anger and not make it evident that I was pissed at this entire situation. My acting as if I wasn't livid about all of this might be the key for me escaping from this. I took a chance and glanced at the door which was still open. Not many people lived in Payne Hall and even fewer lived on this floor, but having someone walk by right now would be amazing.

If I wasn't going to have anyone help me, I could save myself. I slipped off my flip-flops and waited for him to respond.

"Nothing. Absolutely nothing. This is your life for the foreseeable future. This ends when I say I'm done with you."

I had to say that my ability to contain myself and not scream at him or freeze in shock was a miracle. Instead, I bolted out the door as if someone had struck a match and set my ass on fire. In a way, he had. I needed to get out of here and go someplace where I could find someone to help me as soon as possible.

I knew this escape plan was risky and there were many negative consequences to what I was doing. The chances of him catching me were high, but I wouldn't forgive myself if I didn't try to do something.

The first thing I heard was the baseball bat hit the floor. I was scared to look behind me to see where he was. Luckily, due to the creakiness of the floor, I had a good idea of where he was. However, all of my luck wasn't good because, based on what I was hearing, he was gaining on me quickly.

I screamed as I ran down the hall, hoping that someone would hear me. Tears developed in the corner of my eyes, threatening to fall with every step I took. I might have a chance to put some space between us if I could reach the stairs that would lead me to the first floor.

My stalker must have had a similar thought because as soon as I reached my arms out to push the stairwell door open, I was grabbed from behind and thrown up against the wall opposite the door.

"Don't ever try that again. Got it?" He was barely out of breath, and it was another reason for me to hate him.

"Why shouldn't I—"

My words were cut off because he'd bent down and picked me up. I fought against him as he walked back in the direction we'd come from.

"My ass is hanging out!"

"You should have thought about that before you took off running. If you keep squirming, I'm going to throw you over my knee and spank your ass until it's pretty and pink."

I didn't know if I should be thankful that someone hadn't come out to check on what all of the noise was about because now he had my non-panty-covered ass showing for all of the world to see.

He carried me back to my room and closed the door behind him. When I heard the decisive click of him locking the doorknob, I knew I was fucked. No one had bothered to come out and see what was going on so either no one was here or no one cared enough to check.

He spun around and threw me down on my bed. I landed with a small bounce and scrambled to get up. He was on me in what felt like an instant, pinning my arms to the bed, and using his body weight to immobilize my legs.

There was a wicked gleam in his eye as he said, "Now, where were we?"

"I'm going to scream again." I opened my mouth to scream and the look in his eyes stopped any noises from leaving my lips. A tear slipped from my eye, leaving a wet trail in its wake.

"No, you're not." His stare was downright murderous.

I was convinced that if he could have, he'd probably have killed me on the spot. Then again, he wouldn't have had someone to torture so he'd probably keep me teetering on a thin line between life and death.

"The hell I'm not." Another idea popped into my mind. I might be stuck underneath him, but I wasn't out of this fight. I gathered saliva in my mouth and then launched it at his face.

I was proud of myself for momentarily stunning him as he stared me down. Hell, I was too, but my expression didn't give it away. Deep down, I knew that me spitting on him would do nothing to aid in my desire to get away from him, but damn did it feel good.

He used his arm to wipe my spit from his face. "Try that again and I'll punish you. You'll wish the only thing I did was slap your ass."

Something within me cracked. I was beyond tired of all of

this and it needed to end. "You're not going to do a damn thing. You're not going to harm me or my grandmother. What I'm going to do is call the police because who knows how many laws you've fucking violated at this point."

"Every single part of you is perfect."

He'd mumbled the words and I wasn't sure if he knew he'd spoken his thoughts out loud. It was a temporary lapse in the mask he'd decided to wear around me and it took me even more by surprise since I'd just gotten done yelling at him. Nevertheless, my cheeks were red hot and the only thing I could hear after that sentence was the harshness of my breathing as I stared at him.

His eyes drifted between mine and my chest. I finally looked down to see what had caught his attention and, during our struggle, my robe had opened a bit. He was enthralled by the sneak peek of my breasts. It was the first time he was seeing them with the lights on. I couldn't deny that I was confused because of the rush of emotions that were crashing through me. Anger and fear were battling it out for the number one spot, but somewhere, far lower, the intensity of this confrontation with him was turning me on.

What the hell is wrong with me?

"This flimsy robe you have on leaves very little to the imagination. Didn't think that through, did you? That seems to be par for the course with you, isn't it?"

"Fuck you." I thrashed against him again, determined to break the hold he had on me. If I had to choose between modesty or flashing him and getting free, it would be the latter every time. Feeling the heat of his stare on my body sent signals to my brain; signals that I didn't want to have.

"You will be fucking me in due time, petal, and you'll enjoy every minute of it. But until then, you need to earn it."

My head shot back in disgust. "Never in a million years."

"You should never say never that way, when you go back on your word, you won't feel so guilty."

He moved one of his hands from my wrist and for a split second, I thought he might be letting my hands go. I pulled my hand away to hit him, but he managed to grab both my wrists and pin them down with his other hand. I was both amazed that he'd been able to pull that off and terrified of what he would do with one hand free.

My inquiry was soon answered.

His fingers lightly touched the edge of my robe, tracing the lapels before taking them on a journey that I was sure he was only too thrilled to go on.

His hand stopped on my breasts as he played with the edge of the fabric while brushing against my skin. The simple touch made my nipples hard. He'd barely touched me and my body was ready for anything he wanted.

"You're enjoying this."

I rolled my eyes. There was something in me that agreed with him, but I refused to admit it out loud. "So you're a stalker and a liar. A wonderful combination."

His lips twitched, but he didn't say a word. He was enjoying our banter while I was trying to find a way to get away from him as fast as possible.

"And to think that this is only the beginning."

"Get off of me." My voice cracked at the end of my statement. I knew I'd just wasted my breath saying it because it was useless. He was going to do whatever he wanted and I'd be left to pick myself up after. The tears that I thought had vanished were back with a vengeance.

My lips trembled as he drew his fingers up and down my cleavage. It would be mesmerizing, but the anticipation of what he was going to do next kept me on edge.

"What part of get off me don't you understand?" My words had a lot of bite in them, but I could hear the underlying distress within them.

"The part where you don't actually want me to. Your fear isn't that you're afraid of what I will do. You're scared because you think you might like the things I'm going to do to you. I can see it in your eyes."

I hated that he was able to read me with ease. He moved his finger lower as his dark stare stayed trained on my face, almost daring me to say something else. A small, sadistic grin appeared on his face as his hand traveled lower, making a small pitstop on my stomach to undo the belt before coming to rest near my pelvis.

I swallowed hard because I knew what he'd find if he went any lower. My attempts at denying the effect he was having on me would easily be proven to be a lie.

As if he'd heard my challenge, he moved his hand lower and pushed one end of the robe out of the way so that he could get a full glimpse of my pussy. He broke our stare before he dragged his index finger up and down my slit. My heart rate increased with every motion, and he hadn't yet shown any indication that he was going to do anything more than that.

The longer this continued, the more I began to dislike myself for begging him in my mind to do more.

"Look what we have here." His comment was meant to be cocky, but there was something else there. My body might have turned me into a liar, but I could see that he was affected by his discovery.

When his finger slipped inside of me, his eyes darted back to look me in the eyes, as if he were memorizing every emotion that crossed my face. And I gave him a slew of them to see.

I couldn't stop my mouth from dropping open as he sunk into me. The sensations that he caused from just that movement were enough to cause the butterflies in my stomach to flutter. Not only was I not my own biggest fan at the moment, I hated him too.

But what he was doing to me made me want to sing his praises as long as he didn't stop.

A moan escaped my lips, increasing my embarrassment. If there was any question about whether I was enjoying this or not, that noise would have confirmed my feelings on the matter.

My stalker mumbled something else under his breath that I didn't catch, and when I watched him add another finger to my pussy, I gasped loudly.

"Music to my fucking ears," he said. This time, his words were loud enough to interpret, but I still wasn't sure if I was meant to hear them.

The sense of an orgasm grew within me, telling me how this was all going to end. I wanted to push the thought out of my mind and forget who was doing this to me, but I couldn't. Not with the intensity of his stare on me. I could imagine that he wanted me to remember every second of this moment, the way it made me feel and the effect he was having on me.

My legs seemed to move involuntarily on their own, sliding away from each other and to give him more room to work his magic. I'd thrown out any sense of dignity I'd had left when the prospect of having an orgasm came into play.

Was this a form of hate sex? Because I could see how it would be addicting.

That thought fled my mind when he added another finger to my pussy. The grin on his face deepened at my reaction. As I was about to groan, the urge to cover my mouth so he wouldn't hear me was there, but he was still holding down my wrists. I'd forgotten because I'd been so focused on what he was doing to my body. Unfortunately, he once again heard how much I was enjoying what he was doing to me. Which spurred him to continue and he picked up the speed.

The drive to reach nirvana in his hands was all that mattered to me, as the pleasure continued to build. I could feel myself getting closer to my climax and, as I was on the way to letting go, he stopped.

Anger flushed my body as I watched my orgasm slip through my fingers. The only thing I could hear was my harsh breathing and the only thing I could see was him through the figurative red haze that had now blurred my vision. When the smile didn't leave his face, it all clicked into place for me.

"You're doing it on fucking purpose!" I said through gritted teeth. I was outraged by this sick game he was playing, but I wanted this release. No, I needed this release.

"Am I?"

"Yes. Stop it and get me off."

"Is that what you really want? To come all over my fingers?"

"Yes!"

"Too bad," he said as he pulled his fingers out of my pussy.

I watched as he made sure to suck the fingers that he'd been using to play with me clean and I hated that it made me even more aroused.

"Punishments are bittersweet, aren't they? Next time, you'll know better than to threaten me because I always maintain the upper hand."

I wanted to say that there wouldn't be a next time, but I didn't want to tell a lie. Instead, I followed him with my eyes as he got off of my bed. Without waiting another second, I slammed my legs shut. The glare I leveled at him didn't have its intended effect because he went on about his business like he owned this room.

Hell, he'd just gotten done owning my body. He walked over to where my bath things were and grabbed a fresh towel.

"Open your legs, Iris."

"No."

"Do you really want to test me right now? Open up your fucking legs."

Humiliation clouded my judgment as I slowly opened my legs, allowing him to wipe me clean with a towel. When he was done, he threw the towel into the hamper and turned to look at me.

"I'll see you around, petal." He didn't wait for me to respond, choosing instead to leave my room without another word.

I lay there stunned from the events that unfolded. He'd left me in a similar state the last time and I felt like an idiot for letting it happen again. I hated myself for doing what he said I was going to do. I enjoyed what he'd done to me outside of not letting me come.

Fuck.

So many thoughts swirled through my mind and that was when another realization hit me. I didn't even know his name.

15

IRIS

I took a deep breath and let the sound that had been on the tip of my tongue out for whoever was nearby to hear. My scream bounced off the tiles, echoing throughout the bathroom. Tears freely streamed down my face as I let the water from the shower pour down over me. It was a compilation of everything that had happened since the last time I'd left this bathroom.

If I was someone in another stall or in the hallway, I would have been alarmed enough to see what was going on or to call for help. When none came, I was convinced that no one else lived on this floor or that the whole building was abandoned. Nothing else made sense unless someone had secretly soundproofed the walls. The chances of that were basically nonexistent, but it was a passing thought I had.

I wiped my eyes and sniffled as I scrubbed my skin until it turned a light pink. It was all done in an effort to cleanse myself of him, but whether it was having its intended effect was debatable. I couldn't stop myself from replaying the events of this evening in my head.

I'd stared up at my ceiling for who knew how long and somehow, I was able to pull myself together enough to make it back into the shower. Was it a waste of water?

Yes.

But did it make me feel better?

Somewhat.

When I felt as if I was all cried out, I reached a shaky hand out to turn off the shower. I stood there, dripping water, allowing the chill that was in the bathroom to cool my skin after the hot shower. Goose bumps appeared on my skin as I reached out to grab my towel.

Once I was dried off, I put a towel around my body instead of my robe. If I could afford a new one, I would burn the robe because of all the memories it now had, but buying another one would be wasteful.

I made sure to grab all of my things, including the bat, and walked back to my dorm room. This time I'd locked the door and while it took me a few extra seconds to get in, it was well worth the time because I felt more confident that it would be exactly how I left it.

Then again, my stalker hadn't had any issue getting past a locked door before.

None of that mattered, however, because he was nowhere to be found. Thankfully.

Once I'd locked my door behind me, I quickly threw on a tank top and sweatpants. While I got dressed, my thoughts were bubbling over and if I didn't tell someone what was going on, I was going to explode.

I grabbed my cellphone and found the number of the only person I could trust with this. She answered on the second ring.

"Hello."

"Bianca?" I didn't know why I was implying I was unsure if it was her. My voice sounded slightly hoarse, and I knew I could contribute that to the screaming session I'd had in the shower moments ago.

I heard some rustling on the other end of the phone. "What's wrong?"

"I—I have something I need to tell you."

"Do you want me to come over? This sounds like something that needs to be said in person versus over the phone."

I glanced around my room before I shook my head, even though she couldn't see it. "No, I'd rather come to you if you aren't busy."

"I don't have anything going on. Why don't you pack a bag and you can stay with me overnight? We can order takeout and some junk food."

That sounded like a great idea. It allowed me to get out of the room where everything occurred. Plus, it was Friday. I didn't have to worry about classes tomorrow so this was perfect.

"Okay. When do you want me to come over?"

"Whenever is good."

"How about in forty-five minutes?" I could be over there sooner on a regular day, but I wanted to give myself more time today just in case.

"I'll see you then."

I hung up the phone and got to work on throwing my clothes and other essentials in a Westwick University duffel bag that I'd been given during my freshman year. I decided to leave both of the laptops here and to ask Bianca for advice on that too. I wanted to think that by leaving them here, I might be keeping my location a secret, but if he was able to perfectly time entering my room when I went back to grab something I left in the bathroom, he had to be watching me closely.

Thinking about it made me want to crawl into a hole and never come out. So I pushed it to the side and focused on packing what I needed to stay at Bianca's place. She had the privilege of living in an apartment near her college, Brentson University, because her parents paid for it. It was a fancy apartment that I loved spending time at when I had the opportunity, but it did come with a price.

In my experience, she knew how fortunate she was to be born into the family that she had, but she felt indebted to her parents sometimes because of it. Underneath her sarcasm and the urge to push her parents' buttons, she still performed some of the tasks that were expected of her when it came to being a child of a local politician.

She'd been an excellent friend to me over the past couple of years and I was thankful that she was willing to be there for me at a moment's notice. There were sprinkles of shame in there too because there was another thing I was taking and not giving back. I needed to fix that.

Once I'd grabbed a hoodie and thrown it over my tank top and picked up the duffel bag and bat that I'd placed on the floor, I walked out of my dorm room. As I walked down the hallway, I couldn't help but notice that I probably looked as if I was going to play baseball versus going to stay the night with a friend.

When I opened the side door of Payne Hall, I was hit with a blast of cool air. It felt wonderful against my heated skin, but I didn't take much time to stand there and enjoy it because I needed to get to my car as soon as possible. My eyes darted in every direction as I walked through the parking lot. I took inventory of the people who were around and whether or not he was there. When I didn't see him anywhere, it was as if I'd walked into the fresh, crisp air again.

I reached my car without interruption and used my car remote to unlock the doors. Before getting in I looked in the back seat, double-checking to make sure that no one was there. Once I confirmed that I was alone, I threw my duffel bag into the passenger's seat and got into the driver's side. I slammed the car door closed and locked it, securing myself in the vehicle.

I placed both hands on the steering wheel, gripping it for dear life. It wasn't until I was safe and secure in my car that I realized just how much tension had built within my body. It took several rounds of deep breaths to calm myself down, and several more before I was ready to put on my seat belt.

After that was all said and done, I turned my car on, thankful that it started without issue. I typed Bianca's address into my phone just before I pulled out of the parking space. It took another pep talk to get me to put the car in drive and, finally, I was off to Brentson.

The drive to Brentson was straightforward and the only sounds I could hear were my GPS telling me where to go and the soft pop music I'd been listening to in the background. It would have been a peaceful drive if the thoughts in my head weren't colliding with each other, trying to make sense of it all.

Every so often, I looked in my rearview mirror to see if I was being followed, but I didn't see any suspicious vehicles, thankfully.

Soon, I was pulling into the parking lot of the complex that Bianca lived in. I sent her a quick text so she could come down to the front desk and greet me. That was the only way that I would be allowed up to her place, which made me feel even more secure about coming here and hopefully not bringing trouble to Bianca's doorstep.

I sat in my car for a couple of minutes to give Bianca an opportunity to get downstairs. With a deep breath, I unlocked my trunk and then my door before scrambling to get out. I rushed over to the passenger side door and grabbed my duffel bag and the bat. I quickly walked to my trunk and put the bat in there. I didn't think I would need it at Bianca's, and I didn't want her questioning me about why I had brought it with me.

As I walked to the lobby, Bianca appeared. Her long blonde hair was put up into a messy bun and her outfit was similar to mine. It was obvious that we were both dressed for comfort and not to impress.

She stared me down as I walked through the glass door that led to her apartment's lobby. There wasn't a trace of a smile on her face, and I assumed it was because her face was mirroring mine. There was nothing funny about what I wanted to tell her.

Bianca didn't say a word as she opened her arms to let me step into them. Her comforting gesture was my undoing, and a fresh set of tears welled in my eyes.

But I couldn't cry. I needed to focus on the overarching goal of telling her what I could. Then if my emotions wanted to take over, so be it.

"Come on. Let's get you upstairs," she said.

All I could do was nod, because I was afraid that, if I said anything, the dam would break, and my tears and fears would spill out in this lobby.

Bianca gave a small wave to the person working at the front desk as I gave a small nod, and together, we took the elevator up to her apartment.

Her apartment was elegantly decorated, yet felt warm and inviting. It would come as no surprise that Bianca's parents hired an interior designer to work with her to figure out her vision for the apartment. It also gave them an out for having to help her.

Bianca leaned into her love for white, beige, and gold, while several oil paintings that adorned her walls served as a backdrop. Her large windows allowed for so much light to enter into the space, making it a beacon of natural light. Her view of Brentson wasn't too shabby either. Her apartment was literally night and day compared to my dorm room at Westwick.

It suited her because it was a mixture of the things that she liked combined with a coordinated effort between her style and what looked cohesive together. At least she'd been able to work with a designer who had her best interests in mind when it came to what she wanted for this space, because there had been some disagreements over what Bianca wanted for her space and what her father, currently the mayor of Brenston but aspiring for higher office, thought was acceptable.

Bianca threw her keys down on the counter and grabbed my duffel bag. Normally I would have told her not to worry about the bag and that I could handle it, but I was too relieved to let her take the weight off of me.

Any adrenaline that I'd had was wearing off quickly and I

was now beyond tired. I took off my sneakers and walked around her so that I could reach her couch. I sunk down into the cushions and I knew I never wanted to get up. Bianca came over to me and pulled a soft quilt over my body. While the weight of the blanket was comforting, it did little to muffle the thoughts swirling around in my brain.

Bianca left me on the couch and walked toward her kitchen. "Is there anything I can get you?"

I thought for a moment. "Some water would be nice."

"Coming up."

She was bustling around in the kitchen while I reached over and grabbed the remote to find something to put on the television. I needed something, anything, that could help drown out the chattering in my head. I finally settled on a show that I found via one of the streaming platforms that Bianca had. When I put the remote back down on the table, Bianca walked out of her kitchen with two glasses in hand.

"This isn't water, Bianca," I said as she set a glass down in front of me.

"I know it's not. I'll be grabbing those next, but it sounded like this story required something a little stronger." She wasted little time going back to the kitchen to retrieve two more glasses, setting them next to the glasses of wine.

I didn't fault her logic because this story did feel as if it required more than water. It would, at the very least, calm my nerves enough for me to get what I wanted to say out in the open.

I glanced at the wine fridge that had been installed in her apartment. Neither one of us were twenty-one yet, so I wasn't sure how Bianca kept what seemed like an endless supply of wine in her apartment. Whenever I mentioned it, she would sidestep it and try to change the subject.

Bianca sat down next to me and grabbed her glass of wine. After she took a sip, she turned to me and said, "Now tell me what's going on. You have me worried."

I bought myself some time by joining her in drinking from my glass of wine. Whereas she took a sip, I took a big gulp and almost choked as the liquid went down.

I had to admit though, Bianca's taste in wine was excellent. Besides me almost choking on it, the liquid went down smooth. I put the glass down on the coffee table once again.

"Are you ready to talk now?"

I nodded and ran both of my hands across my face. "Someone is stalking me."

I couldn't bring myself to look at Bianca for fear of the expression that might be on her face. Being vulnerable was hard, even if it was to someone you knew and trusted. It was right then and there that I made the decision that there were some things I couldn't tell her in this moment. This wasn't to say that I wouldn't ever tell her, but I couldn't deal with the emotional fallout that would come about as a result of telling her more than I was ready to tell at one time.

"Stalking, as in someone is following you? Tracking your movements?"

"Yeah. He is also the one that sent me the laptop." I took a chance and glanced at Bianca and found her staring at me wide-eyed, while her mouth flirted with the idea of dropping open.

"I have so many questions, but I don't understand why anyone would do that. You keep to yourself and do your best not to attract attention. Have you gone to campus security about it?"

"I wish I knew why. It started at the beginning of the year and he's broken into my room twice now, and yes, I've gone to campus security."

That made Bianca do a double take. She reached over and grabbed me by my forearms and slightly shook me. "What's his name? Screw campus security, we need to go to the police."

"No. He hasn't mentioned his name. I'm afraid to go to the cops because he threatened to harm Gran." The tears that I knew would come were making themselves known. I felt one slowly slip past the corner of my eye. "He knows where she lives, and I know that because he was able to recite her address to me and, supposedly, he took a picture of her home. Hell, I don't know if I'm doing the wrong thing here by telling you right now. I can't afford to have anything happen to Gran."

Bianca moved her hands from my forearms and pulled me into her, hugging me as tightly as she could. Her comfort was enough to make me cry again. There was a lot of sadness from the situation I was in, but there was also relief that I was finally able to tell someone about what was going on.

She held me like that for what felt like forever, and I appreciated every second of it while I released the emotions that had been building since I screamed into the nothingness during my second shower.

"I don't know what he wants, and I don't know why he continues harassing me. I have nothing to give."

"That's not true. You have plenty to give and to the people

that know you, you mean the world to them. Don't let him force you to question your worth."

I pulled back and looked at Bianca, stunned into speechlessness. That might have been the most profound thing she'd ever said to me in the two years that we'd known each other.

Bianca stood up and walked into her kitchen again. I took the time to polish off my wine and when she came back to her couch, she handed me a paper towel to clean my face.

"I still think going to the police is the best bet here. We don't know how dangerous this guy is."

I'd already gone through this same scenario a million times in my head, but his threat of hurting Gran was always at the forefront of my mind. "I can't."

"I had a feeling you'd say that. Going back to campus security is an option. At least maybe they can do more patrols near your dorm room and see if they can spot him. Have you seen him clearly and can describe him?"

I knew I could describe him from memory without issue. The look on his face as he brought me closer to coming before snatching it away would be burned in my mind forever. "I've already talked to campus security and they are supposedly working with the police to find him. And yes, I know what he looks like."

"At least we have that to go on and the police do know," Bianca's voice trailed off as she swiped a piece of hair that had come out of her messy bun behind her ear. "I'll talk to my parents about it. Maybe they know someone who knows what you could possibly do in this situation."

My soaked paper towel felt disgusting against my skin

now, so I used my hands once again to try to dry my face. "If you're okay with doing that."

Bianca wiped her hands on her sweatpants. "I don't like going to them for things if I can avoid it, but you clearly need help, and I want to do all that I can."

"Okay. Is it alright if I go..." I gestured to the bathroom instead of trying to finish my sentence.

"Of course."

I strolled over to her bathroom and every step I took felt as if I was forcing my body to complete the action. I closed the door behind me and leaned over the sink. It was a lot to take in and I didn't know how long it would take my mind to process it all.

I turned the faucet on, allowing the water to get slightly warm before tossing it on my face. The water mixed with my tears then I grabbed a small towel that was hanging in Bianca's bathroom. After patting my face dry, the only way you could tell I'd been crying was by the redness of my eyes and cheeks.

When I was able to calm down and think straight, I decided my stalker was in trouble. Because above all else, I wanted no harm to come to Gran. Even if it meant putting myself in the path of this stalker to do it.

16

SOREN

I brushed my hair back from my forehead and rubbed a hand down my face. It took more effort than I wanted to extend to reach into my closet to grab another black button-down shirt. I looked over at the one I'd had on about twenty minutes ago, or what was left of it. I was slightly irritated that another shirt was ruined because I always made it a point to do what I needed to do as cleanly as possible.

The crumpled shirt on the floor was the perfect metaphor for how messy that last kill had been. It had made me wonder how out of practice I'd become, but this mission was accomplished, nonetheless.

Once I finished buttoning my current shirt, I picked up my old one and held it on the tip of my finger, examining the destruction. The rips in it showed how rough the fight had been, but I only had a single scratch on me and bruised knuckles, while the asshole was dead.

That fact did nothing to soothe my annoyance. Black button-down shirts were a central part of my wardrobe at this point and made it simple for me to always have something to wear instead of fussing over whether something matched. I was able to devote more time to my business and to the Chevaliers because of it.

That now included Iris because she was my business. There was no way I would ever forget about her. I shouldn't be thinking about her as much as I was. Having a twenty-year-old take up most of my thoughts was something I never thought would happen. She was too young and had her whole life ahead of her. I shouldn't be feeling this way, but my desire for her won out over logical thinking.

It's what made the hasty decision to go see her a problem. I hadn't been planning on sneaking into Payne Hall, but I was already in the area, so there was no harm if I stopped by. Or so I thought. It ended up leading me down a path I hadn't expected, including some things I wanted to do since the first time I snuck into her room.

Luck was on my side because she wasn't in her room, allowing me to do what I'd wanted to, uninterrupted. It gave me the opportunity to enable her phone tracking and give me access to her location. As long as she had her phone on her, I knew where she was.

Which was how I knew that she'd gone to stay with Bianca Henson a few days ago, but was now back at West-wick going about her life as normally as she could. Running over to Bianca's place and causing chaos was an option that I considered, but I decided to hold off because I believed she needed space. All of this was a lot to handle and, while I had faith that she would be able to handle everything, it was still a lot to take in at one time. I wanted her to get used to our arrangement and stop this quest she was on to expose the so-called truth about exposing the Chevaliers.

I debated sneaking back out before she came back that night, but then I noticed that she'd bought a bat to defend herself. I couldn't help but pick it up and wait for her to return. If she thought that was going to keep me away, that was laughable at best, foolish at worst.

She could buy an entire arsenal of weapons and that wouldn't keep me away. The second I laid eyes on her, I knew she was mine. The more I learned about her, the more it cemented that this was a fact and not an opinion.

What further complicated things was that I hadn't planned on touching her, let alone fucking her with my fingers. Almost making her come on my hand hadn't been in the cards either. It turned into a punishment for her, to make her see what trying to threaten me would lead to.

I knew she was terrified of me, but I had no intention of killing her or her grandmother as long as she didn't cross any lines. However, she didn't know that, making her fearful of every move I made or didn't make. It was all a part of the process of keeping her on her toes and hopefully distracting her enough that she wouldn't go looking for information about my organization where she shouldn't.

Even I had to admit that, in a fucked-up way, what I was doing was saving her life. If she did find something, Parker would more than likely order her execution. It wasn't a decision I wanted to think about right now.

I tucked my new shirt into my black slacks on the way out of my bedroom. As I strolled through my house, I couldn't help but think about how messed up this whole situation was. If things would have stayed as simple as they were the evening she ran into me, we wouldn't be in this shitstorm. Now that the Chevaliers were involved, layers and layers of complication arose. It would only grow more complicated unless she gave up her quest.

It would be the best for her. Well, good for her as far as the Chevaliers were concerned, and she wouldn't have as large of a target on her back. But because I'd been following her for weeks now, I knew she wouldn't. I hadn't admitted that to Parker yet and I was only choosing to delay the inevitable.

This didn't mean I expected this to end in something resembling a fairy tale. I would have still tracked her every move and that had been my plan before the addition of the Chevalier shit. Following and learning everything about her almost felt like it was a part of my DNA at this point.

I made my way down to my kitchen and grabbed a tumbler. I poured myself a finger of whiskey before walking into my study. I started a fire in the fireplace and stared at it while I sipped on the drink in my hand. Watching the orange flames dance around the logs was oddly therapeutic and provided some warmth to the room. The crackle and popping of the fire's embers along with the smell of smoking firewood, transported me back to another place. Memories of another time where things were much happier and calmer resurrected in my brain, but I needed to tame those reminders because they were never coming back.

Instead, I decided to spend the rest of the evening reading and responding to emails from work. I'd left the office earlier than planned and murdered another man for seeking out Iris. That hadn't been in the cards either, but it was funny how life threw you curveballs.

I tended to prioritize my work over most things, but I saw the opportunity and snatched it. It was different for me — something unexpected—but I had no regrets, outside of my shirt. It was something so minuscule in the grand scheme of things because I had so many shirts and had the ability to buy thousands more if necessary. It was the principle of the situation that was the driving force behind why I couldn't get over it.

I had every intention of walking over to my desk and sitting down in the creaky, old chair, but something stopped me. Rather than doing what I was supposed to be doing, I decided to take a small detour. I opened the top drawer of my heavy wooden desk and pulled out a small key.

I walked over to my bookcase, glancing at the books on the shelves as I walked past them. There was a door on the other side that was partially concealed by the bookcases. It wasn't one of the first things you noticed if you came into this space, and I preferred it that way.

I unlocked the door and was immediately hit with the scent of dust. It was unsurprising since I hadn't been back here in a long while. The glow from the fireplace in the next room gave me enough light to easily find the light switch, and I turned it on.

The lighting in this room wasn't great, but was enough to get the job done. Dust was everywhere, and if you looked at the air at the right angle, you could see flecks of it floating around. There were a bunch of boxes stacked all over this smaller room that I hadn't bothered going through. I dodged all of the other things in my path until I stood in front of what I'd been looking for.

A portrait that had been created of Eden Marsden Grant.

Her dark hair was pulled into an updo and there was a hint of a smile on her face, capturing her essence in a way that only a picture could. The portrait showed Eden's back with her looking over her shoulder at the person painting the picture. The background of the photo was of a lighthouse and the cliff that it sat on, looking over the water below.

I remembered where the picture that led to the portrait was taken. That was because I took it. We'd been driving through Long Island and we'd come across a lighthouse. She was so excited to see one in person that she begged me to stop the car so that she could get out and see it.

I couldn't deny her that.

Eden had been so happy in that moment that it almost pained me to relive it. I knew that this portrait shouldn't be back here, but this had become its home. There were reasons why it was here, but I refused to focus on them because there was no use in thinking about things I couldn't change.

I raised my glass to Eden and brought my drink to my lips. "What happened to you won't ever happen again. I won't let it happen again."

But, of course, no one responded to my declaration. I spent a couple of minutes staring at the portrait before I turned off the lights and locked the door behind me.

As I sat down in my office chair, one of my burner phones lit up. There was a notification that I had a text.

A quick glance at the message told me that Jeffrey Powell, another one of the fuckers who'd targeted Iris, had been found. This was excellent news and would put my kill count for this project now at three, because I had no doubt that his time was limited, and he soon would be lying dead at my feet. The urge to visit him now was there, but I refrained.

I needed to wait and be patient because I didn't want to draw too much attention to these assholes being killed and have the police start connecting the dots. It would only hurt my ability to protect Iris because that would shift me into the spotlight, and I reminded myself that everything would happen in due time.

17

IRIS

I put a fake smile on my face as I saw Professor Hamby. It was coming to that point in the semester where the excitement was starting to wear thin. Homework and projects were beginning to pile up and going to class became a drag. Learning could be fun at times, but with my anxiety, I wasn't thrilled to be back in class again. It meant that my routine had returned and the chaos had been silenced in my world.

Campus security called me this morning and told me that they were still doing everything they could to find him, but he hadn't been apprehended. No news wasn't good news for me and made me feel more helpless. But at the very least, they hadn't forgotten about me, which was good, right?

The days since I last laid eyes on my stalker continued to grow, but at times it still felt as if he were watching me. His presence surrounded me wherever I went. I wouldn't be surprised if he was still keeping close tabs on me, given the last time I'd begun to hope that he'd left me alone, and he hadn't. This time however, the period between his visits was longer than the last time around.

Part of me wanted to think that this was the end and I would never see him again. Another part of me knew better and thought that it was only a matter of time before he came back around and that letting my guard down would be a huge mistake. I used the toe of my shoe to tap the baseball bat I was still carrying around. It was a constant reminder that I needed to stay alert because I didn't know when he might strike.

I pulled out my binder, a pen, and my textbook as I prepared for class to start. Taking notes by hand versus using the new laptop had been the better route for me and I felt less weird about doing so. I glanced at the time on my phone and noted that class would be beginning in about two minutes.

There was some loud chatter near the entrance, and I glanced up. I knew that, without a doubt, a look of surprise covered my face. The widening of my eyes and my mouth dropping open meant I probably looked like a cartoon character, but there wasn't much I could do about it now. I hadn't been expecting to see Sam standing in front of me.

"What are you doing here? Are you in the wrong class?"

Sam gave me a grin as he slid into the seat next to me. "No, I'm not. I needed to add another class to my schedule and this class was interesting. It had open spots and now I'm here. I didn't realize you were taking this class too."

"So far, it's really good." There was a lot of work, but still I would say the class was enjoyable.

"I'm starting to get the idea that this class will go even better than expected."

I looked away from him because I didn't know how to react. None of the vibes I got from him indicated that he was remotely interested in me. I mean I had barely seen him since we met while he was working in the mailroom. It could be that he was just trying to be nice and I didn't want to make things weird.

I turned back to Sam and said, "It has been pretty interesting so far, so I don't think you'll have any issues staying engaged."

Before Sam could respond, Professor Hamby was standing up at the podium and that was the signal that it was time to begin. I'd never been more grateful for class starting in my entire life.

I tried my best to concentrate on Professor Hamby and to follow what he was teaching us. The discussion today focused on the fundamental principles of marketing. I jotted down as many notes as I could in hopes that it would be easy to remember what we discussed later. I knew I was going to have to go over what I wrote in order to better retain what I learned.

The time flew by and before I knew it, the lecture had ended. Professor Hamby dismissed us and I packed my things up just before I stood up to stretch.

Sam cleared his throat and I glanced at him. "I need some help catching up and wanted to ask if you'd be willing to help me? Maybe we can meet in the library and can start by going over your notes and talking through any questions I might have?"

I debated whether this was something I wanted to partake in. Before I knew it, I found myself nodding. "Sure, that shouldn't be a problem. When do you want to meet?"

"Would tonight work? I have a club meeting at around five p.m., but it should be done around six."

I thought about it for a moment. I was hoping to do some more digging around Payne Hall tonight, but it wouldn't be until late at night. "How about seven? That gives you time to grab dinner too."

"Sounds like a great plan."

It was obvious to me that Sam had slowed down in packing his things in order to wait for me to finish packing up. With all of my items back where they belonged, I bent down and picked up the baseball bat. Together, we walked out of the classroom, and it wasn't until we were out of the building that Sam spoke.

"Do you play baseball?"

His question caught me off guard. I was used to getting weird looks when carrying the bat, but I hadn't expected anyone to ask me about it. "Ah... no, but I'm hoping to learn how to play at some point. Trying to find new things to try and all of that."

The words didn't flow as easily as I hoped, but to my ears, the lie sounded convincing.

"I used to play as a kid. I'd be happy to teach you or give you a few pointers."

Fuck. Of course he'd played before. Why did he have to be so fucking nice? "That would be nice... thank you."

"You're welcome." He paused for a moment before he said, "I'm going to head this way."

The direction he pointed in was opposite the one I needed to go in. It took everything within me not to say *thank fuck* out loud. "I'm going this way, but I'll see you tonight at the library."

"I'll see you then."

I turned away first. If I was being honest, I was afraid that he might be standing there, staring at me as I walked away. I refused to look back so it wouldn't look like I was longing for him.

Sam seemed nice based on what I knew about him, which wasn't much. Most of what I knew had come from Aria when we'd had dinner together the other night. Her teasing me about him, both when we grabbed lunch together for the first time and at dinner a few nights ago, was in jest and didn't bother me much, but it did make me think.

My interest in Sam was strictly platonic, but I wasn't sure if he was feeling the same or if he felt more. If it was the latter, I was concerned about it given the predicament I was in with my stalker. That was, if he was still stalking me.

The ringing of my phone brought me out of my thoughts, and I realized that I was only a few feet from Payne Hall. I pulled my phone out of my pocket and smiled when I saw who the caller was.

"Hi, Gran!" I said as I answered the phone. The words came out more cheerfully than I felt, but that was the mask I was wearing for her today. Every time I heard her voice, the panic within me ebbed temporarily because I knew that she was okay.

"Hi, dear. How is everything going?"

"Good. Really good." Guilt crawled up my spine as I lied to Gran, but there was no way in hell I was going to freak her out about everything that was going on with my stalker. It's the last thing she needed to worry about. "How is everything going with you?"

"Great. I wanted to talk to you about traveling up to you

this weekend and taking you out to lunch. Are you busy this weekend?"

I smiled at the suggestion and said, "How about I drive home, and we can spend some time together there? I'd rather make the drive than you." Westwick was about ninety minutes from Gran's home. While not terribly far, I'd rather she not drive all the way here and back again.

"Oh! If you insist, dear." The shock was evident in her voice. I was thrilled to be the one surprising her versus it being the other way around.

"That's fine and it will be nice to sleep in my old bed for the weekend and to have some of your homemade apple pie."

Gran chuckled. "I wasn't planning on making it until you came home for winter break, but I'd be happy to make some for you."

"That would be amazing. Thank you."

"You're welcome, dear. That was all I wanted to talk to you about. I don't want to keep you on the phone for too long."

"Okay, well I have a couple of more things I need to get done before my next class, but I'll talk to you later. I love you."

It wasn't until I hung up the phone and stepped into my room that I realized something else. This would be the perfect opportunity to also reread Margaret's papers and see if I could make sense out of any of them given that I was now living at Payne Hall.

A plan for the evening was forming in my head. Maybe it wouldn't be such a bad idea to go to the library with Sam.

THAT EVENING, I arrived at the library about thirty minutes before seven p.m. I'd decided to come early because I had some work of my own that I wanted to get done before I met up with him. I sat down at one of the cubicles that also contained a computer. While it was awkward for me to be doing this, I needed to get back into researching Payne and his connection to Margaret.

After finding out who'd sent my new laptop, I didn't want to do any of this research on the device. I was also nervous about doing it on a public computer, but I hoped that no one would think to dig into my search history. Plus, I was using private browsing in hopes that it would make it more difficult to find.

It was not a foolproof way by a long shot, but it was what I felt comfortable doing at the moment and I couldn't afford to have my stalker knowing what I was doing. Even if he did find out, he probably wouldn't know what I was talking about, but the fewer people that knew anything about this, the better.

My eyes darted to every corner of the library, wondering if my stalker was here and waiting for me. Seeing no one even looking in my direction was the sign that I needed that I was safe and had nothing to worry about, at least for now.

My research took me through the brief history of Payne Hall. It had been renamed within the last seventy-five years. The installation of the statue came later, within the last forty years.

The reason why the dorm had been renamed was because of the contributions Payne had made to his college after he graduated. That included being heavily involved in offering scholarships to attend Westwick, hosting internships for current students, and having lectures on campus while he was alive. While it wasn't officially listed in the article I was currently reading, I wouldn't be surprised if there had been some money exchanged at some point or another that led to the name change as well.

I also wouldn't be shocked if his co-founding of the Chevaliers also influenced this decision too. While the Chevaliers had humble beginnings, it wasn't long before they held more power than many of the organizations that preceded and followed them.

Well, that was what I was able to put together through inferring from what Margaret had written. In fact, several of the letters she'd written were addressed to Eddison Payne, but she never sent them, for reasons only known to her.

That was, if Payne never wrote about her too. A lot was hinging on stories that had been passed down to me. Deep down, I knew there was no way that Margaret's story was false. I was still determined to prove that it wasn't so. Going back to the house I shared with Gran this weekend to reread the information we had about all of this would be a good thing. I was sure of it.

What I still didn't know was where Payne's letters and writings could be. As far as we knew, his estate said that there had been nothing related to the Chevaliers found in his home or at his office, which didn't make any sense being that he was a part of the organization's founding and stayed involved until his death.

At least that was what we were told. Rehashing the details from that wouldn't get me any closer to the answer of whether Margaret was one of the founders of the Chevaliers.

I checked the time to see how much longer I had until he arrived. When I realized that I had ten minutes left, I took it as an opportunity to look up any books that might be in the library about the Chevaliers. I wasn't surprised to only find one and it was about a bunch of secret societies, but it might still be helpful. Thankfully, it was available.

I made a note of where its location was and rushed to the library's basement to find the book. Today must have been my lucky day because I easily found it and brought it upstairs so that I could check it out. The process took a little longer than planned, and by the time I was stuffing the book in my book bag, someone tapped me on the shoulder.

I jumped and swung my bag, almost hitting the person standing behind me.

"Iris, it's just me," said Sam.

My hand flew to my chest. "You scared the crap out of me."

"That I can see. I apologize." He gave me a warm grin and I couldn't help but smile in return. "Are you ready to get started?"

"Sure. I was doing a little work before you came but let me just shut down that computer and we can find a table to sit at."

With our plans set, Sam and I walked away from each other. I arrived at the computer I'd been conducting research on, glanced up, and saw that Sam found us a longer table to use. I quickly closed out my browser's tabs and signed off, effectively removing my research history to the general user.

I made my way over to the table and sat across from Sam. For some reason, my brain believed that sitting next to him seemed a little more intimate, but that could be me reading into stuff that I shouldn't be.

I took out my things from our marketing class and set them on the table. When I was done, I realized it probably made more sense for me to be sitting next to him so that I could easily show him my notes and explain the different principles and other things that we'd been taught so far. Sam must have noticed this too because he stood up and moved over to my side of the table. Once he was settled in a chair to my right, we got started.

I didn't know how long we'd been working but I heard someone whisper my name. I looked up to find Aria standing in front of our table with a wide grin on her face. I might not have known her for long, but it was easy to tell what she was thinking.

"Hey, what's up?" I asked, leaning back in my chair. My intent was to look as nonchalant as possible, but I didn't know if I had succeeded.

"Nothing," she replied. "I was just in the library and decided to stop by when I saw you guys. I hope I'm not interrupting."

She knew damn well she was interrupting, but I didn't care.

"No. Sam joined my marketing class and I was just helping him catch up on what we were learning. We were getting ready to wrap up in a couple of minutes anyway."

"I don't want to hold you guys up, but I wanted to stop by really quick and just tell you something."

That made me raise an eyebrow. "What's up?"

Aria's eyes bounced between me and Sam. "Remember I told you about a party that I wanted to attend on campus?"

She was being vague on purpose, but I understood what she was getting at.

"Yes, I remember."

"I know who's hosting it."

"Okay..." I let my voice trail off because she could have just sent a text message with this information.

"Let's get together sometime soon and I'll tell you all about it."

Why the hell was she being so secretive? I knew the party supposedly hadn't happened for years, but why did it matter if Sam heard this or not?

I nodded along even though many questions swirled as I tried to piece this together. "We can chat about it later."

"Deal," she said. "I have a group project that I need to get to, so I'll talk to you later. It was great seeing you both."

With that, she walked away, and I was left somewhat dumbfounded by her exit. The cliffhanger she left me on was brutal, but I hoped to get an answer to the hints she was dropping soon.

"Well, that wasn't strange at all," Sam said.

I couldn't help but chuckle. When I glanced down at my binder and flipped through the pages, I realized we didn't have much more to go.

"We should almost be done, Sam. Do you want to just knock this out and then we can leave?" I asked.

"That works for me," he said.

With that, we buried our heads back into the books in front of us. As I predicted, it didn't take long for us to finish our task.

I rose as Sam stretched his arms above his head. Relief flowed between the two of us since this part was done, but for different reasons. I could guess that Sam was happy to be done with work whereas I was glad to be done with this meeting. That thought came out worse than I had imagined it, and I was grateful that I only thought it and hadn't said it out loud. This was out of concern for his well-being versus not wanting to be friends with him. I knew that my stalker was out there, just waiting to pounce and I'd rather not put someone else in his crosshairs.

We both packed our things and as I was finishing up Sam leaned against the table and said, "Can I walk you to your car?"

I froze for a second before I managed to catch myself. I zipped up my bag and said, "Yeah, that's not a problem."

I was grateful for having someone else around while I walked through the dark parking lot that was next to the library. It'd be less likely that I would get approached by my stalker if I had someone else with me. Then again, putting a target on Sam wasn't what I wanted to do either.

"You know what? On second thought, you don't have to walk me to my car. I'll be fine."

"But I want to," said Sam.

I debated arguing with him about it, but I knew it would take longer for us to get over this hump than it would be to have him just walk me.

"Okay," I said. "I'm ready whenever you are."

"Lead the way."

As Sam and I headed to my car, I noticed a dark figure standing on the other side of the small parking lot. His eyes were trained on us, and I felt a chill run up and down my spine. He was leaning against a streetlamp as if he had all of the time in the world, content with just watching our every move.

While I couldn't see him clearly, I knew who it was.

My stalker.

I had no doubt in my mind that what I'd just done was deemed worthy of one of his punishments.

18

SOREN

Sometimes you had to do things you didn't want to do. It was the way that the world worked and sometimes you just had to deal with it.

Tonight was one of these things for me, and Parker was lucky that I was willing to do this for him. I didn't particularly care for socializing. I was annoyed that I had to attend this event because it was taking valuable time away from what I needed to do. What I would say was, it was nice being back in New York City, if only for a few hours.

Taking a second to glance in the rearview mirror, I checked out my bow tie one more time before my car door was opened. A valet was waiting for me to hand him the keys to my Porsche.

"Sir?" He held out his hand and it was obvious what he wanted.

I nodded in return, gave him the keys, and left him a tip as I walked into the hotel where the Cross Family Gala was to be held.

From my understanding, this was an event where mostly

eating and networking would occur alongside presentations showcasing all of the accomplishments that Cross Industries had made this year.

It would also be the first time I'd been around a lavish event such as this in a long time and that was on purpose. I'd sworn off these types of events for years because I didn't see much of a point in them anymore. It was an excuse to network, gain clout, and get drunk off of the top-shelf liquor they had and so I was curious to see what type of reaction I would drum up.

The last time anyone had seen me at an event like this was when Eden was alive. Now, here I was at the Olympus Hotel, one of the fanciest hotels in New York City, attending events like this all over again. As I walked through the lobby, I could feel everyone's eyes drawn to me. What had at first been jovial conversations turned into silence with a side of stares. Sympathy and pity plagued several of the faces of the guests who were in attendance.

I didn't bother acknowledging any of the looks I was garnering. It wasn't worth it and the only thing I wanted to do was make it through this event and go on about my business.

As I signed in and walked to my seat, I could hear the whispers getting louder. I knew I would be the topic of gossip fodder in just moments, but I didn't care. They had every right to talk and spread the "news."

I sat down at my assigned table and looked around momentarily. I noticed Bianca Henson sitting with her family, but I didn't stare at her for too long so as not to draw more attention to myself. It was clear that I'd caught their tables' attention because I could see the Henson family talking with one another and looking over at me every so often.

I was more familiar with Van Henson due to him being mayor of Brentson and me living within the town's limits. I didn't think I'd been officially introduced to anyone else in his family, but I recognized his wife, his son, and his daughter who also happened to be best friends with Iris.

Instead of focusing on them, I pulled out my phone to see if anyone had tried to contact me. No notifications were a good thing. As I placed my phone back in my pocket, Martin Cross, the patriarch of the Cross family, had walked across the stage.

When the crowd noticed that things were getting started, they made a move to get to their seats.

Martin gave a big, award-winning smile before he spoke. "Good evening, everyone. Let me be the first to give you an official welcome to the Cross Industries Gala!"

Unsurprisingly, his comment was met with a round of claps. It was clear that Martin Cross was well loved in this room, which was obviously done by design.

Martin continued with his speech. "Now I want to welcome my family out onto the stage. First, I would love to welcome the love of my life. Without her, I wouldn't be here because there is no way I would be able to do what I do without her. Selena Cross."

Martin joined the rest of the guests in giving her a round of applause. Selena stepped out onto the stage, smiling, and waving at the crowd that clearly adored her as much as, if not more than, her husband.

I watched as each member of the Cross family was introduced and walked across the stage. I held back the urge to check to see what Iris was doing because, if there had been any changes in her status, the men that I'd hired to watch her would let me know.

Things were going to be somewhat slow tonight anyway, not to mention I already had things in motion for my next move. Next week couldn't come soon enough. The look on Iris's face was going to be worth all of the strings I pulled to showcase my next move.

Patience had been a priority for me when it came to her and was usually how I approached most things. Waiting for people when they least expected it gave me the upper hand, but it was clear to me that it had been the wrong approach. When I saw her studying with Sam Wilburn last night, it made my blood boil. It hadn't been difficult for me to look through the large windows of the library and see them sitting together. I hadn't been surprised to see him walking her out to her car either, and that was when I decided to make my presence known. The only thing that saved his life was him not touching her.

That would all change on Monday.

When there was another round of applause, I turned my attention back to the Cross family as they stood up on the stage. When Kingston Cross walked out onto the stage with his date, I was expecting Martin to wrap things up, but when he didn't, I leaned forward to listen more closely.

"Now, as many of you know, there are plenty of other Crosses out there, living all over the world. But we recently found out there was another Cross out there, one that we've welcomed into our family with open arms. Last but certainly not least, my niece Raven."

I knew quite a bit about the Cross family, but I had no idea that Neil Cross had a daughter. Based on the gasps in the room, it seemed as if I wasn't the only one who was surprised.

At least there was something that made the night more interesting.

Raven was looking into the crowd, and I saw when her mouth dropped open. I followed her gaze and looked over at the table where the Henson family were seated. Based on the expression on his face, it seemed as if Van's son was most taken back by Raven being up there.

Interesting indeed.

I filed that away to refer to it at another time.

I stared at the newest member of the Cross family as she came to where I was sitting. She found her seat and took the opportunity to introduce herself to everyone at the table. When she reached me, I stuck out my hand for her to shake.

"Soren," I said.

She didn't respond with her name in-kind, instead choosing to look down. It was obvious that I intimidated her, but I wondered if that had more to do with tonight's event and her introduction to the crowd than me.

The rest of the program for the night went smoothly and once the event ended, I was more than ready to leave. After all, the ride back to my home was relatively long and I wanted to get on the road as soon as possible.

"Soren."

I looked up to see Ioan making his way toward me. By the time he was at my side, I'd stood up and was not so patiently waiting for him to speak.

"What can I do for you?"

"I want to talk to you about one of the things I was looking into before you came back. I should have mentioned it the evening of the Chevalier meeting, but with everything going on..."

I wasn't sure what he was referring to and my curiosity got the best of me. I gestured for him to follow me and together we walked to a corner of the room where no one else was. It wasn't the safest place to talk, but it would have to do for right now.

"What is it?"

"I've been watching some of the comings and goings with several mafia families and other organizations in the city."

"And?"

"I think I might have an idea about who was involved with your wife's murder."

19

IRIS

Exhausted couldn't even begin to describe how I felt. Not even the coffee sitting in the cup holder of my car could give me that spring in my step that I had gotten used to. Thankfully, I wasn't tired enough to pass out while driving, but I knew that I would probably take a nap as soon as I reached my destination.

I was beginning to wonder if it had made more sense for Gran to come to me instead of me going to her. I meant to leave for her house on Friday, but things had grown complicated, and it was easier for me to finish up some of the work I needed to do on campus than to do it off campus this weekend.

I tapped my fingers to the beat of the latest pop song on the radio. It gave me something to do, but it didn't take away the emotions that I was feeling as I drove down the highway.

Guilt swam through me because, by not being there, I was missing out on precious time that I could have spent with her. That led me to decide to leave for home at seven in the morning. It wasn't the best decision.

Nonetheless, Gran was excited to have me home and I was excited to be there. I just needed to get there first. Out of the corner of my eye, I could see the leaves were changing and falling from the trees. This was always a beautiful time of year up here.

There were a few cars in front of me. I assumed it was the early birds that we're trying to get to their destination without any hint of traffic. My gaze shifted to the rearview mirror to see if there were any cars behind me, but they were so small that they almost looked like a speck on the road.

As far as I could see, I wasn't being followed and it was a weird feeling to have. I'd been bracing for retaliation from my stalker after he'd spotted Sam and I walking across the parking lot of the library a couple of days ago. So far, none had come and I didn't know if I should be relieved or concerned.

My tiredness was also due to stress. Not only did I have to deal with school stress, but walking around thinking that at any moment your stalker might jump out and harm you or the people you loved, would take its toll on anyone. It didn't help that the authorities were still trying to track him down last I'd heard. The fear of violence did little to ease the boulder resting in my stomach twenty-four hours a day.

I'd intentionally left the new laptop in my closet on campus. If I could avoid having my stalker know where I was for the weekend, I was determined to do so. I also wanted to keep it away from Gran, who I knew would ask questions once she saw the new device.

That was part of the reason why I stayed on campus an extra evening. Getting the things I needed done that required a computer had been at the top of my priority list. Now, I could do the rest of my homework at home without needing a laptop. I'd also hoped to start reading the secret society book I got from the library this weekend. It would be a great opportunity to read it with Gran nearby because her knowledge about Margaret would more than likely pair well with the things that were written in the book. Well, I hoped so, because who knew if what was written in the book was the truth.

I checked my GPS and saw that I was coming up on my exit and that I would be at my house in ten minutes. I didn't know what had eaten up the chunk of time that I needed to drive, but I was thankful for it.

As I was getting off the highway, my phone rang. There was only one person who would be up this early and calling me.

"Hey, Gran," I said, right after I answered the phone.

"Hi, dear. I was just calling to check to see where you were."

"I'm about seven minutes away now."

"Excellent! I just wanted to check in to make sure that you didn't get held up in traffic or something."

Her excitement made me smile. I couldn't wait to hug her.

"Gran, it's like 8:20 in the morning. Most people are sleeping right now."

"I know. It's just that I'm usually up early because I don't sleep as long as I used to anymore."

A yawn escaped my mouth and was embarrassingly loud. "Sorry about that. My body wanted to let it be known how sleepy I am."

"Well, when you get here, you can take a nap."

"I know, but I hope it won't be a long one because we have a lot to catch up on."

"Yes, we do, dear. Okay, I'll let you go, and I'll see you in a little bit."

"Bye, Gran."

I disconnected the call and made sure that my GPS was fixed. I knew where I needed to go to reach my house, but just in case there was construction or roadblocks, I wanted to be prepared.

Within a few minutes, I was pulling into my driveway. I didn't know how much I had missed home until I returned. Before I could get out of the car, Gran was already at the door. She'd only opened the front door, choosing to keep the storm door closed. I assumed she had been looking for me out the window to see exactly when I arrived.

I was glad the drive was uneventful. I didn't realize how much I needed to be home until I saw Gran standing there. This was what my soul craved, and I couldn't wait to give it what it needed.

I RAN a hand across my face and when I opened my eyes, I was surprised by what I found. Waking up in my old room after my time away was jarring and it took several seconds for my journey to my house to come back to me.

A peek at my phone told me that I'd slept for about two hours, which for me, wasn't too bad. After giving Gran a huge hug and bringing the stuff I'd brought with me for the weekend into the house, I promptly fell onto my bed and went to sleep.

As I was getting up, a smell tickled my nose. It didn't take much for me to recognize the smell of Gran's homemade apple pie. Gran had promised that she would make it and my wish was coming true.

Before heading downstairs to see if there was anything I could do to help, I took a detour to my bathroom to take a quick shower. It would help wake me up and after the nap I desperately needed it.

I smiled when I walked into the bathroom and saw that everything was the same. For some reason, every time I returned home, I was surprised that things hadn't changed. When I left for Westwick my freshman year, I thought that Gran would have made changes to my room or my bathroom. She told me that she didn't want to change anything because this would always be my home and until I was ready to let things go, she would keep things in here how I preferred it.

I'd never been more grateful to wake up and see that at least something hadn't changed. I kept my word that my shower would be quick. As I was putting on a pair of black leggings, my phone buzzed on the bathroom countertop.

My heart stopped. Could it be him again?

I finished putting on my clothes and with a shaky hand, I snatched my phone off the counter. If I didn't answer it now, I would be wondering who it was constantly.

I pressed a button and my screen lit up, showing me a text notification. I unlocked my phone and read the message.

Aria: I didn't know you weren't going to be here this weekend! I knocked on your door and you didn't answer.

The tension that was in my shoulders released as soon as

I saw who the text message was from. It wasn't the fucker who couldn't seem to leave me alone.

> Me: Yes. I went home for the weekend to visit family. Is there anything you needed?

> Aria: I wanted to tell you more about the party! I didn't know how much I should be saying in front of Sam about it. He might think I'm weird for being so fascinated about this.

I didn't know why she cared what Sam thought, but that wasn't my concern.

> Me: I can understand that. What did you find out? Who is the host?

> Aria: The Chevaliers are hosting it. Have you heard of them?

I stared at the device in my hand for longer than was required. There was no way that she'd typed anything about an event that the Chevaliers were putting together.

> Me: I've heard of them in passing, but I don't know much about them. How did you find out it's them that are hosting this party?

> Aria: People talk and I listen. I don't know much about them either, other than it's apparently hard as fuck to get initiated into their organization and that they have a huge house on campus. I wonder if the masquerade ball will be held there?

That was a logical assumption and if I was able to score an invite, that meant I would be on Chevalier grounds. I might be able to find some evidence to prove Margaret's claim. Suddenly, I was interested in this ball.

> Me: Could be, but you have to let me know if you find out more information. I'm very intrigued.

> Aria: Will do. Want to meet up to do homework in the library this week?

> Me: Sounds good. Just let me know when.

I stuffed my phone into my pocket and left the bathroom. Soon I was walking down the stairs to see where Gran was.

It was a safe bet that she was in the kitchen, given that was where I assumed the apple pie was. And I was right. She was currently standing near the sink wiping what appeared to be a bowl.

"Hey, Gran. Is there anything I can do to help?"

She looked over her shoulder at me before she responded. "No, I have everything under control."

"Do you know anything about a masquerade ball that the Chevaliers put together?"

Gran didn't say anything for a moment. "I do know something about it happening when I was there, but I'm not sure if it's still going on."

I folded my arms and leaned on the wall closest to me. "That's interesting because I just heard from a friend that they are planning on throwing it again."

"Huh."

When Gran didn't elaborate, I spoke again. "What? Is that weird?"

She stopped what she was doing and turned around to look at me. "Back in my day, that chapter's rules stated that no one who wasn't an initiated member or had special permission could enter Chevalier Manor. They kept things around that no one who wasn't associated with the organization was supposed to see. The masquerade ball was both an opportunity to open the house up and to have fun. You need to get invited though, or have special permission, or be a date of someone who is either a member or about to become one."

"So, them hosting this event again is a new thing?"

"Well, I haven't been to college in over fifty years so I couldn't tell you if they hosted it in my absence."

I chuckled because she had a good point. I hadn't heard about it since I'd been going to Westwick, but that didn't mean it wasn't a thing. Aria knew about it, so I would assume they started holding the ball again at least within the last two years.

I banged my hand on the wall beside me and said, "I need to go to the ball."

"Yes, you do."

I froze in place because I was taken aback. I hadn't been expecting Gran to agree with me. "You think so too?"

"I do, but I think you, of all people, are going to have a hard time getting in. I want you to promise me that you'll be careful. You're walking further into dangerous territory especially if you do end up getting an invite and attending the event. You'll be on their turf. The rules are different with them."

"What are you talking about?"

Gran walked over to me and pulled me into her arms. "They don't follow the same rules you and I do. They can, and have, gotten away with things that would land anyone else in jail."

I pulled away slightly and looked up into her eyes that were similar to my own. That's when it hit me. "Holy fuck."

I tried to keep my language clean around Gran, but what she was alluding to was scary as fuck. It's not that I didn't suspect it, but having it confirmed had shaken me to my core.

"They'll do anything to protect their status and you unearthing information about Margaret would mess things up. Badly."

Maybe thinking that I would be able to reveal who I was and get my stalker off my back was the wrong move. But I wasn't willing to give up on Margaret either.

"Why don't you sit down at the dining room table and relax? I left something there for you."

Her comment sounded somewhat ominous, much different than how she'd greeted me when I arrived. I walked away from Gran and over to the table. I easily found what she left me.

The table was covered with Margaret's letters and journals but there were more than I recalled studying before. I looked up and found Gran looking at me. She dried up her hands and met me in the dining room.

"This is everything I have in regard to Margaret," she said.

"Gran, this is a lot more than what you shared with me before."

"I know, dear."

This time I looked at her. "Why did you keep the rest of this stuff from me?"

"The first time I showed you Margaret's things it was right before you were going to go to Westwick. It wasn't until you told me that you intentionally decided to stay at Payne Hall and that's when I knew you were serious about finding the truth. I was going to bring it up if we decided to get lunch together, but with you home, this made more sense anyway."

I nodded, seeing her reasoning even though I wished she would have told me about this before. It made me feel as if she doubted my ability to find out the truth about the Chevaliers. "Okay. I have something you might be interested in too. Let me grab it."

I walked out of the dining room and into the living room, where I'd left my book bag. After grabbing it, I retraced my steps and put the bag on the chair nearest where I was planning on sitting. I could feel Gran's stare on me as I riffled through my belongings to find what I wanted to show her. Once I grasped it, I pulled it out of its current resting place and handed it to her.

She adjusted her glasses as she examined the cover. "A book on secret societies. I'm willing to bet there isn't much in here about the Chevaliers though, but I'll look through it while you read over Margaret's papers."

I followed Gran's orders and pulled a chair out so that I could sit at the table, bracing myself for what I might read. I wasn't sure what was to be expected but having even more information about Margaret was a great thing.

I picked up the first letter and realized that while I'd already read it, it wouldn't hurt to have a refresher about what it contained. The anguish in her words about having to beg to be listed as a co-founder of one of the most powerful organizations in the world told me how much this meant to her. I wouldn't rest until I was able to find closure for her.

THE WEEKEND FLEW BY, and I wasn't prepared to be walking back up the stairs of Payne Hall on Sunday evening. Physically, lugging the things that I'd brought back from home to my dorm room sucked because I always managed to bring more stuff back with me than when I left.

Most of that was due to Gran loading me up with home-made goodies and there was no way I was turning those down.

Mentally, I felt drained from all of the drama that had been thrown at me since the beginning of the school year.

When I unlocked my dorm room door, I put my things down and grabbed the things I needed to use to prepare for bed. It had been a long weekend. I was looking forward to going to bed early so that I would wake up refreshed and ready for tomorrow.

When I was done, I climbed into bed, and it was only nine p.m. When was the last time I'd gone to bed at a decent hour?

Not that any of that mattered if I couldn't get to sleep. I turned off the light and settled in. Before I could use some of my usual tactics that I needed to help me fall asleep, I could feel my eyes closing as I drifted off.

20

IRIS

I couldn't stop running. No matter what, I couldn't stop running.

Terror ran up and down my spine, and I continued to tell myself that. All I could do was pump my arms to make myself run faster. I was afraid of being caught because if I was, I knew I was going to die.

I was growing tired, but I couldn't rest. It was waiting for me to give in, but I wouldn't.

I couldn't.

The air was cool and damp and whipped through my hair as I ran. I wanted to look behind me to see if it was gaining on me, but I was afraid. If I slowed down, I was dead.

As if the universe had tossed me a life jacket, I saw a house coming up fast. If I could just make it there, then maybe I had a shot.

Unfortunately, I was growing tired from having run so far. The closer I got, the more the house looked like the haunted house that sat near Westwick's campus. If this was going to be the thing that saved my life, then so be it. It would at least give me an opportunity to catch my breath.

A glimmer of hope radiated through me as I reached the porch and opened up the door. I thought about how several people had entered this house and never were seen again, but it was the only option I had.

I swung the door open and slammed it closed behind me. When I found a way to lock the door, I choked on my breath. It was as if luck was on my side. I hoped that the lock would provide me with more time to find a hiding place.

There was no time to waste, but the lack of light in here made things significantly harder. I walked into the kitchen to look for a weapon, but there was nothing there. Had my luck run out?

I ran through the house, praying that I wouldn't run into anything and stopped when I reached a bedroom. I could potentially squeeze myself under the bed, but I'd seen too many horror movies where that ended in death. As I closed the bedroom door, I quickly realized that the doorknob didn't have a lock and I cursed.

I opened a door to my left and could barely see that it was a small walk-in closet with a bunch of cardboard boxes in it. Maybe I could hide behind one of them and hope that whatever it was behind me didn't have a light they could use to shine in here.

I memorized the path to get me to the boxes and closed the closet door behind me. I could feel myself trembling as I walked across the closet and crouched down behind one of the boxes. Instinct told me to pull another box toward me, hopefully concealing myself further.

And then I waited.

It didn't take long for me to hear banging near the front of the house. It sounded as if wood was splintering, and I knew it was trying to break the door down. Based on the way it sounded, it was only a matter of time before it got in here.

Heavy footsteps sounded throughout the home. Maybe if it didn't discover me, I could make it out of this alive.

Or was that wishful thinking?

I wasn't sure, but I could hear whatever it was searching for me. Its anger could be felt in every step that it took. The walls shook in response, and I wondered if they were closing in on me. The thunderous footsteps continued to grow closer, and I knew with every step my chances at survival dwindled.

My stomach dropped when I heard the bedroom door slam against the wall. It was here. This would be the final test to see if my hiding space was good enough to fool my hunter.

I heard the rustling of something searching high and low for me. If it was being that thorough, I was fucked.

That was when I heard the closet door slowly open. Deep down, I knew that it knew that I was in here. There was no light shining in and, as a result, I was left wondering what it would do next.

There was a moment of silence before everything erupted. Boxes flew around the small space, and I put my hands up to cover my head in self-defense. A hand grasped my ankle and pulled.

I screamed, tried to claw it away, but it was no use. Once I was out of the closet, I was grabbed around the waist until I was thrown up against a nearby wall.

"Did you think you could run from me?"

I couldn't see the hooded figure's face, but I recognized him immediately.

"Let me go."

"No. I think I'll keep you for a while longer." He pulled the hood back and I found myself staring into his dark eyes. I was both afraid and calm at the same time. It was all because it was him.

His gloved hand traveled down my body before arriving back at my face. He ran his hand across my cheek before his lips slammed into mine.

His kiss was so intoxicating, I felt as if I couldn't breathe. It was as if he'd sucked the air out of my body. Just one kiss had taken complete ownership over me, and I was left reeling from his touch.

He picked me up and I involuntarily put my legs around his waist. My body had a mind of its own and wouldn't settle for anything less than an orgasm.

My stalker's hands were everywhere on my body. Each touch heightened the flames within me, and I was shocked by how quickly I reacted to everything he did. He'd scrambled my brain and I didn't know if there was any coming back from it.

When he moved my hair out of the way, he sucked hard on a section of my neck and I screamed. It was both painful and pleasurable as it sent shockwaves through me. What kind of hold did he have on me?

"Put your arms around my neck."

There was no way I was arguing with him because I wanted this just as much as he wanted me. I would deal with the consequences another time.

I did as he said and he used the wall to balance me as he moved his arms from my body. He moved back slightly, and I felt him run his hands up and down my thigh before he made his way to my pussy. He rubbed a finger up and down my slit over my leggings and I moaned in response.

Suddenly, he stopped and grabbed the fabric then pulled. The material ripping sounded like music to my ears. I was one step closer to having him sinking into me.

He moved my panties out of the way, and although I hadn't heard him unzip his own pants, I could feel the head of his cock at my entrance. He teased me briefly before giving us what we both desired. I cried out in pleasure as thoughts of what I wanted him to do to me ran rampant in my head.

Ravage me. Mark me.

I hated myself for wanting it all.

That's where it all came to a crashing end. I woke up suddenly and found myself clutching my chest. My breathing was nothing more than loud panting and I could feel moisture flowing through my shirt. It was obvious that I'd broken out in a sweat and knew why that had happened.

That wasn't the only place I was wet either.

Fuck me.

I was in my bed and, most importantly, alone. I was relieved that it had only been a dream, but damn did it seem real. Almost too real. Was having a wet dream about someone who stalked you a thing now? What the hell was wrong with me?

With the sunlight peering into my window, it was obvious that morning had arrived. At least this dream had occurred at a point where it was closing in on time for me to go to class, instead of waking me up in the middle of the night.

Still, I didn't want to go to class today.

When my phone's alarm blared, I clutched my chest. I didn't know how much more shock my heart could take. At least I was glad to have that backup because I wasn't sure if I would have made it to class today without it.

I'd had a great weekend at home and was determined to start the week off right. Pulling myself together didn't take much and I left my room a few minutes earlier than normal and as a result, made it to the economics building early. As I was walking up the stairs, I looked behind me and found Sam there.

"Good morning," I said as cheerfully as I could muster. It was a struggle, but you're supposed to fake it until you make it right? And I would do almost anything to not be attending class today.

"Morning to you too. Have a good weekend?"

"I did. Went home for the weekend. I'm fortunate enough to live within driving distance."

Sam nodded. "Ah. That is nice. I'm from California so going home for the weekend usually isn't an option."

"That's rough, I'm sorry," I said as we rounded the corner and were within feet of the entrance to our classroom.

"It's fine. I'm used to it. It's why I look forward to the longer breaks we have."

That was fair. I was about to say something as we were walking into our classroom, but all of the words died on my lips.

This couldn't be happening.

Professor Hamby wasn't standing in front of our classroom, but the space was still occupied.

Standing behind Professor Hamby's podium was my stalker. He looked up as we walked in, and his eyes were focused on me. A vicious grin crossed his face as I walked across the threshold.

There was no way this was my reality. I must have still been sleeping... right?

I found my composure quickly, if I did say so myself, and walked to my seat. Once seated, I pinched myself to make sure that I wasn't asleep. The sting was there so this wasn't a nightmare.

Panic surged through me. There was no way this was happening. I was trying to comprehend that this was happening, but my brain couldn't compute. Pinching my skin did little to prove to me that this was real. I wanted to pull my phone out and text Bianca immediately, but I refrained. I didn't want him to know how much he'd freaked me out and trying to maintain what little sanity it felt I had left was of utmost importance to me.

"Good morning, class. Professor Hamby had an accident and had to take a leave of absence. I'm going to be teaching in his place. My name is Professor Soren Grant."

If that was his real name, that opened up many doors for me to figure out my next steps. I pulled out my phone and sent Bianca a quick text.

> Me: I finally know my stalker's real name.

My message was straight to the point. I closed my eyes and prayed that she would answer immediately. As if the universe was taking pity on me, my phone vibrated in my hand. Thank fuck for Bianca having her phone on her.

> Bianca: Holy shit. What is his name?

> Me: Soren Grant. And you'll never guess what else. He is now my new professor.

> Bianca: Wait what?! He was at a gala I was at last week. My parents know him, or at least, of him.

What were the fucking chances? My phone vibrated again.

> Bianca: He's your fucking professor?!?!

>> Me: What happened? And I have no idea... to be honest, I'm worried that something happened to Professor Hamby. He is the one who was supposed to be teaching this course.

I needed every piece of information we could find on Soren.

> Bianca: Nothing happened. Apparently, they were surprised to see him. I got the impression he isn't really at those types of events often.

I thought about what Bianca said when my phone vibrated in my hand.

> Bianca: He doesn't live too far from Brentson. As kids we always thought that the house he lives in was haunted, but I can't confirm or deny it.

"Ahem."

I jumped when I heard the noise and my already fragile nerves bounced around my body. My eyes slowly rose from my phone screen to the man now standing near my desk. I'd been so engrossed in texting Bianca that I hadn't noticed my new *professor* had walked right up to me.

"Is whatever you have on your phone more important than what I'm teaching?"

I could feel my cheeks burning as Soren's eyes were now glued to me as he looked down his nose at me. It was weird referring to him as anything other than my stalker or that asshole, but here we were. The look in his eyes dared me to speak out of turn, but I knew it wasn't wise.

My stalker was now teaching one of my classes and in charge of grading me for said class. I couldn't afford to fail, so I needed to tread lightly.

This entire time, he'd been several steps ahead of me and I didn't know when he'd strike.

But this time, he'd made a big mistake by creating this gotcha moment: he'd given me his name.

My ability to research would be key in this endeavor. I needed to find out everything I could about him and fast. Without a doubt, I had my homework cut out for me in more ways than one.

21

IRIS

The shadows began to creep across my monitor as evening turned to night. If I looked out my window, I could see a few stars sparkling in the night sky. The lamp in my room and the glow from the monitor provided some light, but I preferred to work in the dark.

My eyes began to droop as I leaned my head against my hand, watching the information fly across my screen. I'd been up researching Soren Grant for who knew how long, and I wasn't any closer to finding out who he really was.

He was the CEO of Grant Enterprises, and I was able to find out that he was heavily involved in real estate. It didn't make sense that he was living in what looked like an old house, badly in need of repair, while owning a company that made billions per year, not to mention his personal net worth.

What I also didn't understand was why would he take the time out of his day to stalk me and volunteer to become a professor at Westwick? He clearly had more important things to do, yet here we were.

For my research, I had no issue with using the new laptop he'd purchased for me because I wanted him to know I was researching him. I knew he'd installed some sort of tracker on this device because why would he send me an expensive computer without it? I wanted him to know I was on to him and that I wasn't afraid... even if that was kind of a lie.

It took quite some time for me to pour over the news articles, interviews, and social media posts to see if there was anything I could pick up on, but he came across as charming and polite in all of them. The only thing that stuck out to me was all of these interviews were several years old. It was as if he was everywhere for a moment and then, over the last couple of years, he vanished from the public eye.

What I hadn't been able to pinpoint was why. But I kept digging, more determined than I had been about a lot of things in my life. All I could think about was how much I needed the answer in order to move on. I was addicted to finding out what his history was and the things that made him tick in order to gain an upper hand in this situation. I needed to find a way out of this obsession he had with me because reporting it to the authorities and hoping that I would get justice before he killed me or someone I loved wasn't going to cut it.

As I was digging into another article, something jumped out at me.

Eden Marsden Grant was found murdered years ago. Mr. Grant, who had married his wife just a week prior, has not been seen or heard from in months.

Wait a minute. He was married?

Sympathy hit me hard before it was quickly wiped away when I reminded myself he was stalking me. I felt bad for him, but it didn't give him the right to do what he was doing. The statement in the article made it seem as if his wife's death was sudden, but that was all that I could grasp from that article.

That couldn't be the end, could it? I needed to know more. There was no way that someone just vanished into thin air, but it seemed as if someone had made the effort to do just that with her.

Which made this even stranger. Did he have something to do with her death?

His threats toward me resurfaced and I was pretty sure that if he was willing to threaten a sweet, elderly woman like Gran, then anything was possible, but that might have just been my feelings for my grandmother forcing me to think that.

I performed numerous searches, including on social media websites, looking for his wife, but it seemed as if this woman never existed. When the minutes continued to fly by and I felt as if I was no closer to getting the information I wanted, I sat back in my chair and covered my eyes with my hands. It was obvious that I needed a break, but the urge to keep going was pulling me in a different direction.

A shiver ran up my spine, and I pulled my hands from my eyes and slipped them into the front pocket of my hoodie. The feeling that I was being watched was back, and that was more unsettling than if he'd just been tracking what I was searching for online.

Something flashed out of the corner of my eye and I turned my head to look at it. When I saw a light coming from my closet again, part of me wanted to panic. Freaking out would get me nowhere and I needed to know what the hell was going on.

I pushed my chair back and stood up with my phone in hand. I thought that, in case something happened, it wouldn't be a bad idea to have my phone readily accessible. The anticipation about what I might find was causing me to shake as I walked over to where the light was coming from.

I opened the door and moved my clothes out of the way so I could get a better look at where the light was coming from. This time when I came closer, the light didn't go out. Instead, I noticed there was a hole in the floor of my closet that looked as if it was situated in a way that it gave me a view into the room below mine.

I struggled to remember if I knew what was located on the floor below this one. It could have been more dorm rooms, but I didn't know for sure. If there were more dorm rooms down there, why didn't the light come on more frequently? It seemed unlikely that someone was living down there.

The hairs on the back of my neck were at full attention as I could see a candle flickering, doing its best to light up the room. There was no way this was a dorm room then because most students wouldn't be using a candle to provide light in their room unless it was during some sort of emergency. Did the room not have a light fixture? Couldn't the person who was down there use a phone or a flashlight to help them see?

Based on what I could see, the room wasn't a dorm room at all. It wasn't set up like my room, which should have been the standard for this dorm. I couldn't see a bed or a desk from this vantage point, but that didn't mean that it wasn't there.

All of this was creepy. A million thoughts ran through my

head as I tried to figure out what was going on in the room below mine. Part of me wanted to run away and ignore whatever was going on down there. The other part of me was frozen in place, refusing to move under any circumstances.

A creak on the floor below me forced me to hold my breath. Was I going to see the person who was down there, doing who knew what? The thought freaked me out, but I did my best not to make a sound. The last thing I wanted to do was draw attention to myself.

I watched as someone in a black hoodie with the hood pulled over their head came into view. They stood there for a few seconds before leaning forward to blow out the candle.

The light coming from the floor was gone and I bit back a curse. Just like that, it had all come to an end, and I was left sitting there wondering what the hell I'd just witnessed. I waited a moment to see if I heard whoever was down there make a sound, announcing their departure, but nothing came.

I couldn't sit in my closet all day, so I tried my best to get up soundlessly. With more grace than I'd ever mustered in my life, I backed away from the hole and slowly walked out of my closet. It wasn't until I was near my desk that I stepped on a creaky wooden plank and I winced. Hopefully, if there was someone still down there, they would think nothing of it.

I touched the mousepad of my laptop to awaken it from sleep mode and after typing in my password, I found myself staring at an article about Soren's wife. This wasn't what I had open when I left the laptop was it?

Eden Marsden Grant.

I scrolled down before reading the article to see if there were any photos of Eden included with the article. My jaw dropped and my eyes became as wide as saucers when I was rewarded for my efforts.

The similarities were undeniable. She looked like me.

Freaked out, I couldn't begin to describe how I felt. I wanted to go to campus police with the information I had, but a lot of it would be hearsay. I didn't have a picture of the man that was stalking me and from what I could see, he'd been mostly careful about leaving any traces of him around.

Then it clicked in my mind that I potentially had an opportunity to show that he'd been near me. I cringed about how I did nothing when he'd entered my room and sucked on my nipples. Could that have been used as a way to get his DNA so I could prove that it was him?

I wished I had thought this through before, then maybe I wouldn't be in this predicament.

What could I do now?

22

SOREN

"Does anyone have any other questions?"

The darkness of the room made it slightly hard to see if anyone was about to raise their hand, but I managed. This classroom looked slightly frightened. I was pretty sure they hadn't changed much in here since I attended class in this building years ago and that said more about the college than it did about anything else.

It was the end of my second day of classes, and I looked at each and every student in the room. I was willing to bet that some of the students were daring someone else to ask another question. What they didn't know was that I also hoped there were no more questions so that I could get out of here.

I had important business to attend to and I was done here. I glanced at my phone, confirming the time before I said what I'd been waiting to say since I'd walked in the door. "Class is over for today."

I waited a moment for some of the other students to filter out before I said, "Ms. Bennington."

I bit back a smile when Iris stopped in her tracks. She'd been walking next to Sam, and he, too, stopped when I called her name. None of this had anything to do with him so he had no reason to stay. He gave Iris one last look before whispering something to her and leaving the classroom.

Iris stared at the door and I could tell that she wanted to bolt out of it, much like she'd done at the end of class the day she saw that I was her professor. I'd let her run and have her way last time, but this time, enough was enough. My patience was thin enough to snap. I wanted her in all the ways I could have her and then some.

"Yes?" Her voice was somewhat timid, but I could hear a spark there that at any moment would be ready to detonate. I looked forward to hearing the fireworks.

"I would like a word."

"Professor Grant—"

I could tell it pained her to call me by that title, but she wasn't about to draw attention to herself being that there still were other students in the room. My girl always preferred to remain in the background and be observant about what was going on around her, but not anymore. She was going to take center stage now.

I waited for the rest of the class to leave before I asked my question. "Do you have a class you need to get to right now?"

"Yes."

I knew she was lying because I knew her schedule, but even if I hadn't known, it was easy to tell that she wasn't being truthful. Iris tried to tuck away a piece of her hair that had fallen out of her ponytail and looked up at the ceiling before looking toward me. She refused to look me in the eye, and I wondered if she was afraid of what she might see.

I didn't blame her, because if I were her, I'd be afraid too. But I wouldn't tolerate being lied to.

"Don't lie to me."

"I'm not lying!" Her performance was much better this time, almost award worthy.

I made a note to add it to the punishment tally that I was keeping. "Meet me during office hours today. You and I have some matters to discuss."

"No. What you should do is leave me the fuck alone."

I didn't reply right away. Instead, I walked over to the podium and stood behind it. I folded my arms over my chest, and it took everything not to stop my lips from twitching before I spoke. "That's not how you should talk to your professor. I thought you had better manners than that."

She couldn't stop her eye roll and a smirk appeared on my face. Riling her up was becoming a favorite pastime of mine.

I cleared my throat and said, "Meet me at my office during office hours."

"Where is Professor Hamby?"

I hadn't been expecting her to ask about him, but if she wanted to know how he was, I was willing to tell her. "He had a little accident, but he'll be back to teaching classes after winter break."

"What did you do to him?"

I admired her empathy and loyalty. "Nothing you need to worry about, petal."

"Stop calling me that and attempting to avoid the questions I'm asking." Her eyes were spitting fire and I knew if she could, she would have killed me on the spot.

I moved around the podium, taking her off guard. If she'd

gotten comfortable with the podium between us, she was sadly mistaken. I would knock anything in my path down to get to her.

Iris took a couple of steps back and I followed her until her back hit the wall on the other end of the classroom. I glanced out of the small window on the door to see if anyone could see us, but when I saw no one, I looked back at Iris. I used the back of my hand to brush her cheek. She trembled against my touch.

She might pretend to be unaffected by me, but we both knew that was a lie. There was something else there, floating amongst her baby blues. The fear that I'd grown accustomed to seeing in her eyes wasn't as prevalent as it had been in the past. Instead, there was anger that covered every part of her face. I could see the wheels in her head turning, plotting what she wanted to do next.

"Get away from me." Her voice was just above a low growl, and I'd be a fool not to hear the warning in them.

Rage radiated from her, but where she tried to be intimidating, she failed. Nothing about her made me want to shrink away from her or from what was going on here. I wanted her fire, her every emotion, her every desire. None of the walls that she put up would stand in my way.

"Or what?"

I saw what she was going to do out of the corner of my eye and I reacted. Her hand moved up to slap me in the face, but my reflexes were faster. I grabbed her hand just before the slap was going to connect with my cheek and pinned it over her head. I did the same with her other hand to make sure she wouldn't try the same with it.

I wondered if her thoughts traveled back to when I held

her hands above her head while I finger fucked her. Or when I'd run my knife along her nipples and I made sure to get a taste. Mine surely did, and I couldn't wait to do it again.

Her mouth dropped open in shock. Was it from her almost assaulting a professor or from how quickly I stopped her?

I was amused by her actions, but did my best to restrain myself from showing it. The look on my face remained stern much like the words that came out of my mouth. "We don't hit people around here unless it's me slapping your ass. Got it?"

"I—I didn't mean to try to hit you even though you would have deserved it."

It was a half-assed apology, and I wanted a real one. "We're going to try that again. Repeat after me. I'm sorry for almost hitting you, Professor Grant."

She pursed her lips in an attempt to stop herself from reciting what I said. When I squeezed her wrists, she finally spoke. "I'm sorry for almost hitting you, Professor Grant. Happy?"

"That's a good girl." I watched as she visibly swallowed hard. It was obvious that she liked my praise. "You added a bit extra at the end, but I'll take the apology. Now, when I said that you were to come to my office during office hours, I meant it. I would hate to have to fail you out of this class if you don't show up."

It was a low blow, but I'd do it if I needed to. If she wanted to play hardball, I had no problem doing it too.

"You wouldn't do that." She'd said the words confidently, but the fear was back in her eyes.

"Why wouldn't I? You have an issue with paying attention,

and I think that's the perfect way to get your attention. If you listened to what I wanted you to do, you wouldn't be in this situation."

The lie easily fell from my lips. From the moment we collided, it would have to take an act from the devil himself to take her away from me.

"What do you want from me?"

I waited a beat to think of how I wanted to word my response. I also knew that she was desperate for this answer, so I was willing to wait before I said anything because I liked giving her delayed gratification. "I want for you to be mine for however long I say."

Her eyes widened to comical proportions. That hadn't been what she was anticipating.

Good.

"Absolutely not."

"That wasn't a question, Iris. And now you can't claim to not know what happens if you don't listen to my orders. Now, I'll see you later during my office hours."

I slightly tightened my grip on her wrists before letting her arms go. I took two steps back, giving her plenty of space to do what she wanted. Iris took the opportunity to get away from me and ran out of the room. She didn't even bother to close the door behind her.

I didn't bother with the door either, and instead walked over to the podium to grab my things. I had no doubt that she would be there this afternoon.

Because she had no other choice. I would hunt her down if necessary and that was the last thing she wanted.

23

IRIS

I stood outside of a dark-brown wooden door as my heart pounded in my chest. It was the only thing I could hear even though I was standing in the hallway of the economics department building.

I hated myself for a lot of things that happened over the last few weeks and one of those reasons was for standing here. There were a million different things I could be doing right now and all of them were probably smarter than being in front of this door. Instead of dwelling on what I could have done, I took a deep breath to steel myself, but that failed. I ended up raising a shaky fist and brought it to the door. To me, the sound of my knock echoed throughout the entire hallway. Was I drawing more attention to myself and what I was doing here, even though there was no one around?

I waited a beat and then another for Soren to announce that I could come in. He should have been expecting me, so what was the hold up? Was this part of my punishment, making me stand outside of his office and increasing the risk that someone would come by and see what was going on?

Then again, this all could appear to be completely innocent. I was just a student, waiting for my new professor to
answer my knock. The same professor that had fingered me.
Then again, that happened before he walked into my
marketing course.

This shit was all convoluted. I was left standing here
waiting for this fucker who seemed content to let me stand
outside this door, while he did whatever he was doing. I
wouldn't be surprised if he was fucking someone else in
there.

Startled, I jumped back as the door swung open. There
stood Soren Grant, in all his glory. Gone was the suit jacket
and the tie he'd worn earlier. At some point, he'd rolled up
the sleeves of his black button-down to his forearms and had
undone the top button. It made him look more comfortable,
in stark contrast to the feeling that was pulsing through me.
My entire body was on high alert, and the urge of fight or
flight surrounded me, teasing me with the opportunity to
take either option.

Although this was Professor Hamby's office, Soren looked
right at home here. His dark-colored clothes fit in well with
the atmosphere of the office. The blinds were drawn, making
it darker here than it would be around this time of day. Books
upon books were everywhere and I wondered how Professor
Hamby kept organized in any way. With my brief interaction
with him, he always seemed to be put together, so this was a
surprise.

Unless Soren had caused the mess here, but I doubted
that was the case.

When Soren closed the door behind me, he'd snatched
one of those choices away from me, but the other was still

there, creeping in the background of my mind in case the time came that I needed to use it.

"Have a seat," he said as he gestured to the empty chair in front of his desk.

While on the surface his comment might have seemed polite, I knew there was no kindness in his words. He wasn't giving me a say in the matter. The desire to argue with him about this was high, but I knew I needed to choose my battles wisely with him. I swung my backpack off my back and placed it in my lap as I sat down. It would have made more sense to place it on the floor at my feet, but I didn't want to put another obstacle in the way in case I needed to flee this office.

My eyes followed his every movement as he sat down behind his desk and leaned back in his chair, oozing cockiness with every motion he made. He stared at me for a moment, and I wondered if I was going to have to talk first or if he would.

"Thank you for coming here this afternoon." Sarcasm dripped from every word. He wasn't thankful for me coming here. Being thankful for someone coming or going somewhere meant that they had a choice. I didn't have an option in the matter.

"You're not welcome." My statement came out bolder than I felt, but I was still trembling on the inside. I was irritated I was here to begin with, and I was doing everything to make sure that my annoyance made itself known.

"You can't help but wonder about what I'm going to say or do. The urge to know more is in your blood. Your curiosity is why you're beating yourself up about being here."

I hated that he'd easily read the debate I'd been having

with myself. I took a deep breath to help control my emotions. I tried to repeat the mantra I told myself I would put all of my focus into rather than swinging at him because it would do neither of us any good. What I didn't want was a repeat of what happened in the classroom. "You threatened me to get me to come here, so here I am."

"Since when do you listen to what I say?"

This was pointless. I clenched my bag and made a move to get up because this was nothing but a waste of time for me.

"Sit."

I slowly sat back down, but I refused to relax because relaxing meant that my guard was down, and I needed to protect myself from the man in front of me.

"Did you enjoy that?"

"Enjoy what?"

Confusion muddled my thoughts because it was as if he was speaking in riddles that I couldn't figure out. I didn't know if he was being vague on purpose, or if he didn't fully know what the hell he was doing. I chastised myself for thinking so because it seemed as if he was always in control and fifteen steps ahead of me. This was all a part of his wicked plan, something I didn't have the privilege of knowing.

"There are certain things I want from you, Iris, that you will be prepared to give me."

"I don't know what the hell you're talking about." I cringed at the way I was speaking to someone who was supposed to be my professor, but I knew this was nothing more than him cosplaying to get closer to me.

"I think you do and if I don't get it, I have no problem doing several things to show you my displeasure. That includes failing you on any of the assignments that you submit while I'm your professor in this course and paying your grandmother another visit."

"Leave my grandmother out of whatever sick game you're trying to play."

He leaned forward and put his elbows on the desk before he said, "You can call it whatever you want, but that doesn't change the terms of this agreement."

It took every ounce of control that I had left not to scream at the man in front of me. "I didn't agree to that agreement."

He shifted his body again, crossing his arms over his broad chest. His deep stare captivated me with every second our gazes met. "You will."

"I don't understand why you're so interested in me. I've done nothing to cause any of this to happen." I said through gritted teeth. How I hadn't launched myself at him or fled the room yet, I didn't know.

His eyes never deviated from me, but he didn't reply back right away. It made me wonder if he had a response for my inquiry.

"That's where you're wrong. You've done plenty that has stirred up quite a bit of discord. What I want from you is to put the fucking bag down and stand up."

Hearing him curse shouldn't have sent a thrill through me, and I couldn't tell if it was arousal or fear. Maybe it was a combination of both. I refused to comply. "No."

"Iris..." His voice trailed off and the warning was loud and clear. If I didn't follow what he said, there would be consequences. Instead of waiting for me to move, he stood up and walked around the big wooden desk. Before I could process that he was standing next to me, he wove his hand into my hair and pulled, forcing me to look into his dark stare.

I tried to fight against him, but it was useless. It did nothing but make him smirk. He was enjoying every minute of it.

"Get. Up."

Because of the tightness of his grip on my hair and not knowing what the hell he might do to me next, I dropped my bag to the ground and stood up. He used his hold on me to bring me around the wooden desk to where he'd been seated just seconds before. He let go of my hair and sat back down in his chair.

"I want you to choose a word. Any word that's preferably not the name of someone you know."

Where the hell was he going with this? "Why?"

"Just do it." His tone was serious and left no room for arguing.

I swallowed the things I really wanted to say before I replied, "Diary." It was the first word I could think of.

"Excellent. If you don't like something, that's the word you'll use."

"What if I use it right now?"

Soren scoffed. "You won't."

The smugness in his voice added to the irritation I felt. In fact, I wished he would just run his fingernails along a chalkboard rather than having to deal with the conversation we were currently having. I wanted to say the word, but he was right. I wasn't going to say a thing.

The smirk on his face made me want to curse him out, but that wouldn't be beneficial to me. "Now get on your knees, petal."

His words left me breathless. The harshness of his voice was more of a turn on when I expected to be repulsed. It lit a flame within me that I was easily able to verify was excitement about what might come next. It was the same feeling I'd gotten when I had the dream about him chasing me and then fucking me on the spot in that haunted house.

I wanted to rebel against him, but I found myself wanting to get on my knees for him. With a hard swallow, I slowly knelt down as his legs opened wider, giving me more space to work with.

"Good job, petal. Now unzip my pants."

His command made me tremble in anticipation of what he would say next. Part of me wanted to rebel, but I couldn't deny the power his words held over me. I leaned forward and put my hands on his waistband. My hands shook slightly as I slowly undid his pants. Having to brush my hand against him was enough to further send my brain into a tailspin.

Once I'd finished dragging the zipper down, he put his hands on my shoulders and gently pushed. It was the first time I'd noticed that he seemed to be capable of doing anything tenderly, outside of him being able to go in and out of my room without making a noise.

He lifted his hips up so that the pants could move down his body and I sat there staring in amazement. I wasn't shocked to see that he had black boxer briefs, but I was surprised to see how hard he was.

Nerves danced up and down my spine as I watched him palm himself through his briefs. I could feel him staring at me as he grew harder by the second. I couldn't look up at him for fear of what I might find in his eyes.

Soren lifted his hips up once more and moved the briefs

down his legs and I was left staring at his dick. I wanted to drag my eyes away because it felt rude to stare, but I couldn't get enough. He reached up and pulled my ponytail loose. As I felt my hair cascade down my shoulders, I barely recognized it because I was so entranced by him.

"Put your lips on my cock, Iris."

This was one of the most intimidating moments of my life. It also didn't go unnoticed by me that he didn't call me by his favorite nickname this time.

His hand weaved into my hair as I moved forward. I licked the head of his cock lightly, worried that I might be doing something wrong. I wasn't inexperienced, but sucking off my stalker in his temporary office was a whole new thing for me.

"I know you can do better than that."

His comment pissed me off and I couldn't stand how easily he managed to get under my skin. I glanced down at his cock before looking back up at him and grasping him in my hand. I slowly licked the head again, this time with more force and determination than I'd had previously. If he wanted me to do my best, then he was going to get it.

After playing with his head for several seconds, I opened my mouth wider and allowed him to slip his cock inside. I watched as his eyes shut tight and felt him gripping my hair tighter. He was starting to lose control and I was basking in the joy of it.

A low growl left his mouth as more of his cock made it past my lips. I moved my hand and, when his dick was close to hitting the back of my throat and my gag reflex kicked in, tears sprang into my eyes and his grip lessened on my strands. He shifted to massaging my hair and scalp versus grabbing it.

"You can take it, petal. Every single inch."

This time, I relaxed my throat and mouth in hopes of taking more of him. For some reason, the need to satisfy him had taken over and I was determined to do the best job I could.

As I took more of him in, the creaking of a floorboard made me pause and Soren switched back to gripping my strands once more.

"Did I tell you that you could stop?"

The way he said the words meant that it wasn't much of a question. I shook my head slightly since my mouth was otherwise occupied. He raised an eyebrow as if to say get back to it, and I did just that.

I pulled away slightly and my hand gripped the base of his cock once more. I used my saliva to coat him and moved my hand up and down, finding a tempo that worked for both of us.

"Shit," he muttered, and it ignited something within me. Pride in what I was doing was what I guessed it was.

This time, a knock on the office door made me jump, but unlike the first noise I heard, I refused to stop what I was doing.

"Come in."

He hadn't locked the door? Can you even lock these office doors? Dread crawled up my spine as I heard the door creak open. I looked up at him and saw that he was barely hanging on. From where I was, I couldn't see who was there. I prayed they couldn't see me either.

"I wanted to check in to see how everything was going during your first week."

The voice sounded as if she was near the door. I hoped she didn't come over and come around the desk.

Soren leaned over and started sifting through some papers. "Everything has been great. I absolutely *love* my job, Dr. Glen."

I almost froze again. I hadn't recognized her voice immediately, but there was, now, no mistaking that it was Dr. Glen, Dean of the Economics Department. I tried my best to keep quiet, but I didn't stop what I was doing.

"Okay, well please let me know if you need anything," Dr. Glen replied.

I waited to hear the telltale sign that she'd left us alone once more, but it didn't come.

"One of your students left their book bag here."

"I saw. I plan on sending her an email and finding a way to get it back to her as soon as possible."

"Excellent. Have a good rest of your day."

"I will and same to you."

When I heard the door shut, I breathed a sigh of relief, but that was short lived.

Soren pulled his cock out of my mouth, leaving a loud pop in its wake. He didn't say a word as he lifted me up so that I was standing. Before I could blink, his lips were on mine, forcing me to lean back on his desk. His kiss was even more intoxicating in real life than it had been in my dream.

He broke our connection temporarily to take off my t-shirt and sweatshirt before he was back to kissing me. His hands wrapped around my waist and found the waistband of my leggings and with my help, they ended up around my ankles. If he'd decided to rip them much like he had in my dream, I wouldn't have been upset. That left me in just my black cotton bra and panties.

"Turn around and lean on the desk."

I complied immediately. My rebelliousness was temporarily sated, and I wanted whatever this ended up being. Soren ran his fingers over my ass, taking his time to massage every inch that he could get his hands on. He played with the edge of my panties and lifted them to make a makeshift thong, giving him almost full access to my whole butt.

I heard him make a low moan before his touch left me. I heard some movement behind me before his hand was on my back and I felt the slap hit my ass.

A small scream left my lips, and I hoped it didn't draw any attention to what we were doing in here. Startled, I looked over my shoulder and said, "What is that?"

"Hamby's fraternity paddle. Wonder if he'd ever used it in this way too?"

He slapped my backside again and I didn't jump this time. Instead, a moan left my lips. I didn't know I'd be into being spanked, but what a way to discover it. He repeated his motions, taking care to hit each cheek the same number of times and before long I was leaning on the desk, wondering if I could come just from this.

I heard the paddle drop and his hands were on my ass again. He took his time massaging me, soothing the pleasurable pain from his actions, and said, "I love the way you take this. Your ass looks pink and beautiful. This was supposed to be your punishment for disobeying me, but I can tell that you enjoyed it way too much."

Although I hadn't exerted much energy, I was out of

breath. He turned me around and lifted me up so that I was sitting on the desk. He hadn't bothered moving anything out of the way so the papers that had been strewn about were probably ruined.

I leaned back on my elbows and watched as he stared at me. He leaned over to his left to grab something off the desk, and I quickly saw that it was a condom. He unwrapped it and I couldn't stop watching as he covered his cock.

He stepped between my legs and I looked on as he moved my panties out of the way and lined up his dick with my entrance. I cried out in ecstasy as he finally gave us what we both wanted.

"You're so fucking tight, holy—" The words died on his lips.

I'd expected him to slam into me, but he slowly moved his cock, giving my body enough time to adjust to him. He gave me a couple of warm-up thrusts before he began to pick up the pace. I reached down and grabbed the edge of the desk to hold onto for dear life.

Soren reached up and grabbed the cups of my bra, dragging them down so that my breasts spilled out. He played with my nipples as our groans, moans, and the sound of our bodies slapping against one another, took hold. It was the only thing I could hear. It was the only thing I wanted to hear.

I wanted every part of him that he was willing to give.

I was convinced that this man had the devil within him.

Was this hell? If so, hell shouldn't feel... So. Fucking. Good.

The dark gleam in his eyes sent another shiver through me. His pace picked up and his hands moved to my pussy.

When he found my clit, I nearly yelled out, but bit my lip instead. A metallic taste hit my taste buds and I knew what I had done.

"I'm getting close," I said. The words flew out of my mouth as if they were racing for first place. How quickly my desire had built had taken me by surprise, but I was more than happy for it.

"Come apart for me, baby."

Those words were all it took for me. His hand moved from my clit and grabbed my cheek to steady my face and he kissed me as I came all over his cock. That didn't stop Soren's thrusts as he slammed into me repeatedly.

When I stopped screaming, Soren let me go as determination crossed his face. He wanted to find his release too. He lowered his gaze down so he could watch his cock pound my pussy before dragging his eyes up to mine. He leaned forward again and kissed me. The bellow that came from him would be a sound I would never forget.

His motions slowed right along with our kiss. My brain was nothing but a pile of mush, refusing to process what had just occurred. Soren pulled away from me as he, too, tried to catch his breath and all we could do was stare at one another.

I moved my ass and looked over my shoulder. I saw that I'd leaned back onto a book that might now have issues with closing.

Did I feel guilty about practically ruining a book? Yes, but my guilt was overwhelmingly washed out by the need for him to put an end to my misery.

The slamming of a door in the distance broke our trance.

I hopped off the desk and scrambled to gather and put on

my clothes. Being in his presence any longer than necessary freaked me out.

What the fuck had I done? Was I being a coward by running away? Yep, and I couldn't care less.

"Let me help—"

"No, I'm fine," I said as I yanked my sweatshirt over my bra. I ran around the desk and stuffed my t-shirt into my bag. Taking the two seconds it would have cost me to put it on was too much time.

I glanced at Soren as I put my bag on my shoulder and saw that he was also getting dressed.

"Iris—"

I didn't wait to see what he was going to say to me. Without a second thought, I spun on my heel and quickly walked out of his office. I walked down the hall and braced myself for Soren to call for me. When he didn't, I relaxed a little until I walked past Dr. Glen's office, whose door just so happened to be open.

She glanced away from her computer and gave me a small smile. I returned the gesture and didn't give her an opportunity to get a good look at me. I was convinced that I looked as if I'd just been fucked, and I didn't want to have to answer any questions.

I didn't stop walking until my phone vibrated in my book bag when I could finally see Payne Hall in my sights. I pulled the phone and saw that I had a text notification.

> Bianca: I booked us some much-needed R&R for the day at a spa/beauty salon. If you don't want to go, I'll cancel, but I figured you could use the break.

I was still waiting for my breathing to return to normal from the workout I'd been put through. I tried to type back to Bianca but it was proving to be useless. I'd decide if I'd go on this adventure once I had a moment to myself and could breathe.

24

IRIS

"Are you sure this is something that you want to do?"

I nodded my head without hesitation. Bianca glanced over at me from across the room. Concern was etched into her eyes, but I'd never been surer about something.

I needed this change. I needed to do this to take my mind off of what had happened with Soren. This was something I'd wanted to do in the past, but I always became too afraid or would talk myself out of it. When I saw the photo of Soren's wife, and the events that took place in his office, it only solidified that.

I'd never made a drastic change in my appearance before, but now was as good a time as any.

"Have you decided on a color?"

"Yes. I want this," I said as I showed the photo on my phone to my hairstylist. She studied the photo, nodding her head several times as if she were trying to understand the image in front of her.

"That we definitely can do," she said as she gave me a reassuring smile.

I was still nervous, but I felt slightly more at ease when she confirmed it was something they could do. It was in contrast to the calmness I felt after the massage both Bianca and I took part in earlier today.

"Did you decide on something?"

I looked over my shoulder and spotted Bianca. She was sitting in her own chair, preparing to have her hair done as well.

"I have, but I want it to be a surprise." We could all use a little bit of joy now and again and being able to show off my hair would bring me that.

I tried to relax the best I could as my hairstylist worked her magic on my hair. When she was done with the dye and rinsing my hair, I watched as she blew it out and I couldn't get enough of the color she'd added.

Once she was done, I examined my hair and couldn't believe that I'd actually gone through with it. I had to admit that it looked fantastic. No longer was I the person who blended into the crowd.

I'd asked my hairstylist to dye the ends of my hair purple so that my hair went from being dark brown near the roots to purple as my hair flowed down to my shoulders. This purple hair would more than likely get me plenty of attention, and I didn't know if I was mentally prepared for it.

Fucking anxiety. Shake it off, Iris. You did this because you wanted to, and it looks fantastic.

I also couldn't help but wonder what Soren would think of it. His opinion shouldn't matter to me, but it was obvious that one of the reasons I'd done this was so I didn't look as much like his dead wife.

That was something I never thought would cross my consciousness, but here we were.

My hairstylist gave me instructions that would hopefully keep the purple as vibrant as it was now for a while and how to care for my hair now that it had been dyed. I heard someone say something about the bill and I looked over my shoulder. Bianca was standing at the cash register with her credit card in hand.

"I can pay for my portion, Bianca."

"Don't worry about it. I invited you to this hair salon and spa experience and said you can get whatever you want. I'm paying."

I never wanted Bianca to think that I was using her for her money. We weren't poor, and throwing money at a new hairdo hadn't been a planned expense, but I would have made it work.

"Your hair came out looking amazing, Iris," Bianca said as she walked toward me.

I watched Bianca through the mirror I was sitting in front of as she examined my hair. Her hair looked great as well. She'd gotten her blonde hair cut so now her hair rested just below her shoulders.

As we stepped outside, my eyes were darting in every direction. I was searching for Soren, but if he was here, he was doing an excellent job of remaining inconspicuous because I couldn't find him. What I couldn't decide was if that was a good thing or a bad thing.

Once she'd unlocked the doors, I got into her car and buckled my seat belt. I looked at myself in the rearview mirror before I sat back in my seat. I waited for her to start the car before I spoke. "Have you heard anything about Soren?"

She shook her head. "Nothing that you didn't already know. I've been trying to talk to my parents about him, but talking about anything that isn't about my father's political career means I barely get a response. Which is why I don't like to talk to them unless I have to unfortunately."

I didn't bank on Bianca's parents being helpful with this, but it would have been a more than welcomed surprise. But of course, that couldn't go my way.

"I don't know what else to do. I still don't understand why he's doing this or what he wants from me and it's pissing me off."

"Why do people stalk other people?" She glanced at me before turning her attention back to the road. "Power, control, etc. It could be anything."

"It's more than that, B. At least, I get the feeling that it is, but I don't know what."

"I still think you should go to the police again."

I rubbed a hand across my face, thankful that I wasn't wearing any makeup because if I was, it would have been smudged all over my face. "I can't. I refuse to put Gran's life at risk."

I wanted to get the authorities involved again, but I already saw what happened when I did. I leaned against the passenger window and slammed my eyes shut. It was the only option I had to keep my tears at bay.

Bianca didn't respond right away and I didn't blame her. I wouldn't know what to say either.

She cleared her throat sometime later and said, "Do you

want to go to a football game this weekend? Brentson and Westwick are playing each other. I'll be there with my brother's girlfriend, and it would do you some good to get off campus more."

"Hey! I get off campus plenty." I wasn't really offended. I barely knew that we had a football team, to be fair, but that was mostly because I didn't really follow sports.

"Sure you do."

I knew she was trying to bait me into talking again and take my mind off the impossible task in front of me. I looked over at her and said, "I'm off campus right now, aren't I?"

Bianca rolled her eyes at me. "You know what I mean."

"I do." I threw my hands up for a brief moment and said, "Fine. I'll go to the football game. I don't know much about it but it'll be nice to do something that seems normal for a while."

"Excellent. I believe the game is at your football field, so it'll be even easier for you to attend."

I shook my head at my ability to completely have my head buried in the sand and not know that we were hosting the opposing football team as well. It was obviously a special skill I'd acquired.

"Well, I guess I have no excuse then, do I?"

Bianca glanced at me out of the corner of her eye. "Nope. You don't."

THE LOUD NOISES that were coming from the crowd fed into the energy I felt and that wasn't a good thing. This was supposed to be a minor reprieve from my daily routine and wasn't.

I hated being this nervous. This wasn't my scene but stepping outside of my comfort zone was supposed to be a good thing. Here I was at a football game watching my college's team play against our biggest rivals. I eagerly accepted Bianca's invitation to attend, but I didn't come here only to see her and to be mildly entertained for a few hours.

I wanted to get out of my dorm room and to socialize. The eeriness that surrounded Westwick University seemed to stay at the campus's gates and it felt as if a heavy boulder had been lifted off of my chest. I didn't have to worry about him.

Sports weren't my thing and me veering away from my usual haunts should confuse him. Then again, if he was following me like I assumed he was, me changing my schedule slightly wouldn't mean a thing.

It would allow me time away from his gaze that sometimes rendered me useless. Whenever I was on campus, deep down I knew that he was always there, lurking in the shadows, watching every move I made.

As I shifted through the crowd, it was nice to be just one of many. It meant that I could blend in and not be the center of attention. Then again, the purple tips of my hair drew more attention than I'd been accustomed to, but I'd done that for my own benefit and no one else's. If people wanted to stare, then so be it.

Except for when it came to him.

The way he studied me was very measured and what it made me feel was almost indescribable. I was intimidated because I could never tell what he was thinking as he stared at me. It was as if he was undressing me with his eyes, slowly peeling back every layer of clothing until he had me bare.

But it was more than that. I noticed something in his measured approach. He enjoyed making me uncomfortable, but I could prove none of this. Simply staring at someone wasn't a cause for concern, but it should be when it came from him.

My professor.

And my stalker.

How I'd ended up in this situation seemed to have happened by chance, but the more things happened, the more I wondered if it truly was a coincidence.

I forced myself to look into the crowd to see if I saw Bianca.

This was the first time in I didn't know how long that I didn't feel as if he was anywhere nearby.

And then it happened. My entire body felt as if it were on edge, and that meant only one thing: He was here.

I could feel his presence in this stadium full of people. That sounded strange, I knew, but I also knew what this feeling was. I'd grown accustomed to him being in the same vicinity and the slight shift in air was there.

The coldness in his eyes sent a shiver down my spine even though I hadn't turned around to find out where he was today. No, I wouldn't give him the time of day.

Instead, I saw my friend's profile and walked straight to where she was sitting with another woman.

"Bianca?" I asked although I was pretty certain it was her. When she turned to face me, a wide grin took over her entire face.

"Iris, hey!" Bianca quickly pulled me into her arms before

I had a chance to react. When we broke apart, she gestured to the woman standing beside her. "Iris, this is Raven. She's my brother's girlfriend. Raven, this is my friend, Iris."

"It's nice to meet you," I said as we shook hands.

"Likewise," Raven replied. "I'll move down and you can sit on the other side of Bianca."

I'd never heard Bianca mention Raven, but she seemed pretty adamant that we should meet and this was a perfect opportunity to do so.

I could feel him watching my every move as Bianca and Raven moved so that I could take the seat they were saving. As we got settled in our seats, I looked up and saw Raven look behind us and pause. That was when I knew she'd spotted him.

I hated that my instincts were right in this case. I debated saying something, but what was there to say?

No. I couldn't say a word.

The ringing of Bianca's phone snatched our attention and I was relieved. It would save me from having to speak on something that could mean life or death.

Bianca shrugged her shoulders and showed the message to me before she handed the phone to Raven so that she too could read the message. I stared into space for a moment as I recalled what the text message had said.

> Unknown Number: Be careful what you wish for, B.

My initial reaction was to tell Bianca that we needed to report this to the proper authorities, much like she'd been begging me to do again when it came to Soren. It would be beneficial to have detailed records about what was going on.

But I refrained selfishly because of my situation. It made logical sense for me to report Professor Grant to the cops and to the president of Westwick University. But when you're dealing with a man with as much money and power as Professor Grant, you're walking into a world of trouble and hurt.

Speaking of him, I took a deep breath and looked behind me. Professor Grant was nowhere to be found.

This wasn't unlike him so none of this was surprising. I also didn't feel him staring at me at the moment. The feeling of being trapped in a fishbowl had lifted and I was sure it had all to do with him not being here right now. But he couldn't be far away because there was no way he could have gotten away that fast.

That was when it hit me. There was one thing I had over him that gave me the upper hand in this situation. The one thing that I could control that would probably do nothing but piss him off.

Controlling the ways that I gave him my attention.

A lot of this was about getting a reaction out of me. Whether it was anger, happiness, or something in between. If I didn't give him a reaction or the time of day, it would make him angry and he'd try to do something even more drastic to get my attention.

But I would refuse to give in because that was what he wanted.

I let out a shaky breath as I made peace with my decision. I could still feel him here, lurking around, determined to cause a chaotic storm whenever he felt like it.

In my mind, I was nothing but the center of the storm, expected to take the brunt of the damage that would ensue.

What I needed to do was seek shelter and protect myself because as of now, that was the only way forward. Deep down, I knew he wouldn't like it one bit, but that wasn't my problem.

It was his.

That thought made my body shake and Bianca looked over at me. "Is everything okay?"

I nodded, but I needed to get out of my seat and walk around for a moment. "I'm going to get a drink really quick. Do you both want anything?"

Both Raven and Bianca shook their heads before Bianca spoke up. "Do you want me to go with you?"

I knew that without a doubt she was referring to Soren, but I shook my head. I leaned closer to her so that only she could hear what I was going to say. "I'm not going to live in fear. I'm just going to grab a bottle of water and I'll be right back. If you don't see me in ten minutes, then something is definitely wrong. At the very least, this stadium is crowded, making it harder for anyone to try something."

Bianca looked at me warily as if she didn't trust what I was saying, but she didn't go any further. I stood up and walked in the direction of the closest concession stand. I ordered a bottle of water and looked in my purse to pull out a few dollars to pay for the drink. That was when I felt something clamp down on my hand.

"What the—" My words trailed off as my eyes widened after I looked up. I expected to find Soren there, but it wasn't him. It was a man with pale blond hair and very bright blue eyes.

"What have you found on the Chevaliers?"

"Nothing, get your hand off of me."

He did the opposite and tightened his grip on my wrist. I yanked to release myself, but my arm didn't budge.

"Have you found any of Payne's documents?"

If anyone was looking on, they would think that he and I were engaged in an intimate conversation versus the heated one that was actually taking place.

His grip on me was frightening, but I refused to show it. "No, I swear. Who the hell are you?"

He ignored my question. "When you do find something, call this number. It could be very lucrative for you if you do."

He removed his hand from my wrist to pull out a piece of white paper that was the size of a business card and handed it to me. I looked down at the piece of paper and then looked up again, but there was no one there.

Who else knew I was looking for Payne's things? And what was I going to do now that more people knew what I was doing?

25

SOREN

"Yes, Ms. Clarkson?"

"I'm not sure that I understand the areas of focus for a good marketing plan. Can you briefly explain it again?"

The look in her eyes told me that she'd already known the answer but was trying to flirt with me versus genuinely asking a question. I glanced at Iris and found her looking down, her head in her books as if she wished she could escape unnoticed from this classroom. Too bad she couldn't run away until I dismissed the class.

"We just went over the answer, Ms. Clarkson."

"But I didn't understand it."

I knew damn well that she did, but I went along with it anyway. "Okay. I'll explain it one more time."

All the while I was explaining the concept again, my eyes never left Iris. I yearned for her attention and being denied it wasn't something I was accustomed to. I found my eyes focusing on the new hair color that was flowing from her ponytail. My thoughts revolved around how it would look feathered along a pillow as I pounded into her.

The color popped against her skin and made her look even more ethereal than before. While I hadn't expected her to do something drastic, such as changing the color of her hair, I liked the shift. I wanted to take my time, running my fingers through each strand. The desire to wrap my hand around that ponytail while I was fucking her mouth was overwhelming. Getting a hard-on while I was trying to explain a concept wasn't advisable, but here I was.

Just as I wrapped up my explanation, I checked my phone and noticed that it was almost time to end class for the day.

"Does anyone have any other questions?" I felt as if it had become routine for me to wrap up each class this way, but it seemed to be most effective. Seeing none, I then said, "Class dismissed."

The shift in the mood of the room was obvious as the students shuffled to their feet and pulled their things together to leave. I walked behind the podium once more where I made a show of letting my gaze not stay on any person for too long although my attention was only on one person.

Iris.

I watched as she leaned over to whisper something to Sam. I couldn't tell what she was saying from here, but to say I was happy about it would have been a lie. Observing her giving him any attention was an annoyance, but I would allow it for now. His life wasn't hanging in the balance because he hadn't laid a hand on her.

If he had, all bets would be off.

Iris stood from her chair. I knew she could feel my stare,

but she was making every effort to not give me the time of day. Even with her being feet away, I could feel her nervous energy. She didn't know if she was making the right choice or not, but she was sticking with it.

And I would stay true to mine.

She didn't bother to look back at me and I made a note to myself. While I couldn't see her tonight due to prior obligations, tomorrow night was set. I was determined to do something about this attitude of hers.

"Come in. Sit down," Parker said as he gestured for me to do so.

I gave one final look at his secretary, who'd welcomed me when I entered before following Parker into his office.

"I prefer to stand," I replied. I'd been sitting down for most of the day and wanted to stretch my legs.

"Suit yourself." Parker walked away from me and stood near his window. "Any updates?"

"Nothing has been appearing on her phone or the laptop that I bought her, but I'm hard pressed to believe that she's given up this easily."

It was the next evening and I found myself in Parker's office at the Chevalier headquarters. I'd driven the few hours into the city to check in with Grant Enterprises and to meet with him. It paid to show my face every once and a while, even if I preferred to stay near home.

It had been a while since I'd visited the headquarters of the Chevaliers. Not much had changed since I'd been there last, but that wasn't shocking. Parker was a creature of habit and preferred to have things in a particular order and then not deviate too much from that order. It served him well as Chairman of the Chevaliers in the New York City chapter.

I watched as he folded his hands behind his back and walked slowly. I could tell that he was waiting for me to continue, so I did.

"Do we even know that Payne had journals or letters that he left behind? And if we do, could they be used to prove that their claims are right?"

I didn't want him to think I suspected that Iris had a case against us, but this had been something that had been bugging me for a while that I hadn't had a chance to voice.

"Honestly, there might be something to it. I never thought that the Turner family was off-base with their claims."

I narrowed my eyes at the man in front of me, surprised that he admitted such a thing, yet was content with how things were unfolding. Anger that I'd thought I'd suppressed before I arrived here began to bubble to the surface and I couldn't remove the bite from my words. "Then why the fuck aren't we coming forward with the truth?"

Parker slammed his fist down on his desk, but I refused to show any fear. It had been one of the few times that I questioned him. I didn't care because it needed to be done.

"Because it could change the way the Chevaliers operate forever. It's inserting family into the fold and who knows what that will force us to do. Our job is to keep the status quo and that's what we are going to do. Don't make me give the word."

The words flew out of his mouth as if Parker couldn't control them. I didn't take kindly to being threatened. He didn't know how deep my desire for Iris went because I'd only filled him in on information that he needed to know. It was a lie by omission, but a lie, nonetheless.

If Parker found out, I didn't know what type of discipline reaction I would face. What I did know was that it would be well worth it in my case.

Parker didn't understand the feelings that I had for her. He didn't know how much I urged to burn this whole world down for her if it would force a smile on her face. He didn't know how many men I'd killed because I wanted to protect her. I'd murdered to make sure that they wouldn't even lift their heads to look in her direction and that's more than I could say that I'd done for anyone.

Even Eden.

But he didn't know that. Or he hadn't announced it to me at least.

I shoved the thoughts I was having to the back burner and responded to Parker. "You have no reason to kill Iris and you don't throw around murdering someone who has basically done nothing to you or the organization. I don't know what has you on edge, but calling for that is uncalled for."

"Are you defending her now?"

I fought myself to maintain my poker face. I didn't want him digging into anything about what might be going on between us because that could put another target on her back. "Absolutely not, but you know I'm not one to just agree with everything you say, especially when I feel like you're jumping to conclusions. This is one of those circumstances."

It irritated me that I had to lie to Parker, but I knew it was for Iris's own good. There might have been a better way to approach this, but right now, I wasn't aware of one.

Parker dragged a hand through his hair and pulled hard. I

wasn't convinced that he wasn't about to pull his hair out. It told me that I'd been right in my current assessment of him.

Before waiting for him to speak, I decided to say something to stop all of the bullshit that was surrounding us and this conversation. I didn't want him to focus on Iris and me or try to connect any dots that were there. "What has you so wound up that you're not thinking clearly?"

Once again, he took his time answering. It was obvious that he was trying to choose his words more carefully this time. "There are several moving parts at play that I'm working on, which I'm hoping will continue to sustain the Chevaliers now and in the future. It has a lot of moving pieces and has me stressed out beyond belief. I'm sorry that I overreacted like that."

That might have been the first time I'd heard Parker apologize. Part of that was because he was usually right, and the other part was because we rarely got into spats like this. "I apologize too. I could see your line of thinking, but that isn't the case at all."

There went that lie again, but I didn't feel an inch of remorse for saying it again.

"I think Iris, right now, is the least of our concerns and we should be looking at other external forces that are trying to attack us."

"You mean like Finn Welch? Heard he met his tragic end recently. Do you know anything about it?"

I shrugged. I could admit to being the cause of his demise, but where was the fun in that? "How unfortunate for him, but I think we would both agree that it serves him right."

Parker chuckled. "We can agree on that."

"Is there anything else you need? I'd like to be getting on the road soon to head back upstate."

"That's all I had. Still, keep me informed about Iris."

"I can do that," I said and stuck my hand out to shake Parker's. He returned the gesture before walking me to his office door.

I nodded to Parker's secretary as I left and soon found myself sitting in my car once more. I checked my emails and my messages to see if anything important had occurred while I was meeting with Parker.

Nothing about work needed to be done right away so I ventured over into looking into what Iris had been up to in my absence.

As I waited for an update on her, I thought about how, even though the start to what we had was rough, I had no intention of giving any of it up. There was nothing that I was more absolutely sure about in this world other than the fact that she was mine.

My attention was drawn to the report at hand. It seemed as if she'd spent a lot of time today researching the Westwick chapter's masquerade ball that would be taking place in a few weeks. I wonder where she'd heard about it from.

Based on her search results, it seemed as if she was trying to get an invitation. As I skimmed the words in front of me, it occurred to me why she might want to be invited.

It would give her an opportunity to go to the Chevalier Manor on campus and find what she hoped would be things related to Eddison Payne.

I smirked when I realized she was still trying to prove that her family hadn't made any of this up. I had to give her credit where credit was due, she was determined, and I enjoyed that about her.

She wanted to go?

Then I would ensure that she would.

But first, I was going to see her so that she could pay for admission.

26

IRIS

I threw myself down on the couch in Payne Hall's lounge and sighed. I was ready to slam my head against the nearest thing I was sitting in front of. I'd been walking around Payne Hall to see if I could find anything that would give me a clue about Eddison and I came up empty. I'd been throughout all of the floors, the small library, and, finally, this lounge. The basement was still off limits because I was wary about trying the supposedly sealed door again.

And I'd found nothing. There was no way I was going to continue searching this evening, so I was calling it quits. The Chevaliers secret remained one for now, but I was determined to win this war.

I made my way upstairs to my room and unlocked my dorm door. As I pushed my door open, I wasn't exactly surprised to see Soren sitting at my desk as if it were his.

"Where were you?"

I ignored his question by asking one of my own. "I thought we stopped this whole coming to my room thing when you became my professor?"

"I didn't agree to that agreement."

I smirked when he threw my own words back in my face. Was it weird that I found it cute that my stalker remembered the things that I said? Probably.

"Now, where were you?"

My attempt at deflecting had failed. "I was walking around Payne Hall trying to clear my head."

Soren leaned on my desk as he regarded me closely. "What did you need to clear your head about?"

"Life. School. This situation."

"Is that why you dyed your hair?" Soren said as he stood up from the chair.

I couldn't tell him that one of the motivating reasons for me changing my hair was because of his dead wife. "I needed a change. It's old news at this point since you've seen me multiple times since I did it."

His lips twitched in response as he took a step toward me. "Yes, but I haven't complimented you on it. It looks lovely on you."

"Thanks?" I was unsure of how to respond. What was the proper etiquette when being complimented by your stalker?

"You're welcome." His stride ate up the remaining space between us as he backed me into the nearest wall. He pulled my ponytail back, forcing my head up to look at him. His gaze studied my lips for a moment. "You don't know how much I'm obsessed with you."

Before I could think of a witty response, he kissed me and any thought fled my mind. The kiss was slow and seductive, surprising me with how quickly things had escalated. It was as if being deprived had made me hungrier for him.

Soren let my hair go long enough to unzip my hoodie and

to remove the t-shirt I was wearing. He nibbled on my neck as his hands landed on the white cotton bra I was wearing today. Slowly I felt him move around so that his hand was at my back. He expertly unclasped my bra with one hand and I helped him remove the garment.

My hands ended up in his hair as he played with my left nipple, taking the opportunity to alternate between licking and sucking on it while his hand massaged and gently rubbed my other nipple so that it wasn't neglected. I needed to rest my body against the wall because I wasn't sure if I was going to fall into a puddle on the floor.

When Soren switched breasts, I moaned. He had complete and utter control over me. I had no doubt that he could get me to commit to anything right now, as long as he continued what he was doing when he asked me to do it.

"I don't know how much more of this I can take," I said between large swaths of air. I was starting to feel light-headed because of the sensations coursing through me.

"You'll take all that I'm willing to give you," he said in response.

I could feel my arousal growing as a result and I wanted to shove him and fuck him at the same time because of it.

I cleared my throat and said, "It's pointless for me to remind you that we shouldn't be doing this, right?"

The words I said sounded foolish when I thought of them, let alone when I said them. He paused and allowed my nipple to fall out of his mouth before he spoke.

"What do you think? Do you want me to stop?" I didn't respond to him and he nodded his head. "Didn't think so."

He went back to playing with my breasts as he continued

to complete his quest for making me lose my mind in the best possible way.

Soren made his way down to my jeans where he stopped to kiss me just below my belly button. I watched with a strange fascination as he unbuttoned them and slowly unzipped. He wasted no time and dragged both my jeans and my panties down in one motion.

"Go lean on your bed with your legs about shoulder width apart."

I ran a hand down his chest as I walked away, doing as he asked. I heard him approach me and he ran a hand up and down my slit.

"You're already so wet for me, petal."

"I want you to fuck me now," I said in a breathless whisper.

"Is that right?"

I heard some rustling in the background and the sound of a condom wrapper. Within seconds I felt his cock nudging my pussy, demanding that I give him all of me.

And I happily obliged.

When he sank into me, I screamed out. This had been something I'd been wanting and craving and now my desire was finally being quenched. I fisted my sheets because I needed something to hold on too.

Soren pulled out of me completely before he plunged back inside, the combined sensation making me groan from the pleasure of it all. He did this a couple of more times before he picked up the pace. It seemed as if fun time was over and now, he was all business about getting us both to our climaxes.

I wished I could look into his eyes while he was fucking

me, but that could happen another time. Here I was already thinking about another damn time. *Fuck.*

"I'm so, so, so damn close," I said but I wasn't sure if he understood me. That was until he reached around me and grabbed my neck. Having him wrap his hand around my neck was exactly what I needed to send me over the edge.

I cried out as my body careened out of control. As if he knew what was going to happen, Soren grabbed my waist to keep me upright while he fucked me. When he found his nirvana, expletives flew out of his mouth at such a volume, that I was sure that anyone who was currently in Payne could have heard him.

I thought that the last time we were together, there was no way that this could get any better and my feelings were a fluke. It just hit me how wrong I was.

We both collapsed on my bed for a few moments to catch our breath. Soren moved his body, I assumed to keep from crushing me for too long, but I wished that he was still there.

Although he was only inches away, the sound of Soren zipping up his pants and buckling his belt seemed far away. There was no way that I was going to be able to function enough to get into my bed by myself. As if he'd sensed it, Soren moved and grabbed my pajamas that were near the foot of my bed and a clean washcloth that had been hanging off a rack in my room.

He placed both near my pillow before he wiped me down and helped me redress into a pair of pjs. He went the extra mile of helping me into bed and tucking me in.

"Who gave you this?"

"Wait what?"

He held up a piece of paper that I'd forgotten to put somewhere else besides out in the open on my desk. "What I assume is a phone number, is on this paper. Who gave it to you?"

I slowly moved my head so that I could look at him. I couldn't tell him what the guy said because that contained information about the Chevaliers, but I could tell him everything else. "Some guy with pale blond hair and light blue eyes. He grabbed my wrist at the football game and gave me his number."

Anger flashed in Soren's eyes, and I grew concerned. Why had what I said set him off to the point that he was pissed off and looked as if he was going to wreck the entire world? I watched as he snatched the piece of paper off my desk and pocketed it before walking to the door. He was leaving already?

"Soren?"

My question was met with dead air when he didn't respond. He hadn't bothered removing any of his clothes, so he'd had the advantage over me. It was as if he was in some sort of trance as he left my room, closing the door, and not sparing me another glance. This time, instead of me gathering my clothes to flee the scene, I was gathering a sweatshirt and pants to throw on so that I could attempt to find him and calm him down.

But he was too quick. He'd walked out of my room without looking back at me and I was left staring at the back of my door.

Seeing Soren this angry, although not at me, was troubling. I feared for the person who would be on the other end of his wrath.

27

SOREN

"Are you regretting any of your choices now?"

The man lying on the floor in front of me nodded, but he couldn't speak. I glanced at his tongue on the ground and looked back at him. He was in so much pain and he deserved every ounce of it.

I'd known the reason why he'd approached Iris at the football game was about the Chevaliers. He was on my list of people to visit but had been further down than he obviously should have been. He'd learned his lesson about touching and talking to what's mine too late, but at least the lesson had been taught.

The stab wounds in his body would cause him to bleed out and I couldn't wait. But for now, he had to suffer as his blood dripped from his body, pooling around him. This wouldn't take long, so I had no problem hanging around.

Watching someone bleed out was one of the best feelings in the world. Being able to see his life leave their eyes left me feeling such a thrill that it made my cock twitch from the excitement.

Was it as riveting as fucking? No, especially not when I had the option of having sex with Iris, but the boost of serotonin I felt right now couldn't be denied.

When Kenneth took his last breath, I snapped a photo before I stepped over his body. I didn't bother to clean it up because I didn't care. It didn't matter to me who found his body or in what manner it was in.

He was who Parker warned me about that might be sniffing around when it came to trying to find a weakness within the Chevaliers. He thought he'd found that weakness in Iris, given the talk that was going on, but he turned out to be oh so very wrong.

He bet wrong and now he lost his life to pay the price.

Kenneth might have gotten away with it if he would have been smarter and exercised any patience. I shook my head as I chuckled to myself. There was no way he would have gotten away.

I would have searched every-fucking-where on this planet to make sure that I found him. He had no right to touch her and the fact that he thought about it, let alone did it, was enough to piss me off.

Now, I knew that his death would be a higher profile than the ones that I'd killed before. Without a doubt, Parker would know this was me. I also suspected that he knew about the fuckers I'd murdered already.

Parker would have a ton of questions for me, and I needed to prepare myself to answer each and every one. It would all be worth it in the end but that didn't negate how time-consuming explaining things to him would be.

Thankfully, I was still working under the guise of

protecting the Chevaliers so at least I had that going for me. For now, I still had time before Parker found out the full story, and I wanted to be the one who told him instead of having him find out from his "sources." This meant I needed to act quickly.

I removed any traces of evidence that would lead to me being named the murderer. If the police wanted to sniff around, that was on them, but I had nothing to worry about. It wouldn't be the first time that we'd paid them to ignore a crime.

I hated that the stench of blood was still on me, but I had no time. I took off my suit jacket even though it was chilly outside. I assumed that was what caught most of the blood and guts from Kenneth. I'd deal with buying a new jacket or the dry-cleaning bill later.

While having to kidnap Kenneth was a pain in the ass, I was thankful that it had been easy to kill him in an abandoned warehouse on the outskirts of town. It meant that I didn't have to travel all that far once I got him here and it would make the next few tasks easier to complete.

I drove back to Westwick's campus and parked my car in a familiar place near the entrance of Payne Hall. I tended to avoid walking through the front door, so I made my way to a set of stairs that would lead me into the basement of the dormitory. I quickly walked down the stairs, moved the foliage that covered the door, and turned the doorknob.

The door opened without an issue and I turned on the pocket flashlight that I carried with me. I made my way to the stairs that would lead me to the main floor of the dorm where I could easily slip in undetected.

I glanced over at Payne's statue as I left the basement,

before heading to the stairwell that would take me to the floor I needed to go to.

No one stopped me as I made my way to Iris's floor.

It took me less than a minute to open her door and the first thing my eyes landed on, after noticing her sleeping figure, was the baseball bat that was still near her bed. A whole lot of good that did, but if it kept her under the illusion of feeling safe, then so be it.

What I was happy to see was that she was warm and safe in her bed. No one else had come to visit her and that was all I could ask for right now. I walked toward her sleeping body and pulled the covers up over her. Part of me wanted to crawl into bed with her, but now wasn't the time.

I made a mental note that I needed to check on her Chevalier Masquerade Ball invitation and to make sure that she was prepared for the event. If she wanted to go, I would do everything in my power to make that happen.

With one final look, I left the room in the same way that I entered, content for now at where things stood. I walked out of Payne Hall through the basement, and as I was stepping into my car, I called Parker. He picked up the phone right after the first ring.

"Hello, Soren."

I didn't even bother with the niceties before launching into what I wanted to say. "There are some things that happened tonight that I need to tell you. That includes Kenneth Beard no longer being a problem."

"Funny you called me. I had some things I wanted to discuss with you too."

28

IRIS

"Shit, I need to head out."

I looked up and watched Aria scrambling to her feet. She and I had spent the last couple of hours studying in the math building, having found that the library was too busy earlier in the day.

"Is everything alright?"

Aria nodded as she shoved her things into her book bag. "Yeah, I just have a meeting for another group project. I'm so over working with people."

I chuckled because I could understand that sentiment. Working with others could be a blessing and a curse. Having someone to share the workload was nice, but if they didn't do what they were supposed to do, then the whole group had to deal with how that might affect their grades.

"I'll see you later?"

I nodded my head, confirming that we would. "Hope you have a good night."

"Thanks, and I hope you do too!"

Aria jetted out of the room, and I was left staring at the door behind her. Maybe it made sense for me to leave too.

I rubbed a hand across my face, trying to wake myself up. Studying for hours would do that to a person. I stood up and stretched my limbs. After sitting for so long, it felt well deserved. It was then I realized that I had to go to the bathroom.

I left the desk that I'd stationed myself at and walked to the bathroom. Once I was finished, I splashed a little bit of water on my face to wake myself up before I left the room.

The hallways were empty as I walked back to my seat. I'd expected Soren to jump out behind every corner, but was happy when he hadn't. I still had to deal with seeing him every other day during the week, but because I was seeing him so often, I hadn't seen him so much in my private time, which was a double-edged sword. On one hand, he wasn't visibly around, although I assumed he was still watching me.

Never mind him though. At least I didn't have to worry about him right this second.

As I was entering the classroom, I saw something on the chair next to mine. I thought I might know what it was, but I wasn't sure until I pulled the chair out. There was a book there and I was pretty sure that Aria had left it.

"The History of Payne Hall..." I mumbled to myself as I ran a hand across the cover. What an interesting book to have checked out of the library. There were a myriad of reasons why she probably did, but I couldn't stop my feelings from veering toward it being weird that she also seemed to have an interest in Payne Hall, much like I had.

I flipped through the book and came to a chapter that talked about the various floors in the building. When I reached the section on the third floor, I found out that floor was originally where the old library was.

You've got to be kidding me.

I couldn't waste another moment. I hopped out of my chair so fast that I gave myself a small headache. After packing my things up, I left the math department and marched into Payne Hall with a renewed sense of purpose. I rushed up the stairs, but I stopped short of the landing heading up to my floor.

I was on a mission to discover what the hell it was that I saw through the crack in my floor the other day and I was determined to find it now. Instead, I stopped a floor short of where I would normally go and exited the stairwell.

A gasp fell from my lips as I almost ran into someone that I'd never seen before. It might have been the first time since I lived in Payne Hall that I'd run into someone outside of when I met Aria on the first day. I wondered where she was right now.

"Excuse me," I said apologetically, given how close I was to running into the person.

I expected a response in return, but I didn't get it. The person continued on their way down the stairs as if I hadn't said a word. Maybe they hadn't heard me and that was okay.

I shook off the encounter and started down the hall. I had a general idea of where I needed to go, but I wasn't sure what was on this floor. Based on what I saw through the hole in my closet floor, it made me wonder if there were any more dorm rooms down here. It would make sense if there would be a dorm room right below mine but given how old Payne Hall was maybe the layout was different.

Thankfully, the dorm room numbers on this floor were

similar to the ones on my floor. They all just started with the number three versus the number four.

But when I walked to where the room should be, there was nothing there.

"What the fuck?" I asked out loud to no one. There was no way I imagined what I saw, but obviously the way into that room wasn't through a door in the hallway.

I took a step forward so that I was able to touch the wall where I thought the door should be. Was there some sort of secret lever that would trigger the door to open?

Who the hell was I? A detective?

A small part of me was hoping that my fingers would brush along a button that would cause a secret passage to open. When nothing appeared, I took a step back and examined the area again. A sinking feeling crawled into my brain, but I wasn't defeated. There was something I was missing, I just didn't know what.

I walked away and checked my phone as I reached the stairwell. I still had plenty of time, so I made my way up to my room and closed the door behind me. Since I didn't want to waste any more time, I dropped my book bag near the door and strolled over to my closet. I crouched down and pulled out my phone. With my flashlight app on, I used it to illuminate the room below me.

I could see some furniture covered in sheets much like I had the day I saw the candle lit in the room. I tried my best to shine a light on the walls to see if I could find a door, but either my phone's light wasn't bright enough or I couldn't catch the angle.

Something told me I needed to get down there because it

was important to do so, but it would be a challenge because I didn't know where to begin.

Colorful cuss words fell from my lips as I turned the flashlight off and took a seat on the floor near the hole. Why did everything with this situation have to be so damn hard?

I took a deep breath and stood up, brushing my clothes off once I'd reached my full height. With a heavy sigh, I walked back over to my door, grabbed my bag, and walked out.

I debated what I wanted to do because I couldn't stay in my room for another second, even if it meant killing time until just before class. It took until I walked out of my dorm building before I decided what to do.

I made my way to the mailroom, and I waved at Sam as I passed. I walked to my mailbox. I wasn't expecting anything, but I figured I should check my mail since it had been a while. It took me longer than anticipated to open my box and, when the door finally swung open, I stuck my hand inside and pulled out a black and gold envelope.

My name was written in gold font across the envelope with only my mailbox number on it. That told me it came from somewhere on campus.

But from who? That question could easily be answered I assumed.

I ran my finger along the edge of the envelope flap, touching every inch of the gold on the envelope. With a deep breath I opened the envelope and, as I pulled the piece of paper out, a faint woodsy scent followed. It smelled wonderful, but I couldn't place it. Not that it mattered anyway. The only thing that did was what was on this paper.

I read the words on the piece of paper and shock flew out of every pore in my body.

Why had I received a request for me to attend the Chevalier Masquerade Ball? This was completely unexpected because I hadn't done anything to give them a reason, yet I was standing here with an invitation to the event.

I needed to RSVP to the address listed on the invitation and I noticed that I wasn't allowed to bring a plus one. I found that odd because stepping into the Chevalier Manor alone wasn't what I had planned to do. I didn't know who I'd thought would go with me, but going alone hadn't crossed my mind either.

Nonetheless, this was a step in the right direction for me. An invite to the ball would allow me to uncover any letters or journals that Payne might be keeping.

Or so I told myself.

"Hey, Iris!"

I jumped slightly before I looked over my shoulder. Aria was walking toward me. Nerves began to bubble in my stomach as I wondered whether I should show her the invitation.

It hit me that I wouldn't want anyone to lie to me about them getting invited to an event that I wanted to attend so hiding it from her wasn't the best option.

"Sorry that I ran off earlier."

"No worries. Shit happens. Speaking of you leaving, you left this on your chair." I swung my book bag around and I pulled the book out.

"Thanks for grabbing it for me." Her eyes veered from the book to my hands again. "What is it that you have there?"

"Um... I don't know how else to say this, but I just

received the invite in the mail."

My words came out awkward and jumbled and I could see confusion written all over Aria's face. Instead of trying to explain myself further, I shoved the invitation at her.

"You got invited to the ball. Wow." The disappointment was apparent in her voice, and I didn't blame her. This was something she was trying to figure out how to get invited to and it just showed up in my mailbox one day. I didn't know what else to say after the reveal because I didn't want to be that asshole and the awkward feeling was there.

"Is it supposed to be for one person only? Most events like this allow a plus one."

"I'm not sure..." My voice trailed off as she asked the same question I'd thought about earlier. It was strange that they wanted me to go alone. Part of me wanted to tell her that she could go in my place because I knew how bad she'd wanted to go, but this could be the one opportunity that I had to get into the Chevalier Manor and search for anything that might indicate that Payne agreed with Margaret.

The chances of it just hanging around were slim, but it might give me something to go on and I wouldn't be allowed in there otherwise.

"I mean, I could just take you with me. What are they going to do? Turn us away at the door?" That would be undeniably rude, but it was an option.

"No. It's okay. There are still several weeks before the event, plenty of time for me to get invited. Listen, I'm going to go back to our dorm. I'll see you later."

Aria didn't give me a chance to respond before she walked away, leaving me standing with this invitation and wondering what I should do about this.

29

IRIS

I checked the results of the moisturizer that I'd placed on my face. I was trying to prime my face as much as possible before the onslaught of makeup that I was sure would end up on it. Tonight was the night, and the butterflies in my stomach clearly indicated my feelings about this event. As I took a step back, a knock on my door bounced off of every corner of the room.

"Who is it?"

"It's Bianca. Hurry up! I have too much shit in my hands."

I rolled my eyes when she announced herself. She'd ignored my request for her to text me when she got here so I could help her with whatever she needed to bring up, especially since Payne Hall didn't have an elevator.

For a split second, I wondered if it might have been Soren at my door. Then again, he would have just let himself in.

I rushed to open the door and helped Bianca bring in two garment bags and a duffel bag. "If you would have told me you were downstairs, I would have met you there."

Bianca waved me off and said, "It's fine." Before I could

put on a fake smile, Bianca tilted her head as she studied me. "Is everything alright?"

"Yes, just super nervous about tonight."

"Are you sure you still want to go?"

"Yes. More sure than I've been about anything in a while." I meant every word of that.

"You're in great hands then. Mine. Let's get started so that we can make sure that you're out on time."

I sat down in my desk chair and checked my phone as Bianca busied herself with doing my hair and makeup for the masquerade ball.

We made small talk as she worked. There was a lull in our conversation until she tapped me on the shoulder and said, "Put this on and then use the mirror I brought to look at yourself."

She gestured to the mask and the mirror that were lying next to each other on my desk. I reached for the mask and put it on before I lifted the mirror so I could see what I looked like.

My jaw dropped open as I examined myself in the mirror in front of me. I ran a hand along the edge of the black material covering my face. The difference in textures between the fabric and my skin felt strange under my fingertips. Here was a material that was plastic and felt cool to the touch and my skin that was warm. My nerves were alive and well.

It didn't help that this mask was itchy as hell, but it was something that I would just have to deal with. It was only for a couple of hours, and I had no problem wearing it because this was the only option I had that might lead me closer to my goal. Well, I hoped. I adjusted it for what felt like the millionth time. Having to deal with this on top of being nervous about what was going to happen tonight was driving my anxiety into overdrive.

What was also obvious was that Bianca was growing more irritated with my fidgeting because this time, she glared at me as she walked back over to where I was sitting.

"You can take it off now. I wanted to test the mask out because we would need to find an alternative if it didn't fit. I still need to do your makeup, so feel free to relax."

I bit back the sigh I wanted to release because it would do me no good. What it would do was lead to her questioning me further. She had a good point, and beyond that, I was grateful for her assistance. Without her help, this would've been much harder or potentially impossible. She loaned me a gown for the evening so I wouldn't stick out like a sore thumb and offered to come over and help me with my hair and makeup. She was doing all this without actually knowing the full truth about why I was attending this party.

I felt guilty for having to deceive her, but that was the best option for me at the moment. I longed to tell her everything that was going on, but it was too much of a risk. Hell, I hadn't even told Gran everything that happened.

I was carrying a lot on my shoulders that I knew I didn't have to carry alone. I could've let them in, but the negatives outweighed the positives. If I could avoid having anyone else drawn to this shit, I would. And so that left me on the current path I was on.

I placed the mask on my lap as I waited patiently for Bianca to get started on my hair again.

Bianca pulled a little harder on the strand of hair that she had between her fingers, and I winced. I wasn't sure if that's what she meant to do but damn did it hurt.

"Ouch!"

"I'm sorry. I didn't mean to do that."

"It's fine. Just be a little softer if you can."

"I can. I'm rushing and wasn't thinking. I'm almost done with your hair. It looks stunning with your purple ends flowing down."

I hoped she was right. I knew that the likelihood that I would stand out at this ball was high depending on the likely guests and my ancestral history, but my purple hair made it even more likely now.

Whatever. It wasn't something I could fix now, nor did I want to because it wasn't a problem. But it would draw attention to me, attention that I didn't want or need.

I took in a shaky breath as I tried to compose myself for what was about to come. I had the feeling that this night was going to change my life forever, whether I liked it or not. Without a doubt, I wasn't prepared.

I only had one shot at this and I wasn't going to let my nerves dictate how this evening was going to go.

"And we are just about there," Bianca's voice trailed off as her focus went back to my hair. When she was done with it, she took a small break before turning to my face. Whenever she paused to grab another product, I stared at her handiwork in the mirror. I watched as she slowly transformed me into someone I barely recognized. Maybe not feeling like myself would give me a boost of confidence I needed to pull this off.

I shoved my feelings aside and patiently waited for her to finish up. I couldn't remember the last time I'd been this done up. I didn't go to my prom, so I was leaning toward never.

When Bianca had to pause again to grab the tube of mascara, I checked my phone to see if I had any notifications.

There were no messages.

That was strange.

It was time to push all of the complicated feelings I had about him aside. After all, tonight wasn't about Soren and me or whatever fucked-up thing that was going on between us. It was about getting into the Chevalier Manor and seeing if there might be an opportunity for me to find the papers that they wished to keep a secret.

"Look up for me but don't move your head," Bianca said.

I did as she requested and watched as she put the mascara on my eyelashes. When she was finished, she moved back to admire what she'd accomplished.

"I have to admit, you look damn good."

I ran a hand over my hair, trying to smooth out some of the flyways. "Is that a way for you to say that I looked pretty before or for you to compliment the work you've done?"

Bianca shrugged. "Both."

I shook my head, not at all surprised that she would allude to that. If you didn't have a friend who would half-assed bring you up while complimenting themselves, were they really a friend?

The time on my phone indicated that I had about fifteen minutes before I had to leave to walk over to Chevalier Manor.

"And I finished with plenty of time to spare."

"That you did, Bianca. That you did."

My statement made Bianca cross her arms and narrow her eyes. She stared me down for a second before she said,

"You know you don't have to go to this ball. You know that right?"

"I know, but I'm going. It's going to be awkward not knowing anyone there, but I'll get over it. I'm not missing out on this for the world."

I needed to do this. This might be my only chance to get in there, to scope the place out, at least, or find the thing I was looking for, at best.

"Are you absolutely sure?"

This time I rolled my eyes. "Yes, I'm fine. I can do this, and I really do want to go." Maybe if I said it enough times, I would believe it.

"Okay. By the way, I don't think I told you that you will know someone there. Nash and his girlfriend, Raven, are going to attend the ball."

I'd met Nash before, and I had to think for a split second why the name Raven sounded so familiar. "Oh, yes! We met at the football game."

Bianca nodded her head. "Right."

"But why would they be attending a masquerade ball at Westwick?"

"What I'm about to tell you, you don't know anything about, got it?"

I knew that I'd been keeping things from Bianca, but I didn't realize that she'd also returned the favor. It made me feel both less guilty for my own secrets and sad that she hadn't felt the need to trust me with this.

"Nash is the incoming chairman of the Brentson chapter of the Chevaliers. He's going to attend because it's the first time this event is happening in decades and it's a way to show that the chapters are trying to work together to foster camaraderie because the chapters are supposed to be rivals. Apparently, this generation of leadership is trying to bridge that gap."

"That was more information than I thought I would find out about the Chevaliers." I hated that I was lying, but I needed to continue to act as if I didn't know anything. I still wanted to keep my mission under wraps for as long as I could, and it might be the best way to protect her. When I got back from the ball, I was planning on telling her everything.

"Raven let it spill when I went with her to try on gowns the other day. I was sworn to secrecy and now I'm doing the same to you. If you don't keep your mouth shut, I know where it came from, and I know where you live. That is all I'm going to say."

I chuckled, but I knew she wasn't kidding. I had no plans of revealing what was going on, especially since my focus was on other things related to this organization.

Bianca cleared her throat and said, "Do you want to see the gown I chose for you?"

"Of course I do."

Before Bianca would agree to loan me a gown and do my hair and makeup, she asked that she would be able to pick out the gown that I would wear tonight. I agreed, not because I felt pressured to do so, but because it was one less decision I had to make.

"There's a catch."

I didn't like the sound of that. "What do you mean 'there's a catch'?"

"I brought, not one, but two gowns with me."

I rolled my eyes and involuntarily threw my hands up. When they came to rest again on my lap, I glared at Bianca.

"Why didn't you tell me you were going to bring two? You know I didn't want to have to make a tough decision."

"Well, there was one that I already owned that I thought would be perfect for you."

"So why didn't you just bring that one?"

Bianca held her hand up as if to tell me to stop. "Let me finish. This one showed up just as I was packing up everything I needed to do your hair and makeup. It's brand new and I assume my mother sent it over so that I could wear it to a fundraiser my parents think I'm going to soon. But since I'm not, it's an option for you to wear tonight."

I nodded slowly and stood up, stretching the limbs that had been seated for so long because of this beauty routine. The two garment bags she'd brought with her were currently hanging in my closet. She grabbed one and I grabbed the other and together, we brought both of them to the two hooks that were hanging behind my dorm door and placed them on it. At the same time, we both unzipped the bags and then I gasped as my eyes darted between the two gowns.

One gown was black with a neckline that showed quite a bit more cleavage than I was used to and had what looked to be a split on the side. The other dress was navy blue, with a higher neckline and without the split.

"Are you going to tell me which one is the one your mom had sent to your apartment?"

Bianca didn't say anything for a second and I noticed when the proverbial light bulb went off above her head.

"Why don't you try both on and then once you pick one, I'll tell you which one was the one my mom sent."

I sighed. "I don't have time for this. I need to head out soon."

"Well, I suggest you get moving then, huh?"

But I knew something that she didn't. "What if I already know which one I would pick?"

Bianca's eyes widened slightly before her lips shifted into a smirk. "By all means, let's put you in the gown that you want."

I reached for the gown that Bianca hung up. The all-black gown fit my mood perfectly, and I knew as soon as Bianca unzipped the garment bag, it was the one I was going to choose. Bianca and I worked in silence as we removed the dress from its protective casing and maneuvered it so that I was able to slip it on with ease.

I couldn't help but run my fingers up and down the fabric, as I enjoyed the way it felt on my skin. The split in the dress over one leg was much higher than I thought, but I would manage.

"Stand still," Bianca said as she toyed with the zipper on my gown. "I don't want to scratch you while trying to zip this thing up."

I looked down before moving my hands to my chest, slightly pressing against my breasts. Bianca zipped up the dress easily and I let my hands drop. I was worried that I wouldn't be able to breathe in this thing, but it fit perfectly.

"It looks stunning on you. I think this is the one," Bianca said.

I didn't even want to bother with the other dress because this one fit as if it was made for me. I pulled up the top of the gown so that I had more coverage and noticed a small 'S' stitched into the top that would be resting near my heart.

There was only one person who could have achieved this,

had the money to throw at this item and whose name began with a 'S.'

Soren.

Of course, he'd known my dress size. What didn't he know about me at this point? Not to mention, he'd just *had* to have the dress branded with his initial.

But that wasn't what made my heart skip a beat. It was him knowing that I needed a dress for tonight's event. How had he pieced together that I would be attending the Chevalier Masquerade Ball tonight?

30

IRIS

I f I'd thought I was nervous while I was getting ready, that was false. It was nothing compared to the feelings I had now. My heart was racing as I walked up to my destination. With every step that I took, bile rose in my throat, and I wondered if I was going to puke all over this stunning gown and ruin all of Bianca's hard work.

It took a lot to keep myself together, including the light sweat that had developed on my brow that I assumed was from the mask. Somehow, I managed to do so as I walked up the concrete steps in front of the building. When I reached the big wooden doors, there was a guard standing there, checking IDs to make sure that people were who they said they were.

"Are you attending tonight's event with someone?"

I shook my head. "No, I'm here alone."

The guard studied my face and then looked behind me as if to prove that what I was saying was true. "Well, enjoy your time at the ball."

"Thank you," I said as I walked into the building. I'd

almost dropped my clutch as I was walking in, but thankfully my quick reflexes were in full effect and didn't make me look like a complete idiot in front of everyone. Once I knew I had a firm grasp on my bag, I began to take in my scenery.

To say that I was impressed was an understatement. The Chevalier Manor had similar architectural characteristics to Payne Hall, and it made me want to research whether they were built around the same time. The dark gray walls were an interesting choice to say the least, but who was I to judge? The gold fixtures popped against the paint, however, and I could admit to liking that.

"Ma'am, may I take your coat?"

I turned to the man who was standing to my left near a door that I assumed led into a room that was where they were storing everyone's outerwear. I stared at him for a moment longer than necessary before I began removing my coat. While it would have been nice to have someone to help me with it, I managed.

I handed my coat over and shivered slightly as a light breeze hit my skin. I hoped it would be warmer when I walked further in, or I'd be freezing most of the night. With a quick thank you, I walked away from the coat check in order to walk further into the house.

I nodded my head in acknowledgement as I walked past several people on my journey through the house. The next room I ended up in made my mouth drop. I was sure I made it to where the evening's festivities would be held. The walls were painted a lighter brown while the archways that led into other parts of the house were painted white. The carpet on the floor was red, as if someone had rolled out the red carpet for tonight's guests. A golden chandelier hung from the ceiling and was the centerpiece of the room. It was as if I'd walked into a fairy tale, and I was the star of the movie.

However, that was where the fantasy ended. I was still at this party with no one that I knew, and I was nowhere closer to finding any of Payne's letters or journals. With that thought in mind, I studied the room, trying to figure out how I could escape to investigate the rest of the house.

Across the way, I could see there was another room that was filled with tables, and I assumed that was where dinner, or whatever food they planned on serving would take place. I assumed they would make an announcement when we needed to head that way, but as of now, I was staying where the music was playing for as long as possible.

If I were special documents, some options for where I was hiding would be in a safe or a safety deposit box. A library was another obvious place because there would be nothing but papers in that room. There was a good chance it wasn't even here given how much it might be worth and what could happen if it got into the wrong hands, but I needed to keep the faith.

"Iris?"

My examination was halted as I heard someone call my name. There were very few people here who knew who I was so when I turned and found Raven standing behind me, I wasn't surprised. I took a moment to calm my nerves and steel my spine in an attempt to appear as if none of this was freaking me the fuck out.

"Raven, it's good to see you again."

"I thought it was you, but I wasn't sure. You look stunning."

"Thank you so much and you look wonderful." The red

dress that Raven had on fit her like a glove. She also had the confidence to back it up, something I was trying to develop in this moment. It was obvious to me that she knew that she looked damn good tonight.

I moved my head slightly so that I could look around Raven and I found Nash talking to someone behind her.

"He's been getting stopped by multiple people as he walked in. I'm convinced that this now happens everywhere we go."

I was aware that Nash was a football player and a local celebrity in addition to his father being the mayor of Brentson. With all of these things combined, it didn't surprise me that everyone would be hoping to have some sort of connection to him. He'd developed this persona that he had no problem turning on at the drop of hat. Nash was handling it all with grace and I'm sure a lot of that came from being trained when it came to speaking in public. On the other hand, my introverted self would have probably run to the nearest exit.

Raven and I made small talk for a bit until Nash came over. I couldn't help but grin as they embraced. It was as if he'd been away for several months versus the few minutes that it took for him to walk toward us.

Something casted a shadow on us and I knew who it was before I turned around. The smell of his cologne betrayed him, making it easy to pinpoint who he was. When I did look, I found a man in a black suit standing close to me. He was wearing a mask that was identical to mine and suddenly I went from being nervous to being afraid.

Soren.

What the hell was he doing here? Only current students

of Westwick were allowed, or so I thought. The only way it made sense for him to be here was in his capacity as a professor, but I'd formed the idea in my head that this event was only for students. The only other possible answer I could think of was that he was here because he was a... Chevalier.

Fuck everything.

He noticed when the realization hit me because he nodded and stuck his hand out. "Dance with me."

"But we haven't eaten yet." It was a halfhearted stalling technique that didn't make any sense. No shit we hadn't eaten. It was because they hadn't called us for dinner yet.

Out of the corner of my eye, both Nash and Raven were watching our exchange, probably wondering what was going on and if any assistance was needed.

"I assure you that dancing with me is something that you want to do because I have what you want."

Days ago, I would have taken what he said as something sexual, but the look in his brown eyes told me differently. There was no question or room for debate. If he knew what I now thought he did and was alluding to telling me what I wanted to know, I was willing to take the risk.

I nodded at Raven and Nash, letting them know it was okay as I turned to face Soren. My hand trembled as I put it in his and together, we walked out to the dance floor. He wrapped his arms around me, and we danced for several seconds before I dropped the bomb on him.

"Are you a Chevalier?"

"That's quite the question to ask right out of the gate? No hello, how are you doing today? Aren't we having lovely weather?"

"Don't be a dick."

His lips twitched in response. "I wouldn't dream of it, petal."

We danced together for a while in silence, enjoying each other's company. To be honest, I was somewhat shocked that Soren could dance. Then again, based on the limited knowledge I had on him, I thought that he would never let a skill conquer him, so of course he would learn how to do this. And it was weird, because this might have been the first time I'd felt normal in his presence, outside of when the only thing on our minds was fucking each other.

"Come with me. There's something I want to show you."

"You're lying." The words flew out of my mouth before I could stop them.

He pushed my hair behind my ear and said, "The last thing I would do is lie to you. I'm here to help you. How do you think you got invited to this event?"

He'd made an excellent point, one that I accepted. Soren had ensured that I got invited to this and made sure that I had a gown to wear so that I could attend. This was what I'd been waiting for, but I also didn't trust him as far as I could throw him. If this was a trap, I needed to make sure that my guard was up because there was no telling what he'd do.

He was, after all, a Chevalier first and foremost. Just like all the rest of them.

"I'm serious. Come with me," he said, and his breath tickled the shell of my ear.

I turned to look at him and asked, "Why? Where do you want to take me?"

He stopped dancing and placed his hand just under my jaw, as if to hold me in place. "Somewhere we can be alone, without the prying eyes of everyone in this room."

His words sent a shiver down my spine as I could feel a blush creeping up my cheeks. The urge to take off this mask grew because my face was heating up. What was unexpected about this whole encounter was that I felt safer in his arms than I had the entire evening, including the lead up to this event.

There was a chance that Soren knew where anything related to Payne might be. If he knew where the documents were, that must have meant he was higher up in the organization than I'd originally thought. I nodded as we danced again, allowing Soren to guide me to the edge of the room. It took some maneuvering, but we walked through one of the white archways and ended up standing in front of a door. He looked back at me briefly before opening the door and pulling me inside. What a way to get a tour of this place.

The lighting in this room was somewhat dull, but still enough that I could see. I didn't know where we were, but I could see that we were in a room filled with bookcases, so it would be easy to assume that it was a library or den of some sort. I couldn't believe that this might be it. This could possibly be where Payne's papers were located.

But all of that flew out the window when Soren's lips landed on mine. He backed me into a bookcase, which lightly shook due to the impact of our bodies, but none of the books fell. If they had, it would have put a damper on this.

"Wait, what are you doing?"

"Kissing you," Soren replied matter-of-factly. He kissed me again and I felt his hand drifting up my bare leg.

"We're going to get caught."

The smirk that I was slowly coming to love appeared on his face as he shook his head. "No, we aren't. Trust me."

I had my reservations about this being a good idea, but I went along with it. I wasn't sure if I could say that I trusted him, but I was willing to see where this led.

His lips were back on mine, and I moaned into his mouth. That was all the encouragement he needed because his hand moved up my leg once more. I moved my leg and wrapped it around his waist with ease due to the split in the dress. I had him to thank for that access.

My purse dropped on the floor, but I didn't look in the direction that it fell in. All I wanted to do was get closer to him as quickly as possible.

"We don't have much time," Soren said as he moved on from my lips and down to my neck. I sighed into him as he found a spot on my neck that made me want to explode in his arms.

I wasn't sure what he meant by that, but I assumed it had to do with us stepping away from the party temporarily. People who noticed we left, like Nash and Raven, might start asking questions.

His fingers found my pussy, moved my thong out of the way, and he groaned. "You're always so wet for me, aren't you, petal? Can't let any of this go to waste, can we?"

He took that comment to heart because he wasted no time before thrusting a finger into me. I cried out as my fingers clenched his suit jacket. It was as if I was holding on for dear life and maybe that was because it felt as if I was.

I tried to find the words to say to voice my pleasure, but the only thing that came out was noises that were inaudible. Nothing made sense, but in the current state of my world, this was the only thing that mattered. He slid another finger into me and whatever adjustment he'd just made almost made me want to cry happy tears.

"And there she is," he said with a smile on his face.

"W-what?"

"Your G-spot."

I nodded my head, not caring what he said anymore because I couldn't process it anyway. I wanted him to continue fucking me with his fingers, but I also wanted him to fuck me with his cock. I wanted to pull him to me and stay like this forever, but I also wanted to put some distance between us for making me feel this way.

What a conundrum to be in.

"Fuck," he muttered as I moved to unzip his pants. He made good use of our time by pulling out a condom. He stared me down as his cock was waiting by my entrance, I nodded my head and braced myself for the onslaught of feelings that would come as a result.

And even with me knowing that it was going to happen, I still wasn't prepared.

"You don't know how long I've been waiting to do this again," Soren said.

He took pity on me as he adjusted my leg so that it was tighter against his waist. I was so thankful for the bookcase now because there was no way I would be able to keep standing with these heels on plus what was about to happen.

His repositioning was the only warning I received.

Soren slammed into me, and I swore I saw stars. He didn't move for a moment. The intensity of our connection was bearing down on me, and I couldn't look away.

"Do you feel that?"

My gaze never strayed from Soren, but his question hung

in the air. All I could do was nod because I still didn't trust myself to form words.

"You're going to remember this moment forever. The way I've fucked you in this house with people just outside the door. You're going to remember every damn second."

I knew he was right. There was no way I would ever forget it.

He moved his hips and thrusted into me again. However, this time he didn't pause, quickly finding a rhythm that would bring us both to completion.

The noises that fell out of my mouth were indiscernible, but I had no issue piecing together the thoughts that were smashing into one another in my mind. Gone was the desire to prove that my family wasn't a bunch of liars, or anything related to school. The only thing that I cared about in this moment was the two of us and the euphoria that we were going to reach together.

His stare became too much, and I closed my eyes as I embraced the feeling of losing control. That's how I always felt around him. I didn't think I could want something from someone that I once feared, but here I was. Living proof that it was possible.

"Petal."

His nickname for me forced my eyes open and it was the first time I didn't hate the term of endearment. It also set off a chain reaction that shoved me to the edge of a cliff that I couldn't wait to fall off of.

"I'm s-so close, Soren." It felt as if those were the first words I'd spoken in hours.

"I love hearing my name come from your lips."

I wanted to give him what he wanted. That was all I needed to fall apart in his arms.

"Soren, I—"

The rest of my sentence ended in a loud moan as I released the pleasure that had spent its time building up within me. It seemed as if Soren was waiting for me to reach my climax because, as I was quivering under his touch, he came as well.

The euphoric expression on his face didn't last long before his face became stoic. The change almost broke me because I couldn't imagine what he would be frowning at. I wanted to ask him what was wrong, but he leaned forward to hug me against the bookcase. That was where we stayed.

It took some time for my heart rate to return to normal and Soren stood there and held me until he was sure that I could stand on my own. He shifted his body weight so that he could move back before he helped me fix my gown. While he did that, I fluffed out my hair. I didn't know what state my look was currently in, but I could fix it later. Soren stepped away from me and threw out the condom. When he came back, I rubbed my lipstick off of his face when there was a knock on the door that we'd walked through.

Both Soren and I turned to face the door before he walked over and opened the door a crack to talk to the person. I couldn't hear what was being said, but Soren turned to me and said, "I'll be right back. Stay here."

It was as if someone snapped their fingers and woke me up from the hypnosis I'd been in. This couldn't be real. I couldn't have the possibility to search this room all by myself. I nodded and said, "Go on. I'll be right here."

Soren jetted out of the room and closed the door behind

him. I grabbed my purse that ended up on the floor. It only took a second for me to react before I was looking around the room, trying to decide where to look first.

I walked over to one of the desks in the room and started searching through it. I found nothing of importance on the table. If there was something in any of the bookcases in this room, I was going to need more light.

I walked over to the light switch and flicked the light on. What greeted me almost made me scream because horrified couldn't begin to describe it.

Someone had taken the time to make a collage of photos of dead bodies, brutally murdered. Who the hell would do this, let alone take pictures of it? Although I wanted to, I couldn't take my eyes off of everything in front of me. I needed to close my eyes because the longer I stared at it, the more sure I was that I was going to vomit.

"Found what you were looking for?"

I gasped as I spun around and covered my mouth. Either Soren had entered the room again silently, or I'd been so stunned by the collage in front of me that I didn't hear him.

"Look at this! I think someone committed numerous murders."

Soren's gaze narrowed at the display, but he didn't seem surprised by any of it.

"We have to go to the police."

"No."

My eyes scanned the photos until I came across one of the bodies that looked oddly familiar. "That kind of looks like the guy who walked up to me at the football game."

"That's because it is him."

That was when it all clicked. "Did you kill him? Did you kill the rest of these men as well?"

"Yes."

He didn't wait for me to react to his news. Instead, he grabbed my wrist.

I attempted to pull away, but to no avail. "What the fuck are you doing? Let me go!"

I screamed in hopes that someone would hear me. He didn't respond. Instead, his grip got tighter before he started to yank me toward another part of the room.

I hit his hand with my purse, tried to use my nails to dig into his skin to make him let go, but nothing worked. "Soren, let me go!"

"Keep screaming. It's not like anyone will hear you, anyway."

"Help! Help!" I screamed at the top of my lungs. I'd gotten caught in a lust-filled haze and let my guard down and now he was doing what he'd intended to do all along.

Kidnap and kill me.

31

IRIS

I continued to yell as Soren dragged me through what seemed to be an endless hallway that turned into a tunnel. Tears stung my eyes as I tried to both fight against him and keep up with how fast he was walking. The walk down this tunnel was long and my feet were starting to ache in these shoes. An idea quickly formed in my head about what I could do, but I knew I might only have one opportunity to do so.

I gave nothing away as I continued to struggle against him, all the while looking for an opportunity to escape. Deep down, I knew that coming here was a bad idea. It was laughable that I would receive an invitation to this event on my own merit. Instead, it was a way to force me into a trap, yet I fell for it.

Soren was within feet of another door, and I knew this would probably be my only chance to escape. He would need to slow down even for a split second to open the door, and that could give me some leverage to maybe get away. But without being able to take off these heels, this plan was as good as dead.

Maybe so was I.

When I thought I would have an opportunity to escape, the door opened without Soren having to do anything. I saw my opportunity to flee flash before my eyes and all that was left in its path was dread. It felt as if I was being dragged to a jail cell and who knew what could happen once I was in there.

The door slammed behind me, and I was pulled up a set of stairs that led to the main floor of what looked to be a small house. Then a dull light flickered on because I could see what looked to be a tiny kitchen nearby. It reminded me of the dream I had about the haunted house across the ravine. What I hadn't noticed was that there were two other figures standing in the shadows, but I couldn't get a good look at them. Being surrounded by strangers in a place that I didn't know was nerve-wracking by itself, but I'd heard about what the Chevaliers were involved in and capable of. I was in way over my head, and it might just cost me my life.

There was no way that this whole circus came together this seamlessly, this quickly. "How could you do this? This was all a part of your sick plan to make sure that I came here so you could do whatever you wanted to me."

None of the men in the room replied and I took that to mean that my assessment was correct. I was trying my best to maintain a level head as I went through the options I had, but the problem was that I didn't have many.

I looked at each man, wondering who I could appeal to. While the one with lighter hair seemed somewhat sympathetic, the person who I had the closest relationship to was

Soren. It pained me that he looked more closed off than usual, but my only hope was that there was a shred of empathy there that might get me out of this shit.

"Is it alright if I take off my shoes? My feet are killing me."

It was an interesting choice of words to say the least, but Soren nodded once and walked over to me. I trembled as I held on to his shoulder and removed my heels one by one.

Thump.

Thump.

The sound of my shoes hitting the ground bounced off of the walls in this cold, empty room. The pointy heels could also serve as a weapon if it came down to it and I needed to keep that in mind.

"What can I do that will ensure that you'll let me go? I promise not to tell anyone about what happened tonight."

"You not telling a soul about any of this isn't going to help you here." This time it was the man with darker hair who spoke. He looked slightly less intimidating than Soren, and he almost looked bored by the whole exchange.

"Then can I at least ask why I'm here?" Maybe if I kept them talking, something would arise and give me the opportunity to escape.

"Eddison Payne," Soren said.

I schooled my face to not show any emotion. After all, it's what I suspected and the only reason it would have made sense to invite me, a descendant of Margaret Turner, to this ball.

"Where does this all end then? Do you want me to stop digging?"

Soren's gaze didn't leave my face as he said, "You won't ever stop digging, Iris."

"Then where does that leave me?"

"There's only one option."

It didn't take much to know what he was getting at, but I refused to go down without a fight. "What, you're going to kill me? Do the same thing you did to your dead wife or to all of those men?"

Soren raised an eyebrow at me and said, "Watch your fucking mouth."

Warning had taken hold of each of his words and had woven a tight web around it. I was treading on thin ice, but at this point what did I have to lose? If what had happened to his wife was true, maybe he was the one responsible for her death.

"Do it then. As long as you promise to leave Gran alone. She stopped searching for the truth long ago, and after everything she's been through, she deserves to live the rest of her life in as much peace as she can. I also want you to tell her that I love her. Please."

While I hoped that this wouldn't end in my death, I had to prepare for the worst. If I did die, I knew that my death was going to crush her, but if I could guarantee that she didn't suffer physically, I would do it in a heartbeat. Gran was a strong woman, but after losing her daughter and son-in-law, and now with my possible death, I didn't know if she could survive much else.

Both of the other guys in the room seemed to lean into the emotions they displayed earlier, but Soren's facial expression remained unchanged. I wasn't sure if I'd gotten anywhere with him and that troubled me. If the person you'd not only spent a significant amount of time with, and who was your stalker, remained unfazed, the chances of me getting out of this were slim to none.

"What do you want to do with her?" the man with the lighter hair asked.

I couldn't tell what he looked like due to how dark this room was, but it was obvious to me that his hair was closer to sandy blond than brown. What I also didn't know was whether he was asking Soren or the other man in the room about what my fate should be.

The other guy in the room held up a hand and said, "Ioan, we are going to let Soren handle this. After all, this seems to be his project, not ours."

That's what the guy with the lighter hair's name was. Interesting.

Soren looked at the man whose name I didn't know out of the corner of his eye before taking several steps toward me. His stare was more terrifying in this light and the darkness in his eyes was anything but warm. I never thought I would long for the way he looked at me while we were having sex, but here we were.

Soren brushed past me and grabbed something that was sitting on a ledge. It looked like a glass with a dark substance in it, lending even more evidence to my theory about this all being planned before I'd arrived for this party.

"Drink this," Soren said. His tone was no nonsense, but I didn't care.

I shifted my body to put more space between us. If he was going to tell me to do something, he was going to have to make me do it. "Absolutely not. Fuck you."

"Iris, don't fucking play with me. I will pour this liquid down your throat."

"Then that's what you're going to have to do, because I'm not willingly putting whatever the hell that is into my body."

"Fine."

I took a huge step back, almost tripping over my heels as I backed myself into a wall. Nothing changed about his footsteps as he walked toward me. While my heart was beating wildly and panic shot through my body, he seemed very much in control. None of that was surprising because the only time I'd seen him lose it completely was when we were fucking.

Soren grabbed my cheeks and tried to force my head forward, but where he'd made an error in his judgment was not ensuring that he had a firm grip. I was able to yank my head free and I knocked the drink away. While I'd wished he dropped the entire thing, I was pleased when I saw some of the liquid leak out of the cup. I darted back to where my shoes were as Ioan and the other man came toward me, and just as I was able to grasp one of the straps, I was grabbed from behind.

I struggled against my human binds and tried to step on the person's shoe or kick them in the dick, but luck wasn't on my side. I couldn't get enough leverage to cause any real impact, so I was left helpless as I watched Soren walk up to me with the drink in hand.

"Watch how you handle her," he said. His voice was low enough to the point where I wondered if he'd said anything at all. I felt the pressure on my arms lessen, but nothing would deter Soren from what he'd decided to do. He once again grabbed my jaw, forcing my mouth open, and poured what was left of the liquid down my throat. I tried to spit it out but once he closed my mouth, it became too difficult not to swallow.

Whatever I'd drank was thick with a slight metallic taste. I screamed after I swallowed most of what was in my mouth. My heart felt as if it were beating out of my chest. My brain was beginning to feel fuzzy, and I couldn't focus on one thing. I tried my best to keep my thoughts together, but with each second that ticked by, that proved more difficult.

Once Soren had finished the job, whoever was holding my arms back released me and I felt mostly fine—physically. My first instinct was to run to the door that I was dragged through because that was a way out. If I could make it, maybe I could alert someone like Nash or... what was her name again?

I couldn't believe that I was unable to recall Nash's girl-friend's name off the top of my head. I'd just seen her less than an hour ago. I knew it began with a 'R,' but...

When I took a step, I immediately felt wobbly, and the world started spinning. It was as if my body couldn't figure out a way to get coordinated so that I could move in the direction of the door.

Please don't do this. Please.

I hoped I was begging to myself because I didn't want to give any of the men in this room the satisfaction of hearing me beg. What was in that liquid?

I tried to take another step, and I fell to my knees. It was too much effort for me to lift my eyes up from their place on the ground. Before I could do anything about it, I found myself laying on the ground and the only thing I could focus on was the pair of expensive black shoes that were directly in my line of sight.

My tongue felt heavy, but I was able to get one word out. "Why?"

"It's for your own good."

Before I could say anything else, my world went black.

MY EYELIDS FELT TOO heavy to move. My fingers touched something rough, but I wasn't able to make out what it was. What I did know was that I was lying down on something cold and hard. I managed to move one of my feet but failed to move the other. It was then that I realized that my foot was weighed down by something that was cold and heavy.

The desire to know what it was is what forced my eyes open. I was staring at a dark ceiling that I'd never seen before. I turned to my left and saw nothing on the walls outside of a couple of small windows. When I turned to the right, I gasped when I saw what looked to be a figure standing in the darkness. Startled, I jumped in surprise as adrenaline kicked in and I realized that my ankle was chained to the wall. My eyes darted between my ankle and the person standing in the dark as I decided what I needed to focus on first.

I pulled at the chain lightly, not yet trusting that I had enough energy to do anything more. When I couldn't do anything else, I turned to the only other person in the room.

"What are you doing? Who is there?" My words sounded scratchy as if it had been months since I'd last spoken.

The person walked out of the shadows and I saw who it was. "Nothing, just watching over my little prisoner as I contemplate what to do with her."

"I'm not *your* anything." It took more energy than I was used to exerting to get that comment out.

"But you are. In fact, I'll be nice and answer a question I'm sure that you have. Do you want to know why I have you chained by your foot instead of by a hand?"

Out of all of the questions I had, that wasn't even close to making the top ten, but okay. "Sure."

"Because I want to see you try to crawl to me, begging me to let you go."

I watched as the man who'd scrambled my emotions every which way, was breaking any trust that I'd had in him. Whatever this was had started under nefarious circumstances and I should have kept it locked in that category. There were so many signs that this was wrong, and I let my desire to find the truth get in the way of common sense.

Now. I was in a worse situation, that I had no idea how I would be able to get out of. Or *if*.

I locked eyes with Soren, hoping that it would convey every emotion that was pulsing through me. "Never." My voice was weak, but I meant it with every fiber of my being.

"Oh, but you will." I watched as Soren turned on his heel and walked to the door. He looked behind him briefly before opening the door, allowing the light from beyond the doorway to shine into the room before closing the door behind him.

Just like that, I was shrouded in darkness, wondering what the future held for me.

∿

THANK you for reading The Lies Beneath! Iris and Soren's story will continue in The Truth Between and it's available for preorder now!

WANT to read Nash and Raven's story? Keep reading to find a sneak peek of Devious Game!

WANT to join discussions about the Westwick University duet? Click HERE to join my Reader Group on Facebook.

PLEASE JOIN my newsletter to find out the latest about the Brentson University and my other books!

DEVIOUS GAME BLURB

I left Brentson in the dead of night and made a promise that I would never return.

I was determined to leave my past behind, but here's the thing about it:

It always has a way of hunting you down.

Now, I'm face-to-face with Nash Henson, my ex-boyfriend, heir to the Henson fortune, and crowned king of Brentson University.

He'll never forgive me for what I've done.

And when he's done playing his game with me, there won't be anything left.

Because he's determined to destroy me.

SNEAK PEEK OF DEVIOUS GAME

My hand tightened on the steering wheel as I drove past a familiar sign.

Welcome to Brentson

The elaborate sign was meant to offer a warm embrace and show Brentson's hospitality. Except I felt anything but welcomed.

The only thing keeping me calm was the cool breeze that felt like a gentle whisper on my face as I drove through Brentson. Late August into early September was always one of my favorite times in the town. With the leaves already starting to change, it painted a pretty picture of my hometown. What should have been a time to bask in remembering the good times I spent here was anything but. I spent many afternoons during high school at Smith's Ice Cream Parlor—still standing and as popular as ever. Many of my memories there included Nash Henson, someone I tried to forget over the years. And I failed every single time.

A few minutes later, and with a heavy sigh, I steered my old Toyota Camry onto Brentson University's campus. Another welcome sign beaconed me home. Butterflies collided in my stomach as I took in my surroundings. What once had been my dream school was now my living nightmare. As a kid, I'd hoped that I would one day enroll at BU. Now that I had the opportunity, it felt as if hell had swallowed me whole.

Transferring to Brentson had been a lot simpler than I thought it would be, and for that I was grateful. Not having to deal with that on top of everything else was crucial in helping me prepare for this move across the country.

I looked at the map on my phone before turning off the GPS. I knew where I was now. Some things had changed in the last three years, but most of what I remembered about this town had stayed the same. Recalling the last couple of directions from the GPS, I navigated to a small home and pulled into the driveway. It looked well maintained, which wasn't surprising given that it was owned by the university.

Before I had an opportunity to move, the front door swung open and out popped a petite woman with a huge smile on her face.

"You're here!"

I nodded and gave her a small smile through the windshield. Seeing Izzy Deacon did nothing to calm the nerves building in my body. With a shaky hand, I stepped out of the car, locked up, and took a deep breath. She bounded down the stairs and pulled me into her arms.

It felt wonderful to be reunited with Izzy again. We had seen each other in person a couple of times over the years, but it had been months since we last hung out.

"Glad you made it here okay. I've been dying to hear more about why you decided to transfer here for our senior year."

There was only so much I could tell her because I needed to do my best to make sure that no one else would be affected by this mess. "Izzy, I'll fill you in. I promise."

That seemed to satisfy her as a smile reappeared on her face.

"We have to get you settled. You mentioned that you were having trouble finding a place and I wanted you to know that you could always stay with me. I know there is no way in hell you'd go back home."

"I appreciate the offer, but I know I'll find something near campus."

Izzy crossed her arms in a huff. "Well, you should stay with me until you do."

I shifted my weight from one foot to the other. "Okay."

"Yay!" Izzy exclaimed with childlike glee. "It's been way too long since we've spent time together. I've been waiting for this ever since you said you were coming back." Without another word, Izzy pulled me into another hug.

"I've been looking forward to this, too." That wasn't a lie. I had looked forward to spending time with Izzy since I knew I was coming back to Brentson.

"Oh, no."

Izzy whispered this in my ear because we were still hugging. It was clear that something was wrong. When her arms loosened, and I regained the ability to move, I looked over my shoulder before doing a one-eighty. Standing across the street was the last person I was ready to see again.

My breath caught in my chest when his eyes landed on me.

Nash.

He still looked as handsome as I remembered. Any hope I had that he might have forgotten all the things I did was dashed when his eyes narrowed. And he glared at me. If he could have snarled at me from where he was, he would have. He wasn't alone, and soon the guy with him drew his attention away from me. But, as he left, he gave me one final stare.

I watched him walk away, not blaming him one bit for his reaction.

My name might be Raven Goodwin, but I was far from good.

Devious Game is available now!

ABOUT THE AUTHOR

Bri loves a good romance, especially ones that involve a hot anti-hero. That is why she likes to turn the dial up a notch with her own writing. Her Broken Cross series is her debut dark romance series.

She spends most of her time hanging out with her family, plotting her next novel, or reading books by other romance authors.

briblackwood.com

ALSO BY BRI BLACKWOOD

Broken Cross Series

Sinners Empire (Prequel)

Savage Empire

Scarred Empire

Steel Empire

Shadow Empire

Secret Empire

Stolen Empire

The Broken Cross Series Box Set: Books 1-3

The Ruthless Billionaire Trilogy

The Billionaire's Auction

The Billionaire's Possession

The Billionaire's Vengeance

Brentson University Series

Devious Game

Devious Secret

Devious Heir

The Westwick University Duet

The Lies Beneath

The Truth Between

The Shattered Trilogy

Shattered Sinner

Printed in the USA
CPSIA information can be obtained
at www.ICGtesting.com
LVHW041732261123
764962LV00047B/783